# THE WOMAN BEFORE YOU

Carrie Blake works in real estate and lives in Manhattan. This is her first novel.

# THE
# WOMAN
# BEFORE
# YOU

CARRIE BLAKE

A division of HarperCollins*Publishers*
www.harpercollins.co.uk

Harper*Impulse* an imprint of
HarperCollins*Publishers*
The News Building
1 London Bridge Street
London SE1 9GF

www.harpercollins.co.uk

This paperback edition 2018

3

First published in Great Britain in ebook format by
HarperCollins*Publishers* 2018

A catalogue record for this book
is available from the British Library

ISBN: 9780008279479

Typeset in Birka by Palimpsest Book Production Ltd,
Falkirk, Stirlingshire

Printed and bound in Great Britain

# Prologue

On the day he finally asked me, I knew. This was where everything had been leading, all along. I didn't ask: What happens now? I didn't ask: Why me? I didn't ask: What will I have to do? I didn't ask: How bad will I have to be? How evil?

I waited for him to speak.

He smiled at me across the table in the restaurant where he'd just shown me something that had changed everything. Something that put the last part of my life—or maybe my whole life so far and my immediate future—in an entirely new and different light.

He didn't have to explain. He didn't have to tell me what I'd just seen. He took my hand in his and gently stroked my palm. His hands were smooth and icy cold. As cold as the devil's, I thought.

'You're perfect,' was all he said. '*Perfect.*'

# Isabel

It's always a nasty shock to learn that what you believed was your deepest self, your inner core, was, all along, only your surface. It's even more shocking to discover how fast that clean, pure surface can crack—and reveal the darkness and dirt beneath.

On the surface I was a nice girl; the girl you want to have coffee with after yoga class, the girl whose shoulder you cry on after your break up, the girl you call to watch your kids when the babysitter cancels at the last minute.

My senior year in high school, they actually tested us for compassion—to see how much sympathy we had. Our principal's wife taught in the college psych department, and everyone said that the test was part of her research. We knew that this was probably not approved by the Iowa Board of Education, but no one objected. If you refused to take the test, it meant you had no compassion. You weren't a nice person. You failed.

The school guidance counselor, Mr Chambers, took us

one by one into a side room off the gym, a windowless cubicle that reeked of disinfectant and old sneakers. He asked a lot of questions. I aced the test without trying. Would I risk my life to save someone? Sure. If I won the lottery, how much would I give to charity? Fifty percent. Did I usually assume that a person was telling the truth or lying? Mostly, telling the truth. It depended on who the person was.

Mr Chambers put his hand on my knee. Beads of sweat popped out on his forehead. He stared into my eyes. His eyes were liquid and brimmed with fat tears under his dark bushy eyebrows.

I ignored his hand inching up my leg. I pretended not to notice.

I answered his questions truthfully. I said what I thought. I didn't have to think. I didn't mention the fact that, all through the test, his hand kept edging further up my leg. Did he think he was being encouraging and supportive? Affectionate and kind?

Finally, I slapped his hand away, like a pesky mosquito. He raised his hand, and shook it from side to side, as if he were waving goodbye to me. After a few minutes, he put his hand on my leg again. I wanted to say something, to yell at him, to scream. But I didn't. I just sat there, answering his questions.

To be fair, he never got further than my lower thigh. And maybe that was the *real* compassion test, underneath the fake one. Question: Did I think Mr Chambers was a disgusting perv who should be locked up for the rest of his life, or did I think he was a sick man who needed help? Answer: I thought he was a disgusting perv who needed help.

My friends and I never talked about what happened in that cubicle, and I think I learned something from that, though I couldn't have said what it was. At least not then. Not yet.

Later, after everything had happened, I thought back to that day. And I thought I knew what the lesson was: *Be careful. Trust no one.* You never know the secret reason behind what seems to be happening. When (and if) you find out, it's usually more sinister than whatever you could have imagined.

I'd always taken people at their word. Once, I ate a giant spoonful of cayenne pepper because a mean girl told me it was cinnamon candy. I dove into a slimy pond that a cute boy told me was clear. Everyone laughed when I came up for air, slicked with algae and mud.

For years the joke was on me. But what saved me was that I always somehow knew what people were thinking and feeling. It wasn't anything weird, like telepathy or ESP or anything like that. But it was a little like that. I looked at the person and I *knew*. I could feel what they felt.

It was strange, I could almost *see* into their hearts

and minds. It was like a new window opening up on an electronic device, a tablet or a phone. There was me, and there was that other person in a corner of my consciousness.

I sat with the kid at the party who needed someone to talk to. I stuck up for the bullied. I comforted the kids with problems at home. I wasn't afraid to do the right thing, though I didn't always know what it was. Even the cool kids came to like me for it. I was like their conscience, so they didn't need to have one. Doing the right thing was a service they paid me for, with their friendship.

I never told my super-nice high school boyfriend that our hot romance bored me. Why would I hurt his feelings, telling him how often I was thinking of something else—a movie I'd seen, what Mom was cooking for dinner?—when we had sex in his bedroom after school while his parents were off at work? I was always relieved when he made that funny little snorting noise after he came. It meant that the sex part was over, and I could lie with my head on his chest and think my own thoughts, which I actually sort of liked. I was good at playing the girl in love for the time being.

After we graduated high school he went off to Oberlin. I could have gone to Oberlin, too. I got into all of the schools I applied to. And yet, despite the objections and fears of my mother, who thought that New York was a dangerous and scary place, I was going to New York to be an actress. Theater was the only place I felt at home. But this didn't fit in with the kind of girl I was supposed to be—the one who went away to college to study hard, and then went to grad school to study harder, until I became a lawyer or a psychologist or a director of marketing at some startup company. Thankfully, my mother had raised me to be an independent person, to believe in myself, to be strong and not to let anyone make decisions for me. My dad had been killed in a car wreck when I was four, and she'd supported us since then, without a man to help her. She was an inspiring example of how a woman could be her own person and follow her own lights. And now she had to stick by her own principles, even though she worried about me.

My boyfriend and I pretended to be really sad about the fact that circumstances beyond our control were separating us. I could tell that what he was feeling was mostly relief ... and happiness that he was leaving town to start over somewhere else. Maybe he'd meet a girl who honestly thought that he was interesting and sexy. We broke up with a long lingering kiss and hug. We were Midwesterners. We were nice.

On the day I met The Customer, that niceness began to crumble. That do-the-right-thing conscience started to peel away, like the papery skin that flakes off after a sunburn, and you can't stop picking at it because it hurts so much and it feels so good. When that clean, pure surface was burned away by sex and need and desire, I was left with my true self: all body, all skin, all touch, no soul, lustful, depraved, and corrupt.

# Isabel

I'd always wanted to be an actress. It was where I could use my ability to see what other people were feeling, what other people were thinking and make a crowd of strangers see it, too. I could even make them feel it. It was like a superpower. There was no limit to what I could do in these pretend worlds. That should have raised a red flag; pretending is never too far from reality. But I saw no flags. I loved the feeling of not being me, of being someone else. I loved the attention. I loved making my whole school cry when I did Emily's 'Goodbye, World' speech in *Our Town*, at the end of senior year.

By the time I was in high school, my mom had finished school (she'd put herself through college working as a waitress) and had a job she really liked as an administrative secretary in the English department at the college in our town. I could have even gone there for free. But I needed to leave. I loved the small Iowa town where, it seemed, I knew everyone and everyone knew me. But that was another reason why it was time for me to get away.

When I moved to New York, I had about six hundred dollars of my own money—money I'd made when I'd worked every summer, babysitting and minding the neighborhood kids. And Mom had given me a fraction of the money she would have spent sending me to college— money that I knew she didn't really have—in one lump sum. I dreamed of late-night rehearsals, smoke breaks on fire escapes, stacks of scripts piled high on dusty Turkish rugs in my bohemian penthouse. There'd be bottomless brunches and dinners till dawn with the crew. *My* name in lights. My glorious stage and film career.

I went to a few auditions. It took me a couple of weeks to realize this wasn't high school anymore. I stopped going to auditions. I took a drama class at the New York School of Theater, which is where I met my two closest friends in New York, in fact my only friends in New York, Marcy and Luke.

I tried out at a few more auditions. I quit again. Everyone was better than me. I could hear them through the walls as I sat in the corridor, waiting for my name to be called. And when I got through the door, I could see the casting directors' eyes glaze over. I was pretty, but not pretty enough. I wasn't *this* enough, I wasn't *that* enough. I looked like a million other girls who'd come to the city with the same hopes and ambitions. And boy, were they ever *not* interested in hearing me do the tragic monologue from *Our Town*.

Thanks. We'll call you. Next!

I was running out of money way faster than I thought I would. If I wanted to stay in New York, I would have to make some changes. It wasn't easy to give up on my dreams. And when I finally called my mom in Iowa to tell her that maybe I didn't want to be an actress after all, it was as if I'd somehow made it official. Even though I knew my mom loved me and believed in me and wanted only the best for me, it made me furious when I heard, in her voice, that she'd always known how small—how ridiculous—my chances were.

She said, 'Maybe you should consider something else, dear. Maybe you should think about becoming a psychologist. You're so good with people, so sensitive. So intuitive. So caring.'

That was when I almost told her what the school guidance counselor had done in that dim cubicle off the gym. But I didn't.

'Thanks, Mom,' I said. 'I'll think about it.'

That night, I cried myself to sleep. Could it really be this easy to give up on so much of myself?

Maybe that was part of what I saw in The Customer.

He gave me a chance to act, to pretend to be someone else—someone hotter and sexier than the nice girl I'd always been. But he knew I wasn't pretending.

And he *believed* in me. He believed that I could become someone else, that I could do something else. And he let me show him how.

The week I got to New York, I found an apartment in Greenpoint, Brooklyn, a studio which was super cheap because it was tiny and had hardly any light and because everyone knew that it was directly over a giant toxic dump site that had never been properly cleaned up. I didn't care. I wasn't planning on staying there long enough for it to hurt me. I bought a plant—a cactus. I named it Alfred, I don't know why.

The cactus shriveled up and died. Too little light, I guess.

I got jobs that paid almost nothing but that I was grateful to get. I helped people figure out how to use the copy machines at Staples until the flash of the machines started hurting my eyes and I got scared that it was going to damage them. I was a receptionist at a nail salon. The Korean girls were friendly and sweet and really brave in the midst of their terrible lives, but the only English they spoke was about nail shape and length and polish, and it made me feel even lonelier than I already did.

I guess that's how I wound up selling mattresses at Doctor Sleep.

The place was named after Steve—my boss's—favorite Stephen King novel. Steve lent me a tattered paperback copy of the novel and told me to read it. I got through the first two hundred pages, but it was too scary. It gave me insomnia—and when I finally fell asleep, I had nightmares. It seemed odd to me that a store designed to help its customers sleep better had taken its name from a book that would keep them awake. I thanked Steve for the book and told him that it was my new favorite novel, too.

Obviously, I'd never once in my life said: I want to be what Steve refers to as a 'mattress professional.' Believe me, I never thought: Oh, if only I could know everything in the world there is to know about memory foam and pillow tops and coils. If only I could work for a guy named Steve who looks like an aging groundhog, who has creepy, secretive habits and a pitiful business model, and who always stands way too close when he talks to me. Though in fact he never touched me, except once, to shake my hand when he hired me.

I could tell what Steve was thinking and feeling. I saw how he imagined himself: as the king of a vast mattress empire with branch stores all over the city and suburbs.

I decided that Steve was harmless, which didn't mean that it wasn't a little disturbing when, on my first day at work, he explained his theory: insomnia is not a psychological problem but an actual disease that only the right mattress can cure.

The showroom had touches—white tile walls, a weird little machine that blinked and beeped like a heart monitor, and to one side, a gurney on which there were stacks of fancy duvets no one ever bought—designed to look like Steve's sick fantasy of a hospital or operating room. Steve even wore a white lab coat. At first he said that I should too, and he lent me one of his, which smelled of cologne and sweat and said 'Steve' on the pocket. But after a week he told me that it was a pity to hide my pretty legs under a uniform.

So he got me a short white medical jacket that came just down to my hips, the kind of jacket an outcall hooker would wear, a prostitute hired to play Naughty Nurse.

Maybe that's why The Customer got the wrong idea. Except that it was the right idea. The right idea that went very, very wrong.

My name was stitched on the pocket of the medical jacket. *Isabel.*

I felt like sobbing when I saw it. It was like a threat: I'd be working here forever, at least for a very long while. But I could tell that Steve was proud of the jacket. That little corner of my mind that had Steve's feelings in it lit up like a Christmas tree. He was so happy when he gave it to me. I smiled and said, 'Thanks, Steve.'

'I can write it off as a business expense. It improves the look of the establishment,' Steve said.

Was I supposed to say *thank you* for that?

My friend Marcy, from drama class, had worked at

Doctor Sleep for a few weeks. She said it was easier than waitressing: better hours. But she preferred waitressing. I wondered if she'd left because of Steve, but I couldn't ask a friend, even a friend I saw more rarely now that I'd quit drama class, if she'd set me up to work with a total creep. I didn't like how Steve looked at me when I tried on the starchy white jacket.

On my second day at work Steve announced that he was in an open marriage, but that workplace romances were strictly forbidden for professional reasons. I was the only person he could have had an office romance *with*, so I assumed he was telling me something. That was a relief. As I said, he never once touched me, or did anything perverted. If I wanted to keep my job, it seemed like a stupid idea to ask my boss to stand back when we talked. I wouldn't have been at all surprised if he took it the wrong way. So I didn't say anything. I let him breathe his hot breath on me.

Whenever Steve left for his lunch break, he had a furtive, weaselly air. Through the window, I watched him scurry away. I always had the feeling that he was going to see a dominatrix. But weirdly, the part of my brain that told me what someone else was experiencing stayed empty—no picture, no sound—when Steve left for his lunch break. I'd always had an almost telepathic sense of empathy, but now I realized the foolishness of taking any gift for granted, of thinking you would have it forever.

I told myself that it wasn't fair to blame Steve for being the person he was.

On the day Steve hired me, a Friday, he gave me a large binder full of papers from the International Mattress Retailers Association. He told me to study it over the weekend. On Monday he would give me a test.

I had a bad feeling about this 'test,' but I studied just in case it was real and not some euphemism for getting groped by Steve—like the 'compassion test' at my high school. I learned about the science of sleep and the fine points of mattress construction. There was even a section about *feng shui*—the ancient Chinese system that told you where and how to position your bed in your room for the soundest sleep and maximum good health.

The manual instructed me to look friendly, concerned, professional, like a doctor. I was dealing with one of the most intimate aspects of my customers' lives. I should keep that in mind when I asked about slumber positions, back problems, sleeping difficulties, what they wanted in a mattress.

On Monday Steve handed me a multiple choice test and told me to fill it out at his desk. I scored one hundred.

'Good girl, Marcy,' Steve said.

'I'm Isabel,' I said.

'Right,' said Steve. 'Marcy was the last girl.'

'My friend Marcy,' I said.

'Right,' said Steve. 'The redhead. You're the blond.'

I did what the mattress experts suggested. I acted concerned, sympathetic, professional. Like a kindly family doctor. I'd guide the customers to the most expensive mattress I thought they could afford, murmuring about why it was perfect for them. I even talked about *feng shui*, if I thought a client was the type to go for it. I never once tried to make clients buy something that I knew was beyond their budget.

Almost always, customers wanted to try out the mattress. Then my role would shift from that of the diagnostician to that of the tactful nurse who leaves the room or turns away when a patient undresses.

It was surprising how many people lay like corpses. On their backs, arms crossed. Even young couples, in love, lay there like statues on a tomb. Staring up at the ceiling, they discussed the mattress. Too hard? Too soft? You would never suspect that they might ever have *sex* on that mattress. Watching them, you couldn't imagine the thought even crossing their minds.

The day I met The Customer was one of those weirdly warm, swampy September afternoons. An unusually quiet Saturday. Lately, business had been slow, even though Steve said it was usually his best season, when NYU students were moving into their dorms and convincing their rich parents that they needed a better mattress than the one the school provided. I could feel Steve's gloom, his disappointment. He'd stopped talking about opening a second branch in the East Village.

Steve had gotten me a small cheap desk, at which I sat, looking out the window at people whose lives were more fun and exciting than mine. Everyone had somewhere to go, someone to be with, shopping to do. I wished them well. Someday I could be one of them. One of the lucky ones. I was determined not to feel sorry for myself—not to give up hope, no matter what.

A mom with a stroller came in and asked if we sold mattress covers for cribs. Steve sounded impatient when he told her to try Babies 'R' Us. When she passed me I flashed her a smile that I hoped said, *what a cute baby*, though I hadn't actually seen her child under its milky plastic awning.

I tried to concentrate on my book, an anthology of poems based on Greek myths. I was obsessed with Orpheus, on how he could have gotten his beloved Eurydice out of hell if he hadn't turned around to make sure she was there. What was *that* story about? Trust? Love? Fear? Stupid faithless men who would ruin everything in a heartbeat if something upset or scared them? Or women who think they can overpower fate and end up trapped forever?

I read the poems till I thought I understood them. Which I never did.

But I guess those poems prepared me for how I would

feel about The Customer. For the sheer terror that I would turn around—and that he wouldn't be there.

I pulled out my phone and scrolled through to a folder of apps I'd labeled 'auditions.' It hadn't been easy to abandon acting. But the truth is I'd found a small workaround, for the time being at least. One drunken night, Marcy, Luke, and I all downloaded Tinder on our phones. It started out as a joke. We would each go on three dates and report back. 'Come on, nice girl,' Luke said. 'Join the modern world. You're not in Iowa anymore.' We'd spent the rest of the night swiping left and swiping right, laughing out loud, screaming every time we had a match. I'd be lying if I said it didn't feel good when a hot guy matched with me. We switched to beer and took a sip every time we landed on a picture of a guy with a puppy or a guy with a guitar. We were all hungover the next day.

I was surprised by how little effort it took to 'match' with somebody. But when I actually started texting with one of these so-called matches, I understood the old 'plenty of fish in the sea metaphor' on a whole different level; it was a big sea filled with a lot of creepy fish. The first guy made a joke about how cheesy dick pics were, told me he liked butt play, and then sent me a dick pic. Then there was the guy who sent me a picture of a paddle and asked me what I wanted to do with it. Or the guy who opened the conversation with 'do u like to be choked?' Finally, I matched with a guy who had just moved from Connecticut to work in marketing at some greeting card company in Midtown. He missed his mom and had a dog (the adopted, shelter variety—included in his Tinder profile) and lived just a few blocks away from me. Pretty vanilla. But after so many conversations with gross guys about the size of my chest and euphemisms for penises, I could do a first date with Mr Vanilla.

The date was pretty basic. We met at a bar around the corner from his apartment in Williamsburg that had just opened and he'd been meaning to check out. The bar was dog-friendly, so he could have brought his dog, he told me, but he didn't want us to 'move too fast.' I wore a yellow knee-length dress and he wore a button-down shirt and khaki shorts. I could tell he'd gotten his hair cut for the occasion.

We talked about his hometown of West Orange; about what he studied in college, and his favorite TV shows. But when he started to ask me about my life a funny thing happened. I told him I grew up in Ohio, had two brothers, and two parents who were crazy in love. My dad was a historian and my mom was a lawyer. Dad was a total romantic and my mom was a real-life superhero. I had a grandmother I was really close to (actually my great-aunt, but I called her Nana—'a long story,' I told him), who passed away last year. The best Christmas present I ever got was my Labrador-mix named Juno, when I was nine. I met my best friend when we were in kindergarten, and I lived with her now.

I watched his eyes light up as I pulled out the props for my character. I could feel how excited he was to know me—this girl with so much potential who knew where she had come from and where she was going. I had written a different script for myself. I became the girl he would want to see again, someone who *would* meet his dog, his mom, his best friends from home.

After a chaste kiss at the corner, I walked home alone. I deleted our conversation from the app on my phone. I didn't want a second date. I wanted to preserve that moment. The look on his face when he thought he recognized me, when I became the perfect girl. It was almost like acting except better. I wasn't just memorizing lines, I was writing them, too. And in real time for an audience of one.

I wanted to feel that way again. To meet someone, figure out who they were and what they wanted, and become the person they needed, then watch them fall in love. Now I was the one not giving callbacks. I'll admit, it felt good to finally have some power. When Tinder started to feel stale and flooded with perverts, I made profiles on Bumble, Thrinder (even more of a challenge), OkCupid, Coffee Meets Bagel—and each with a slightly different character. On Bumble, I was Riley from Portland, Maine. On Thrinder, I was Lorrie from the Bay Area. On OkCupid

I was Amanda from Manhattan. All I had to do was make a new email, and a new Facebook profile (back when Facebook made it easy to do such a thing). I never went on more than a first date—and never took more than a sweet goodnight kiss on the cheek. I was still a good Midwestern girl, after all, and one date wasn't enough time for anyone to get hurt. I thought of it as more of an ever-evolving character study game. I loved keeping all the scripts in my head at once, remembering which app I met so-and-so on, which backstory to pull out.

That day, I was going on a coffee date with a Mr Matthew from Bumble. I pulled up Bumble and scrolled through his pictures. From what I could see, he was tall with broad shoulders, and dark hair. There were no puppy pictures. There was Matthew on the beach in a tank top and American flag shorts, all square chest and tight, tan quads, Matthew sitting at the center of a group of guys, his thick shoulders wrapped around the two closest to him. But the one I kept swiping back to was a picture of Matthew standing on a pier, the sunset behind him framing his face. His head was thrown up to the sky and his eyes were closed, like he was in the middle of the greatest laugh. He had the best jawline I'd ever seen.

I grabbed my stuff and prepared to leave for my lunch break date. Steve told me to 'have fun' as I walked out the door. As I was walking to the coffee shop to meet Matthew,

I kept thinking about that laugh, that jawline. I didn't know why, but something about this date made me want to ride the line—maybe show him a little more of the 'real' Isabel. A new character challenge, or so I thought.

When I walked into the coffee shop, I spotted him immediately. Our eyes locked and we both grinned, mirroring each other's delight as we moved closer to each other. When I got to his table, he stood up and gave me a kiss on the cheek. He smelled expensive—all sandalwood and vetiver—and my knees buckled as I tried to remember what he thought my name was.

'Excited to meet you, Riley,' he said, watching me as I sat down.

I laughed and said something about the pleasure being all mine. This was a new role for me—the fumbling girl who couldn't get the words out of her mouth in the right order. I blushed every time I looked at his smile, and had to look away.

He glanced at his watch and said something about having to be back to the office for a meeting later in the afternoon, then asked me what I did. I opened my mouth to start talking about my uncle's lobster boat on the coast, but I couldn't bring myself to do it. I had this strange feeling that telling Matthew who I really was would make him like me even more.

'Okay, so here's the deal,' I said. 'My name isn't Riley, and I'm not from Maine.'

He smiled but didn't say anything. And so I did. I told him about growing up in Iowa and about moving to New York to be an actress and about failing at being an actress and about my 'acting game' with the dating apps and finally my sad life working for creepy Steve at Doctor Sleep, just down the street.

I laughed as I finished my confessional monologue, and leaned back in my chair, waiting for him to react.

He was quiet for a beat but his eyes were bright and working fast to take me in.

'So that's it? Any recent ex-boyfriend killing sprees? Any fetishes you want to confess?'

I laughed. 'No. No. That can wait for our second date.'

'Well then,' he said, smiling as he leaned in closer to me. 'I'm excited to meet you, *Isabel*.'

It was liberating to let someone in on my secret game. I had gotten the feeling that he would be okay with the story, but I was still surprised to realize that he was not only okay with it, he was *thrilled* by it. I was working hard to look cool and unfazed, but the way he said my name made it hard to stay composed.

'Now your turn.' I said. 'Is your name really Matthew?'

'No, no,' he said. 'That can wait for our second date.'

We both laughed.

He looked at his watch. I looked at my phone. My lunch hour was up and I had to be back at Doctor Sleep in a few minutes.

Before I had a chance to say anything, Matthew said, 'Hey, I have a crazy question.'

'Go for it,' I said.

'I'm sure you're about to tell me you have to go back to work. But I feel like I've only just met you, Isabel-formerly-known-as-Riley. And the truth is, I don't want to stop being with you just yet.'

I was floating. I definitely didn't want to leave him either. 'So what do you suggest we do?'

'Well, I don't feel it's fair to deprive the poor mattress shoppers of their favorite Sleep Doctor, so what if I came back to the store with you and pretended to be your customer? I'll wait for a minute to come in so your boss won't suspect a thing.'

I smiled and shrugged. 'Sure. Why not?' I knew Steve would be going on break when I got back from mine, anyway. It was probably the first time I had ever been excited to race back to the store from lunch.

When I walked back my whole body was buzzing. I was kind of okay with the idea of slipping on my uniform today.

I walked into the store and Steve said, 'I'm going on break.' The timing was too perfect. I wondered what Steve did when he left. I didn't ask and I didn't complain even though his breaks were getting longer and more frequent.

'Fine,' I said. 'Take your time.' The truth was, I usually

hated being alone in there in plain view of every passing maniac who might think, Hey! Look! A young woman all by herself with a cash register and a lot of mattresses! But today, I was excited to be alone. Today, I wanted him to take his time.

The doorbell rang its fake sleigh-bell chime. I looked up. Matthew—or should I say, The Customer—stood in the doorway, back lit. Tall, thin, broad-shouldered.

I walked toward him, slipping into character; welcoming and friendly, but not pushy, hungry, or aggressive. That was what the mattress professional instruction manual said to do.

Close up, he was so handsome I had to look away—but not before I noticed his glossy dark hair, dark eyes, eyelashes longer than mine. His features were chiseled. He looked a little like Gary Cooper, a little like Robert Mitchum—like old-school movie stars used to look before actors began to look like the guy next door who's going to get fat and bald and jowly the minute he turns forty.

In other words: *He was hot.*

I said, 'Can I help you?'

He said, 'I hope so. I'm moving soon, and I don't see any point in taking my old mattress with me.'

If I had ten dollars for every time I heard someone say those exact words, I could have quit and lived on the money for the six months it might take me to find a better job.

But sex and beauty change the conversation. Things you've heard a million times sound interesting, fresh and new.

I wanted to know everything. Where did he live? Why was he moving? Who would be sleeping on the new mattress? I loved this adaptation of my game—for two players now instead of one.

'What sort of mattress are you looking for?'

He smiled and shrugged. He had a beautiful smile, a charming shrug.

'A comfortable one,' he said.

I said, 'Okay, let me ask you.' This was on script. 'Do you like your current mattress?'

'My mattress is ten years old, what would *like* mean?' He smiled again.

I smiled back. So there we were.

I asked him the standard questions. Side sleeper? Back sleeper? Skeletal problems? Sleep issues? He slept like a baby. He closed his eyes and fell out, slept straight through the night. I wanted to lie next to him, with my head nestled on his chest.

I had never felt quite like that before. Certainly not about any other mattress store customer. It threw me off script.

'Lucky you,' I said.

He didn't respond. He was making me do all the work.

'I think I know what you might like. We have one on the floor that I can show you. Please come this way.'

'Thank you,' he said.

I walked down the aisles lined with mattresses, looking back from time to time, as if to make sure that he was still behind me. I thought of Orpheus—don't look back!—mostly to avoid thinking about how self-conscious I was, how aware that a man was following me, looking at me, at my back, my ass. Sometimes I wondered how a customer was responding to Steve's weird medical decor, but now I wished The Customer would actually look at the gurney, at the bizarre medical stuff—at anything but me.

I stopped at the foot of the most expensive and luxurious mattress we had, twelve thousand dollars' worth of organic German cotton, French wool layers, inner hand tufting. The celebrity movie star mattress, the Executive Deluxe Comfort Natural Pillowtop Set. As far as I knew, Steve had never sold a single one of them, but he insisted on having it on display. He said it improved the look of the 'establishment,' like my shorty jacket, I guess.

I could read The Customer's mind well enough to know that this was the mattress he would want. But I also obviously knew he wasn't going to buy it. I had no idea what he was thinking right that second. It was as if those circuits—my mind-reading window—were jammed by how sexy and handsome he was.

He asked, 'Is this the best one you have?'

'I think so,' I said. 'I mean yes. Would you like to try it?'

'No. You. I want *you* to try it. I'd appreciate that very much. If you wouldn't mind lying down for a moment.'

It wasn't that this never happened—that people asked me to lie on the mattress. But mostly it happened with very old people, or people with some physical damage, who came in with their caretakers. They couldn't, or didn't want to, risk being a spectacle, struggling to lie down. Or they couldn't lie down without help. In that case, they might want to see *me* lie on the mattress, to see if I looked comfy.

'Comfortable?' they'd ask.

'Totally,' I always replied, though nothing could have been less comfortable than I felt at those moments.

In the ten months I'd worked at Doctor Sleep, not one—not one!—young, handsome, hot guy had ever asked me to try out a mattress for him.

Actually, I *did* mind. I felt sort of queasy and flushed. I wanted to say that this wasn't my job.

I could tell that he wouldn't have insisted. He was too polite. But I was a nice Midwestern girl. I wouldn't want to be rude to a customer...

And besides, I wanted to do it.

'Lie down,' he said. 'Please. Let me see.'

That *please* did the trick. 'All right.' I couldn't look at him.

I climbed onto the mattress. My white jacket rode up. I had to lift my ass to tuck the hem of my dress around me. All this time I was conscious of how intently he was watching me. I saw myself through his eyes. The mind-reading corner of my brain was glowing red.

When I saw myself through his eyes, I realized that I was already shaking.

I lay the way all the customers did, on my back, with my arms crossed, like a mummy.

I was so nervous that I started babbling. 'Do you know anything about *feng shui*? It's an ancient Asian ... I don't know ... science, I guess you could say. What matters is not only which mattress you buy but also how and where you set it up in your room. It's important for how you sleep and how healthy you'll be. There are principles, guidelines...'

I stopped. I sounded like an idiot. He didn't seem to be listening, and I didn't blame him. Why was I blabbing on about all this to the last guy in the world who would be interested? I lay back and stared at the ceiling.

'No one sleeps like that,' he said. 'Like you're lying now. On your back with your arms crossed. Do *you*?'

'No,' I told the ceiling.

'Good,' he said. 'Show me how you really sleep.' His voice was low, gentle but firm and insistent.

I rolled over on my side. I reached back and yanked down my skirt. He walked around to the other side of the bed so he was looking straight down at me.

Was I ashamed? I was ashamed to think that I would *never* have done this if The Customer hadn't been drop-dead handsome. I thought: What a shallow person you are, Isabel.

'How does it feel?' The Customer asked.

'Comfortable,' I said, automatically.

'I think not,' he said. 'I don't think you look comfortable at all.'

'Okay, not really.'

'You don't have to lie to me,' he said. How did he know? I was the mind-reader here.

'It feels weird,' I said. 'But good weird.'

'That's a step in the right direction.'

He just stood there, looking down at me. I heard my breath get slightly ragged. I willed it to stop, but it wouldn't. My breath came faster.

'All right,' he said. 'Good. Now roll over on your back.'

I rolled onto my back.

'Lift your jacket,' he said.

I tried. It was awkward and clumsy.

'Beautiful,' he said. 'You're very beautiful, do you know that?'

'Thanks.' How stupid I sounded.

'Now spread your legs a little,' he said. 'Just a little.' His voice was so calm, so even, considering what he was asking.

I moved my legs apart, just a few inches.

'Okay. Now I want you to do you one more thing for me. I want you take your underwear off,' he said.

31

I didn't think: *What?* I didn't think: *Who is this sicko and what sick game is he playing?*

Here's what I thought: What underwear am I wearing? I couldn't remember. I couldn't stop myself from reaching up my skirt. I felt an edge of lace. Thank heaven.

'No, wait. Stop. Keep your hand there, where it is,' he said. 'Put your finger inside that lace edge, just underneath...'

'I can't,' I said.

'Why not?' he said flatly. 'I know you can. *Please* don't tell me you can't.' We were almost whispering now. He leaned closer down over me, to hear.

'Steve could be back any minute,' I said. 'My boss.'

I didn't say: I don't want to. I didn't say: Are you crazy? How can you ask me to do this? I didn't say: Go fuck yourself, pervert.

I said: 'Steve could be back any minute.'

'Just a little,' he said, even more softly 'Just raise your knees and spread them a little. And touch yourself.'

I closed my eyes. It was the only way I could do it. I couldn't look at him. I could feel my face burning. I wanted to hear his voice with my eyes closed.

'Please.' His voice had a funny sound, not pleading exactly, but almost.

I pulled my knees halfway to my chest and let them slowly drift apart. My body felt hot and weirdly sleepy, as if I were dreaming, as if I'd lost my power to resist.

I didn't care if Steve came back. I didn't care what happened. It was the not caring that let me say, 'Want to join me?'

I had never said anything like that in my life.

Even though most of my dating in New York had been of the online-dating game variety (with no sex, only chaste first-date goodnight kisses), I'd still managed to have my share of brief sexual affairs, and thought of myself as someone with a little experience—certainly I'd had experience taking my clothes off in front of a stranger, which, if you ask me, is a big part of what hangs people up about sex. I could count the number of guys I'd slept with: seven. But none of them had made me feel what I was feeling now in the middle of a public place, a mattress store, alone on a bed with all my clothes on.

Even then, right away I knew that I would do whatever The Customer told me. The pure electric pleasure flooding every nerve—I wanted to feel it forever. Exhibitionism, voyeurism, consensual, harassment. There were no words for what I was doing, for what was happening to me. It was just a feeling.

'Sit up,' he said, sharply, suddenly.

I sat up just in time to see Steve outside, slithering into the frame of the window. I was surprised to notice that I was on the edge of tears. What was *that* about?

I jumped up, slightly dizzy. The blood was taking its

time, flowing back from between my legs to my brain. I stood beside the bed. The Customer stood beside me looking down at the mattress. We both looked at it. There we were, for anyone—including Steve—to see: a mattress professional and her customer engaged in a simple business transaction that might or might not occur.

I put my palm out toward Steve. Stay away. But Steve didn't. He couldn't. This customer, this mattress. It was like showing honey to a bear. This was the big fish Steve had dreamed of reeling in.

'Have you made up your mind?' I asked. I wanted to keep my job, so I included Steve in our conversation. 'Do you think you might be interested in making a purchase today?'

'No,' said The Customer. 'Not yet. For the moment I'm just looking. I need to think it over. Can I have your card?'

Steve was gloating, triumphant. He'd insisted on printing up business cards for me and making me carry them in the pocket of my little white jacket. I didn't want strangers having my name and the phone number of the store. I'd fought against it, but he'd won.

Now I was glad I'd lost. I took a card from my pocket. It flipped out from between my fingers. Steve and The Customer watched me scramble to pick it up from the floor. I felt my short dress ride up, and I yanked it down. With Steve there, nothing was sexy, just pitiful and clumsy.

'Thank you,' The Customer told me and Steve, his gaze focused midway between us. 'I'll call when I've thought this through.'

'Perhaps you'd be interested in something that was less of a ... financial commitment,' said Steve.

'No,' said The Customer. 'I wouldn't.'

And with that, Matthew left the store.

***

The weather turned drizzly, a chilly, watery taste of the winter ahead. I sat at my desk at Doctor Sleep and read a novel about zombies. Sometimes I stared out the window, past the fat cold drips blurring the world outside.

I wished I had never met Matthew.

Until that day he walked in, I'd made my peace with life. No boyfriend, no real job, no career track, a crappy walk-up apartment in Greenpoint next door to my landlord, who screamed at his wife all night. But still I had no major complaints. Hope for the best, my mom always said. Look on the bright side. Something will come along.

Now something *had* come along, and I'd let it slip through my fingers. I should have done any sex-maniac thing he wanted. I should have made him promise to call me. I should have humbled myself—right in front of Steve—and begged Matthew to stay.

The days dragged on. I could hardly fake the interested smile for the few customers who came in. Once I practically nodded off in the middle of a sale.

Steve hissed, 'Isabel! Look sharp!'

Look sharp? How sharp did Steve think *he* looked?

I worked Saturday and got Sunday off. I slept till eleven, then sat in a café and read, like I did at work. Every so often I thought: I am the loneliest person in New York.

I was about to call my mom in Iowa when I got a text from her that said, 'Faculty potluck. Yuk. Talk later.' Even my mom had something better to do than talk to me.

At five I met my friend Luke, and we got mojitos at Cielito Lindo, the Mexican restaurant in the East Village where Marcy worked. If we got there early and left early, Marcy let us drink for half price. She'd sit with us for a few minutes, taking sips of our drinks when no one was watching. But around six-thirty she got busy, and after a while she gave us a look that said, 'You guys better leave.'

Luke was still going to auditions. He'd gotten so thin and dyed his hair such a flashy platinum-blond color that it limited the parts he could get. But I couldn't tell him that. It wasn't my place.

We sat in Cielito Lindo, with the late afternoon leaking into the windows, a salsa beat thrumming, everything revving up for maximum deliciousness and fun. But just when things began to get good, Luke and I would have to make room for people who could pay actual money.

On his second mojito, Luke said, 'Audrey got me an audition for the older brother in a cereal commercial. I didn't get a callback. I guess they figured out that I'm twice Cereal Boy's age.'

Three times Cereal Boy's age, I thought, but didn't say.

'How old do I look?' Luke asked.

'Hard to tell,' I white-lied. He was twenty-six, a year older than me. He looked fifteen. He looked thirty. He looked awful.

How old did Matthew think *I* was? I liked having a secret. Luke, can I tell you something? Promise not to tell. I played weird sex games with a stranger in the store when Steve was out to lunch.

'Hey, are you in love or something' Luke said. 'You have this ... glow. Promise me you're not pregnant.'

'I promise,' I said. 'I'm the same.' I loved that Luke noticed something different about me. It made me feel almost hopeful. Maybe it was the mojitos kicking in, but suddenly I realised Matthew knew where I worked. He could stop by the store, maybe he would...

'Are you hungry?' Luke asked. 'I know a pretty good Thai spot near here.' *Pretty good Thai spot* was his not-so-secret code for *even cheaper than Cielito Lindo*.

'That's okay.' My stomach heaved at the thought of chopsticking up the gummy, stuck-together, greasy Pad Thai that Luke would want to split. I wanted to go home and think about The Customer and what we'd done—and jerk off and fall asleep.

I said, 'Next time, okay? I don't know why I'm so tired. I think I'll call out for Chinese and watch TV and pass out.'

Walking to the subway, I felt the mojitos wear off within minutes, and I got sad again. Why was I so stupid? Why couldn't I just text Matthew? But I would never text Matthew first. Back in my apartment, I called my mom, who had gotten home from the faculty picnic.

'Honey,' she said. 'Is something wrong? I can hear it in your voice.'

'No,' I said, 'Really, I'm fine. I've been out with my friends. I had a couple of mojitos, maybe that's what you're hearing.'

'As long as you're having fun,' Mom said.

'Oh, I am.'

What a liar I was becoming. And the lies were only just starting...

On Tuesday, the store phone rang. Steve answered. There were no customers. He put the phone on speaker.

I heard Matthew's voice from across the store. I would have known it anywhere. I closed my eyes for a moment. Then I went closer to the phone.

I heard him say, 'I'm calling to order the mattress I looked at in your shop a few days ago. That nice young woman helped me ... Isabel, is that right?'

He was taking this whole role-playing thing to a new level.

Steve gave me a thumbs up sign. He switched the phone off speaker, put on earphones and began typing into the computer. Numbers came up on screens that dissolved into other screens.

Steve said, 'Sure thing. You'll have it tomorrow. Thanks for doing business with Doctor Sleep. Yes, certainly, I'll tell her. Goodbye.'

'Tell her what?' I said.

'Nothing,' said Steve. 'I can't remember.'

I could have tortured him to find out. Steve walked over to me, so close he was practically standing on my toes. I shrank away.

'Good work, Isabel,' he said. 'That was your friend from last week. He went for the Super Deluxe. He said that the floor model would do, if that was all we had. I think the guy has the hots for you. Otherwise it doesn't make sense. Guy like that should have an assistant ordering for him, he doesn't do shit like that himself. You know what I think? I think the guy was hoping you'd answer the phone. I'll bet you would have liked to talk to him, too.'

I wanted to smack him. But he was right. Why wouldn't Matthew text me? Maybe he lost my number and this was the only way he could reach me? Maybe that was my last chance. I would never get another.

Steve said, 'Am I right? Huh? Am I right about you and

that guy? Something ... funny? As in, funny business? I definitely got that vibe when I walked into the store that day he was here.'

That Steve noticed made me blush, and it made me strangely happy. It was all I could do not to ask what made him think that something *funny* was going on. I liked having evidence that whatever happened between me and Matthew wasn't entirely in my imagination.

I said, 'I have no idea what you're talking about, Steve. Maybe the guy just wanted to buy a mattress. Maybe he's got more money than he knows what to do with.'

Who was I angry at? Steve? Matthew? What had Matthew done except play a fun little game and leave me more unhappy than I was before I met him? It's not like I hadn't done the same thing to countless guys before him.

'Whatever,' said Steve. 'And FYI ... *No one* has more money than he knows what to do with. People with that much money know what do with it.'

'I wouldn't know,' I said.

'I don't suppose you would,' Steve said.

The next day the guys from the trucking company took away the mattress. They carried it away ... bye bye.

It left a giant gap on the sales floor. Steve let the spot stay empty for a while, to remind himself of the amazing deal that he (already taking credit) had made. I couldn't stand to look at the bare space, the only evidence of my hot, five-minute scene with The Handsome Customer. Now I

40

would grow old and sell mattresses until I retired and died.

I looked up Matthew's order on the store computer. There was no name, just an address in Brooklyn Heights, a charge to an Amex card listed to the Prairie Foundation and a note (in Steve's writing) that said, Contact assistant.

The next day the phone rang. I knew it was for me before Steve said, 'Isabel?' He put his hand over the receiver. 'It's your rich boyfriend.'

Somehow, I'd known who it was. My friends never called on the store phone. None of them had that number. My mom would have called on my cell.

'Isabel, it's me.'

I didn't have to ask who *me* was. I couldn't speak. Or breathe.

He said, 'The mattress is set up. I'm wondering if you would be willing to come over to check out the *feng shui*. I would hate for it to face in the wrong direction.' He laughed, meaning it was a joke and not a joke. The *feng shui* line was a joke. But my going to his place wasn't. After all, we had a history. We were more than friends.

'I could do that,' I said.

'Isabel?' he said. I loved the way he said my name. 'Excuse me. I think we may have a bad connection.'

'I could do that,' I repeated. Maybe I'd been whispering, or maybe he wanted to make me say it again. Our connection was fine.

I felt something warm and moist and unpleasant on the back of my neck. Only then did I realize how close Steve was standing.

'When?' I said. 'Where?'

'Is tomorrow evening too soon?'

I should have said, *yes, way too soon*. I should have invented dates I couldn't break. A boyfriend I was seeing. But what if this was my last chance? I wasn't busy tomorrow evening. If I were, I would have cancelled, no matter what it was.

'Tomorrow evening would be fine,' I said.

'What time do you get off work?'

'Six?' Why did it come out as a question? Why was I asking *him*? I could probably leave any time I wanted if I told Steve where I was going. But the following day, Steve might try to make me tell him everything we did.

'Perfect. Come straight here,' Matthew said. 'We can watch the sunset.'

'Great,' I said. 'Can you text me the address? On my cell.'

'No need for that,' he said. 'It's in the system at your store.'

Suddenly, it was as if I heard Mom's voice. Put the phone down. Don't talk to this man again. Don't go there tomorrow night.

Sorry, Mom, I thought. I have no choice. After my dad's death, my mom never remarried or even (as far as I knew) dated. So there was a lot my mother didn't know about the modern world. Anyway, I wouldn't have listened if she had been standing beside me. The desire made everyone else disappear.

When I hung up the phone, Steve said, 'You're not supposed to get personal calls on the store phone.'

I said, 'This was business, Steve.'

I'd never felt that I had the power to make Steve step back. Yet now something—some new note—in my voice made him take a big step backward. Something in me had changed just from talking to Matthew.

I should have taken that as a warning, a hint of changes to come.

I couldn't sleep all night. I obsessed over what to wear. Sexy but not so sexy that it would look weird in the store—and send the wrong message, first to Steve and then to Matthew. But what message was too sexy after what I did on the mattress?

I bought new underwear, black lace with a slim red ribbon threaded through the bra and panties. I wore a short denim skirt and a black T-shirt. I carried a jacket, just in case. The weather seemed changeable, low clouds, wind. Stormy weather. I went light on the make-up. At the end of the day, I could put on more in the broom closet that Steve called 'the staff lounge.'

'You look nice,' said Steve, when I got to work. 'Nicer than usual. Going somewhere?'

I didn't answer. He knew.

Maybe I should have dressed up every day. Business was booming, for a change. There had been a bedbug scare in the NYU dorms, and the place was jammed with kids using their parents' credit cards to (they hoped, ha ha) fix the problem. They bought the cheapest mattresses, but so what? In Steve's words, we were 'moving product.' I liked the college kids, mostly. Their needs were simple. Their purchasing decisions were all about price. Not one of them wanted to act like a jerk trying out a mattress while a stranger (me) watched. Fine, they said. I'll take it.

Steve felt good about the day, and when I asked if I could leave early, he said sure, if I was willing to come in early a couple of mornings next week and open up. That sounded fair to me. I would have agreed to anything.

I redid my makeup. And when Steve was in the toilet, I put on high heels and skittered out of the store.

I spent a big chunk of that week's paycheck on the cab fare to Matthew's apartment in Brooklyn Heights. Google Maps said that it was blocks from the station, and my heels were too high to walk that far. Besides, I was eager to get there.

I had four condoms in my purse, just in case. I was a nice Midwestern girl, but not *that* nice. Hey, this was New York, 2016.

From all the way down the block I knew which building was his: the luxury high-rise designed by a famous architect. There had been a battle between the Landmarks Commission vs. the architect and the developers. The outcome—who was going to win—was never in doubt. The structure was a twenty-four story middle finger raised to the city.

That was where Matthew lived. The house of the neighborhood destroyers. Though (to be honest) I knew that I would live there too if someone offered me an apartment.

The lobby reception desk was raised, like a throne. Seeing it from below added to the height and size and heft of the two enormous doormen, both in olive green uniforms. What if they asked me for Matthew's last name? I didn't even know it.

I gave them the apartment number. Could they ring Penthouse Three, please? I was asking them to ring someone whose name I didn't know.

'And you are?'

'Isabel,' I said. 'Isabel Archer.' I hardly recognized my own name. It sounded like two nonsense words. What did it even mean? Part of me had left my body. The nice Isabel, the cautious one, was trying to understand why this reckless new Isabel was here—doing this.

The doorman hung up the house phone. 'Go on up,' he said. 'This elevator goes as far as the tenth floor, where there's another desk for our premier floors. They'll tell you what to do from there.'

A double layer of doormen.

The elevator whisked me through a column of air and let me off ten floors up, where a second pair of doormen directed me toward another elevator. I pressed PH3. This elevator was glass on all sides, so I could watch the roof-tops of Brooklyn fall away beneath me.

There was only one apartment on the floor. I rang the bell.

A middle-aged housekeeper opened the door and took my jacket.

She said, 'The Señor is out on the terrace.' Did I want a cocktail? Absolutely. *Bueno*. Already poured. A young man, also Hispanic, also friendly, brought me a martini glass on a tray. Balancing the glass—filled to the brim with orange-golden liquid—I followed the maid through a huge living room that looked like a modern art museum, with white couches, white marble floors, walls whose perfect whiteness was defiled only by the violent splashy energy of the large abstract paintings. Was that a real de Kooning?

The glass wall to the terrace was open. The Customer stood with his back to us, looking out over the edge. I gulped down half my drink.

'Thank you, Maria,' he told the maid, without turning around.

The maid—Maria—asked me, 'Are you all right, Señora?' I wondered how many girls she'd watched stop dead in their tracks, barely able to move.

He didn't turn around or acknowledge me in any way. I went and stood beside him. He was wearing jeans and a crisp white shirt, open at the neck. He looked even more handsome than he had at the store. I grasped the edge of the low brick wall and hung on. The view made me dizzy, or maybe it was being near him. Or just possibly it was the drink. It was all very confusing, but I loved it. I loved the last rays of daylight twinkling in the windows, the giant red ball that was the sun bouncing on the water.

Now I knew what it meant to feel like you owned the city. The Manhattan skyline spread out before us, lay at our feet, begging us, its rulers, to tell it what to do. Though maybe I was confused again. Maybe that was how *I* felt. Like a queen.

I took another sip of the cocktail. It was intensely delicious. Tequila, I thought. Edge of chili, edge of something fruity but tart.

'Hibiscus flower,' The Customer said.

The strong drink went straight to my head, especially since I'd skipped lunch. I'd been too nervous to eat. But now I kept drinking till it was done. I'd never tasted anything so amazing. I felt tipsy, terrified, and happy.

The sun dipped into the river. Matthew moved closer to me, and like a reflex or afterthought, as if he wasn't paying attention, he rested one hand on my ass.

'Lovely,' he said. 'No?'

'Yes,' was all I could say. But what was I agreeing to?

The loveliness of the sunset, or the lovely warmth of his hand?

'Come take a look at the bed.'

He smiled as he stepped back and let me precede him into the apartment. He took my arm and guided me down a long corridor lined with small vitrines, cut into the wall, displaying classical Greek and Egyptian statuettes. I paused in front of a figure of a human with a dog's head.

'Anubis,' he said. 'The lord of the dead and the underworld.'

I wanted to say I'd been reading poems about the underworld, but I was afraid of sounding pretentious. And I'd dated enough to know that too much anxious chit-chat could kill the sexual buzz. And there was plenty of buzz.

The bedroom was as stylish as the rest of the apartment. There were windows on three sides, so it seemed to be perched, like an eagle's nest, above the city below. Could you have sex in a room like this without thinking about all the strangers who might be watching? Or maybe that would be part of the fun, the excitement.

Was it really *me* thinking that? I was shy about my body. I'd always preferred to have sex with the lights out. But now I was ready to do it any way, anywhere...

In the center of the room was the bed: the mattress from our store. Not that I would have recognized its organic cotton and hand-knotted tufts covered by a simple but beautiful midnight-blue silk bedspread and a half dozen matching throw pillows. Was he married? Would a single guy have a bed like that?

Maybe this was how rich men lived, men who never made their own beds. It shamed me to think of my bed at home, a tangle of rumpled sheets and blankets piled with books and, right now, with the entire contents of my closet, clothes I'd tried on for this evening.

Why had I bothered? I could read his mind, sort of. And I had the definite sense that he wasn't getting ready to throw me down on the mattress. He wasn't even going to ask me to repeat what I'd done in the store. We stood there in the doorway, looking into the room. He was still holding my arm.

He said, 'Do I have to have it moved?'

'What?' I said.

'The *feng shui*,' he reminded me. 'Does it work?'

*Was* he serious? I didn't know him well enough to ask. I was ready to have sex with him, but I wasn't comfortable enough to find out if he was joking.

From a strict *feng shui* point of view, the bed should have been diagonal to the door, which it wasn't. But I wasn't going to say that. There was really no place else in the room that the bed could go.

'It's fine,' I said. 'Perfect.' If he had bad luck, or got sick, or developed insomnia, it would be my fault. Fine. Anyhow, I didn't even believe in *feng shui*. It was just a way to sell mattresses.

He said, 'That's odd ... I had the impression that the bed was supposed to be diagonal to the door and facing the other direction.'

My face burned with shame. 'Probably,' I said. 'That's probably right...' Then why had he even asked me?

'But I think I'm going to leave it where it is,' he said. 'Live dangerously, right?'

'Right!' I said. 'That's right.'

Standing beside me, he reached around and put his hand under my T-shirt, on my bare skin, on my back, just above my waist. My breathing quickened. It didn't take much. He could feel it.

'What now?' I said. It was up to him. I would do whatever he wanted.

He took his hand out from under my shirt.

He said, 'Thank you, that's great. I can't tell you how grateful I am.'

'But...' I couldn't help myself. Something could still happen.

Or did I fail some sort of test when I'd lied about *feng shui*?

Only later I would learn that I'd *passed* the test when I lied.

He said, 'I'm looking forward to getting to know you better, Isabel.'

Was he trying to make me beg? Maybe I would have, if I could have figured out how to beg a man for sex without humiliating myself. I was ready to humiliate myself, but I didn't believe that it would work.

'Could I ask you a question?' I said.

'Ask me anything,' he replied. But I could feel him tense. What did he not want me to ask? What was he hiding?

'Well. I suppose we might call this our second date. And you haven't confessed to any other names. But what's your last name?' I said. 'I was terrified one of the doormen would ask me for it on the way up tonight.'

He laughed. 'I assumed you knew.'

'I don't,' I said.

'Well, I'm Matthew,' he said. 'Matthew Frazier.'

'Pleased to meet you, Mr Frazier,' I said, and stuck out my hand.

He looked down at my hand but didn't take it. My arm dropped back to my side.

He guided me back down the hall and through the living room towards the front door. Halfway there, he handed me on to Maria, who gave me my jacket and opened the door.

'Thank you,' she said. 'Goodbye.'

I stood outside the door in the hall for a long time, though I was pretty sure that I was being watched on a security camera. Let them watch. I couldn't move. Why had The Customer—Matthew—brought me there? What did he want from me? Why had he even called? He couldn't have meant that he cared about the *feng shui*. And then when he caught me in a lie ... I didn't know him well enough to know if my tiny white lie had been a deal breaker.

Well, I told myself, I would be better off if the whole thing ended right here. I'm a truthful person. I don't need a relationship with a man I'd started lying to, even before I had met him.

Over the next few days, even Steve could tell that something was making me miserable. He seemed weirdly pleased about it. Luke and Marcy treated me like a person who had a life-threatening disease but who didn't want to discuss it.

When Marcy and Luke and I met at Cielito Lindo at our usual time on Sunday, Marcy made sure that my drinks from the bar were double strength and doubly delicious. But that only reminded me of the cocktail I'd drank at Matthew's apartment. Nothing would ever taste that wonderful again. Nothing else would ever get me high in that same way. I'd been offered magic, and I'd lied and spoiled everything. I should have told him to move the bed. Maybe I'd be *in* that bed right now. Did he ever think of me when he lay on the mattress?

One night, after not having heard from him for days and not having thought of anything else, I dreamed I gave him a present. It wasn't clear in the dream, what the present was, but I woke up remembering his smile, how in the dream he'd hugged me, how warm and happy I felt.

I thought: It's a sign. I'll send him something. A little thank you present. Thanks for the lovely drink. Thanks for buying the (I wouldn't need to say 'most expensive') mattress. Businesses sent thank you gifts all the time. They showed their appreciation. That's how you built customer loyalty, which was something Steve talked a lot about, though no one had ever bought anything from us twice. So what would customer loyalty have meant?

But what could I give The Customer? *Matthew*? What did a man like that need? How could I base my decision on a coffee shop exchange, a sex game in the store, and a chaste drink on the terrace? And a dream I only half remembered.

Every day, on the walk from the subway to Doctor Sleep, I looked in every window. I was shopping for The Customer. For Matthew. But nothing seemed right.

Then one warm afternoon—on my lunch break—I was going to meet Luke for a quick picnic in Tompkins Square Park. I passed this funny little store, part joke shop/part kids shop, the kind of place you hardly see anymore in New York except in the East Village. In the window was one of those Mexican card games, Loteria, like bingo but with pictures, beautiful old paintings of the world, the sun, the musician, the jug, the cactus, the tree, the heart— and words in Spanish on the card and the board.

The image that caught my eye was *El Melon*. A cantaloupe, sliced open, pinkish orange, juicy and full of seeds. A picture of a cantaloupe. A picture of sex.

I bought the set, and sent the card to Matthew's penthouse, in an envelope addressed to Matthew Frazier. I hoped that he would open it himself, rather than the assistant he'd listed on his sales receipt—whom I'd never met—or the housekeeper.

Nothing happened. No reply. I imagined him throwing my card in the trash. What a stupid gift I'd chosen. Why would a hot rich guy who sipped cocktails on the terrace want a funky old picture of a cantaloupe?

A week later the package came back to me. The stamp on the slightly battered envelope said that no one by that name lived at that address. Why had he done that? Did he not want to hear from me? Why had he gone so far as to pretend he didn't live there?

Meanwhile, I couldn't stop thinking about Matthew. His hands, his body, the way he smiled at me from across the table at the coffee shop, the sound of his voice when I'd lay on the mattress at the store. I got interested in sex—obsessed, you could say— in a way I'd never been before.

Now, when Steve went out to do whatever he did at lunch, I watched porn on my computer. I'd found a little clip in which a guy who looks like Matthew is interviewing a girl for a job and he somehow persuades her (I watched it without sound) to have sex on his desk in many different positions. I'd come every time I thought about Matthew's voice saying, 'Lie down. Please. Let me see.'

# Matthew

Sooner or later everyone wants a do-over. Sooner rather than later, everyone reaches a point when they say, Okay, guys, roll it back. Let's try something else. Begin again. Give it another ending.

Especially if you are like me. If your life, like mine, took a turn for the worse early on, and nothing can get you back to that place you were before the bad thing happened.

I'd had money and comfort, high hopes. All the advantages, as they say. I'd grown up on the South shore, south of Boston. In a big house near the water—not right on the beach, but close enough so I could hear the ocean from my bedroom.

I'd made a mistake. I'd fallen. I wanted to climb back up. I longed for it like some people long for their childhood home.

My childhood home was comfortable. My dad was a bank executive and amateur photographer. He took lots of arty shots of my beautiful mother, who didn't work, and who every so often had to be sent away for mysterious reasons. Only later (after both my parents died) did I figure out that Mother had a little problem with alcohol and pills and went, occasionally, into rehab.

The summer before I was supposed to go to college, my younger brother Ansel and I stole our neighbor's car. Not just any car. A Mercedes convertible. Our neighbor didn't deserve a car like that. Not just any neighbor. Doctor Graves. Graves was his actual name, I always said when I told this story. The Doc was a total dick. He'd called the cops on us, twice, when my brother and I accidentally drove over the edge of his lawn. What was his problem? We were kids, just learning to drive.

To get up the nerve, my brother and I got trashed on some candy-sweet alcohol drink concocted selectively from the back of our parents' liquor cabinet. We cut holes in tube socks and put them over our heads and told Doctor Graves we had a gun. He knew we were the boys next door, but the papers were full of rich suburban psycho teens committing murders. He could see the headline about the killer prep school boys. How did he know we weren't like that? He handed over the keys.

I won't pretend it didn't feel great, taking the car out on the highway. We knew the back roads better than the cops. We had a big head start. We parked near the beach. My brother leaned down and felt under the back of his seat and said, 'Holy shit. Why does Doctor Graves have a gun? What does he need a hand gun for?' Maybe the doctor thought he needed a hand gun to protect his Mercedes from punks like us.

Even drunk, I was the big brother. I grabbed the gun from Ansel. The gun went off. The bullet grazed my brother's hand. A scratch. I freaked and called 911. Ambulances and cop cars came screaming up to where we were parked. It must have looked really bad, there was so much blood all over the front seat.

We both knew that it was an accident. Ansel made a complete recovery, with only some minor nerve damage in that hand.

But he hasn't spoken to me in the fifteen years since the accident. Maybe he saw something in my eyes when the shooting happened. Maybe he knew that I always believed our parents loved him more.

Ansel has been the family success, the success I was supposed to be. Or maybe he was always the one who was supposed to be successful. Last I heard, he's an architect, with an extremely profitable residential practice on Eastern Long Island. A cousin who gets in touch with me every couple of years (last time he was tracing some kind of genealogy thing) told me that Ansel had had a few serious relationships, but he'd never married. No wife, no kids. You had to wonder why what that was—maybe because Mom and Dad provided such an uninspiring example of marital bliss.

Anyhow, when we had our little ... accident, I fell on my sword for my brother. My dad and mom had excellent lawyers who pleaded the grand larceny charge down to probation, a huge fine, and a class D felony on my permanent record. The college counselor at St. Andrews wasn't thrilled about being bothered in the middle of summer vacation, just when he thought the whole college mess was sorted out. He called Dartmouth, where I was headed, to ask if a felony conviction would be a problem. Yes, in fact, it would be a problem. A gigantic problem.

That was the start of the slide. My friends went to college. Mom and Dad suggested community college, the only place that would take me, but I decided to move to New York and live on my own in the world's most expensive city, which meant a counter job in a gourmet take-out fried chicken stand and a walk up on a pre-gentrified block in Crown Heights. I would really have gone under if I hadn't lucked into a series of brief affairs with generous older women.

A few years later, Ansel was the one who got to go to Dartmouth. Having a bad boy as an older brother wasn't a stain on *his* permanent record.

My high school friends graduated from good schools, got jobs on Wall Street. Against all odds, we stayed friends.

One Friday night those same friends and I were drinking at a downtown dive bar we liked, despite the bar's newly acquired hipster chic. Even though a few of the guys had girlfriends and were moving on in the direction of separate, grown-up lives, our partying had gotten more intense— more desperate, maybe—now that we sensed that our stay-out-all-night years might be drawing to a close.

That night we saw, at a table across the bar, Val Morton. We looked and tried not to look, and we looked again. Was it or wasn't it him? Those clean sharp features, that cool confidence, that authority, those looks—all pretty impressive in a man pushing sixty—were hard to mistake. But still... When we finally decided that it was him, and not someone else who looked like him, we felt that charge in the air, that fizzy vibe, the way that someone famous changes the atmosphere in a room.

It was Valentine Morton, the craggy movie star turned politician turned one-term Governor of New York, defeated in a run for re-election after the newspapers broke the story of how Val Morton and his wife were never in Albany. They stayed there at most four days a month.

At the table with Val and a few guys around my age was Val's wife Heidi, a tall former supermodel who had spent her twenties watching her rock star boyfriends snort coke and destroy hotel rooms. Then she grew up, scaled back on the runway appearances, appeared in a couple of straight-to-video movies, married Val, and settled down. She'd traded the thrill of watching flat screens fly out of hotel windows for the comfort (and the thrill) of traveling the world in Val Morton's private jet.

What did the Mortons do now? In the past few years, Val had become a high-profile Manhattan real estate developer. His name appeared quite often in the papers, mostly in connection with some battle that his real estate development company (named The Prairie Foundation, as if it were some public-interest group dedicated to helping Midwestern farmers) was waging with the city or the Landmarks Commission or the residents of the neighborhoods which his projects were about the destroy. For some time, he'd been fighting to develop a huge stretch of the waterfront in Long Island City, overlooking the Manhattan skyline. A lot of people hated Val Morton, a lot of people tried to stop him, but he always won. The Prairie Foundation had more than enough lawyers, time and money to beat the local block associations. And Val seemed to enjoy these fights; that is, he enjoyed winning.

When Val wasn't too busy razing brownstones or throwing a block of mom and pop stores out of business, he and Heidi went to parties. They appeared in *People* and the other celebrity magazines. If you got your hair cut or went to the supermarket, you saw Val and Heidi hanging out with Hollywood stars and the Clintons. The Prairie Foundation did give to some worthy liberal causes: literacy, the public library, prisoners' rights, rebuilding disaster sites. Val still acted in films every few years, mostly sequels to pictures he'd made when he was young. It didn't matter if the films did well or not. He had lifetime celeb-rity status. Lifetime celebrity money.

The dive bar got warmer and brighter. Across the table from Val, who was playing to his entourage of young guys in suits, Heidi sat checking her phone and grabbing waiters who passed by, pulling them down to whisper drink orders in their ears.

Val was doing all the talking. His boys all laughed explosively at everything he said.

Meanwhile Val kept looking over at me, the way a girl would look at you in a bar. Was he gay? You heard that rumor about every actor, but I hadn't heard it about him. I'd been cruised by guys before, but this didn't feel like that.

My friend Simon said, 'I think the governor likes you, Matthew.'

'Ex-governor,' I said.

One of our guys swung by Val's table en route to the men's room and came back and said, *Yeah, definitely him*.

Duh. No one else looked like him: the aging, handsome, slightly debauched Hollywood warrior. His eyes kept tracking to me.

Fine with me. I was straight. I'd had two serious girl-friends and lost count of the not-so-serious ones. I'd slept with all my female friends. They'd slept with each other's boyfriends.

But hey, I'm a practical guy. Open-minded. Finding

an aging sugar daddy before I got too old seemed better than taking orders at Fries and Thighs. I didn't much want to get fucked in the ass, but we could work around that.

Val Morton was handsome and rich.

I went and stood by his table. He watched me walk across the room.

I said, 'Mr Morton, I'm sorry to bother you, and I know how creepy it is to say I'm your number one fan, but...' My voice trailed off.

I laughed. He didn't. He'd heard it before. There was nothing to do but go on. He was listening.

'I'm a huge fan. I've seen all your films. I voted for you for governor.' That last part wasn't true. I hadn't voted in that election.

'Guys, give us a minute.' His posse rose obediently and left. He put one hand on Heidi's arm, meaning *stay*. She was staying anyhow. She was poring over the cocktail menu. She didn't even look at me.

He motioned for me to sit down but not get *too* comfortable.

He said, 'Do you know that *sorry* was the fourth word out of your mouth? Don't start off apologizing, okay? Not to me, not to anyone.'

'Okay,' I said. 'Sorry.' I laughed. He didn't. He'd heard that before too.

'Valentine Morton.' He put out his hand.

'Walker Frazier,' I said.

'What kind of parents name their kid Walker?'

'A photography fan and his bullied wife,' I said. He watched me deciding not to ask what kind of parents name their son Valentine.

'Guess what lovers' holiday in February I was born on,' Val said, answering my unspoken question for me. 'So what do your friends call you? Walk?'

'Matthew. My middle name. My friends call me Matthew,' I said.

'Ah, right,' said Val. 'The friends. I can see them from here. So let me describe your evening to you ... Matthew. You're going to drink quite a bit more than your friends, and when someone pays, or when they split the bill, you're not going to be putting your credit card in with the rest. Am I correct? In the ballpark, maybe?'

'More or less in the ballpark.' *Fuck you*, I thought.

'More,' he said. 'More than less. But that's not a problem. For me. From my point of view, it's the opposite of a problem. It's actually an advantage. I'm looking for someone like you.'

'To do what?' Somehow I could tell that this was about business, not sex. If it was a sex thing, Heidi would at least have checked me out.

'What do you think I want you to do?' he said. 'Blow me? Christ. Don't flatter yourself. You think you're hotter than Heidi?'

64

At the sound of her name, Heidi looked up, then went back to the cocktail menu.

'To work for me. To do stuff.'

'Stuff?'

'A *range* of stuff,' he said. 'For which you'll get paid in cash, if I may. No boring tedious social security and tax deductions. No problem. And no record of your having worked for me. At the end of the day, should we decide to part company, no fulsome recommendation letter. No bright spot on your CV. How does that sound?'

It sounded great, but I kept waiting for more ... for some sense of the weird 'stuff' he would be paying me to do.

He said, 'What I mean is, how does a hundred and fifty grand a year sound?'

'Amazing,' I said, taken aback. 'But ... why me? You've never met me before. You know nothing about me.'

'I saw you and your friends. You're the hungriest guy at that table.'

He motioned for his entourage to come back. He told me to give my contact information to a tall, gym-buffed guy in a pale gray suit who typed it, lightning fast, into his phone.

'My office will contact you,' Morton said. 'Have a fun evening.'

I went back to my table.

The guys said, 'What was *that* about?'

I said, 'I was just telling him how much I liked his films.'

My interview with Val Morton was two days away. I spent them on the internet. I read the puff pieces about the good works that the Prairie Foundation was doing, and some shorter pieces, mostly from political sites that weighed the fact that Val Morton was helping to ruin New York City against the fact that he'd built houses in the 9th ward after Hurricane Katrina.

I read about his fights with the Landmarks Commission and other city agencies regarding his plans to turn some of Manhattan's oldest, most beautiful structures—the counting house off the Battery, a hall at Ellis Island—into condos. It was Val Morton's position that he would preserve these places, which the cash-strapped city was letting decay.

Of course, I wondered why Val was hiring me. The way he'd said *hungry* scared me, partly because it was true. What had he meant by *stuff*? If the job wasn't about sex, then what was it? To be his hired goon. To go to meetings and threaten the neighborhood associations. To make it clear that the sweet little old lady who said that her river view was being blocked by Val's condo would come to wish she'd shut up and let Val do whatever he wanted.

I read the details of how his building on the waterfront in Brooklyn Heights had involved a battle. About how his co-op board was up in arms about Val's plans to combine two Upper East Side apartments in order to double the size of the prewar Park Avenue palace in which he and Heidi lived. And about the ongoing war over his plans to take over Long Island City.

At the Prairie Foundation office, on the thirty-sixth floor of a high-rise in Tribeca, I had to run through a gauntlet of security guards, receptionists and secretaries before one of them finally gave me a form to fill out. There were several dozen questions, mostly having to do with my education, my health, my background, my previous employment.

It was just the kind of thing that made me conscious of how dismal my resume was. I worked in a fried chicken place! At the end, the form asked if I had a criminal record. I considered lying. Did one mistake I'd made as a teenager mean that I was supposed to spend my whole life asking, 'Will that be light meat or dark?' But something about my talk with Val Morton made me think this might be the rare case: a straight job for which a sketchy history would actually count in my favor.

Val didn't bother seeing me. A secretary said, 'Oh, Mr Walker, you're hired.'

'Matthew,' I said. 'Matthew Frazier.'

'Yes,' she said. 'You can start Monday.'

* * *

The job was never boring, though I didn't always know what I was doing or why. I got paid enough to rent a nice one-bedroom apartment near Central Park, where I ran either before or after I went to work. I didn't ask a lot of questions. I found out the answers later, if I found out at all. Sometimes I felt like a high level, well-paid errand boy. Once I hand-delivered a laptop to a lawyer's office in Kansas City. It was assumed that I wouldn't look at what was on it. I was sort of like Val's personal assistant, though (at least I told myself) the work was a little more challenging and demanding than that. I never understood the black and white rules for being a 'good guy.' I liked working for Val because for Val—everything is grey.

I managed Val and Heidi's apartments in Brooklyn Heights and on the Upper East Side, so he and Heidi could stay wherever was closer to where they were spending the evening. I worked with Val's decorator, Charisse, to fix up the Brooklyn Heights condo.

Charisse and I trusted each other. When I told her that Val needed a new mattress, even though he already had one, she let me pick it out.

The real explanation was that I had found Isabel, and she was working in the mattress store.

But that was a secret between Val and me. Charisse didn't have to know that.

\* \* \*

One day, not long after I went to work for him, Val Morton called me up to his office. He always sat in front of a vast, explosion-proof picture window so that the Statue of Liberty seemed to float in the air behind him. He always gave everyone a moment to be wowed by the view. Then he got down to business.

'I need you to do something that you may not understand, at least at first. But it has to be done. There's something I need. You will need a partner. An accomplice, if you will. A woman. A young woman. Pretty but not too pretty. Sexy but not too sexy. Not ridiculous. A smart girl who isn't crazy but who will do *anything* you say. The Bonnie to your Clyde. The Sissy Spacek character to the Charlie Sheen character. Dude, relax. I'm joking. I'm not asking you to rob banks or commit serial murders.'

I looked over his shoulder at a helicopter hovering over the Hudson.

'Does this involve sex?'

'Not with me,' Val said. 'I don't even want to watch. I've got Heidi. Remember?'

As far as I knew, Val and Heidi were more or less happily married. A few days before, Val had taken me to lunch at Michael's. He'd ordered the Cobb salad, as always.

He said, 'I don't know if you know this, Matthew, but I've been married three times. I must believe in the institution. I've got four kids, two from each previous marriage. Everybody gets along, loves everyone else. I'd say okay to one more kid, but that's not on Heidi's agenda. So at the moment we're good.' He knocked lightly on the table and gave me a version of the smile that had made him a movie star.

Now, in his office, Val said, 'Don't be an asshole, Matthew. This is not about the porn film of your dreams. Sex with this … accomplice would be your call. Sex, I need hardly point out, is one of the most reliable forms of mind control. Especially useful with young women.'

It was an odd thing for an older guy—my boss—to say. Was he saying that Heidi was his personal mind control sex slave? I'd assumed their connection was about Morton's money and power. If power was the greatest aphrodisiac, money and real estate were right up there along with it.

'That's not very feminist,' I said. 'Very retro.'

'Mea culpa,' said Morton 'Please. Take it easy. This is supposed to be fun. You're getting paid to seduce a pretty girl of your choice. Thank me. There's no rush. Let's give it to the end of the fall. Find the right girl. Get her ready. Maybe hold off on fucking her. Make her wait for it. Make her beg. Keep me posted. Let me know how it's going. Tell me when she's ready to do what we need. What I need. Then I'll tell you what comes next.'

Actually, it was intriguing. What a cool assignment. All I had to do was find a girl who would do anything I said. I could have sex with her if I wanted to, but I didn't have to. And it would be fun to make her wait. Val was right. I was getting paid for what most guys would pay to do. And somehow, in a funny way, that qualified me to do it. It was a job. Compared to the jobs that were out there, this was beyond sweet. I'd be nice to the girl, court her, tease her a little. She'd never have to be the wiser. And— at least as far as I knew—no one would get hurt.

I felt a little guilty, not telling a woman the truth, but, let's face it, I'd done it before. It was something guys did all the time, even when they were married. *Especially* then.

I'd had several relationships. They always ended badly. Freud said, *what do women want?* I could have told him: Whatever they want, it's more than you want to give.

Val Morton made it a challenge. An assignment. I began to look at women in a different way. A more ... specialized way. More ... practical.

Dating apps made it too easy. I went on Bumble—where sweet girls who want to feel empowered by doing all the work go to meet guys who supposedly want more than one fun night. Maybe for the first time ever, I knew what I was looking for. And now all I would have to do is swipe right and wait for her to make the first move. That was how I found her.

*Isabel.*

Later, *too late*, I asked myself: Why her? I never figured it out. I guess people just know things about each other.

They pick things up on their radar. They know how far a person will go.

I don't know how I knew about Isabel, but I did. Even when I thought her name was Riley.

That was an added twist—something that made her even more perfect, for some reason.

Right away I could feel it between us. The heat. When she walked into the coffee shop and told me about her little game. When she said yes to my own game. When I asked her to lie down on the overpriced mattress she was pretending to sell me. Well, good for her. It was pure inspiration. It was fun, and it was hot. By the time I left the mattress store, I knew I had found my accomplice, my partner in crime. My creature.

Who knows how far I would have gone if her creepy boss hadn't shown up at the store? Or maybe we'd gone far enough. For the moment.

That night, alone in my bed, I thought about her and jerked off. I hoped she was doing the same. I would have liked to call her the very next day. But I knew better. I made her—and myself—wait.

# Isabel

One slow morning at work, I looked up from my book and saw a white business envelope on the floor, just inside the door. I jumped up to get it before Steve did. I had a feeling about it.

The thick, expensive, cream-colored envelope was addressed to me. Inside was a printed invitation, the letters embossed in an elegant, old-fashioned cursive.

*You are cordially invited for cocktails at the home of Valentine and Heidi Morton.*

Val and Heidi Morton? Me? Why was my name on the envelope? Someone must have made a mistake.

There was something else in the envelope. I reached in and pulled out a Loteria card. *El Mundo*. The world. A picture of the world. On the back it said, in neat block letters, *I'll meet you there at seven*. It couldn't have been a coincidence. I knew it was from Matthew. But why had my own letter with the melon card come back to me? Had he opened the envelope and resealed it and returned it to

Carrie Blake

the postman? Why would someone do something like that?

I would find out, or I wouldn't. I was meeting Matthew at a party at the Upper East Side apartment of Val and Heidi Morton.

What did you wear to a fancy uptown Upper East Side cocktail party when you were a failed actress and mattress professional living over a toxic dump site in Greenpoint? I went to one of the last vintage clothing shops in the East Village and asked Melinda, who'd owned the store for years, what to wear to a cocktail party given by (I didn't want to name drop) a famous older celebrity actor and politician on the Upper East Side.

'Oh,' she said. 'Val Morton.'

'How do you know?'

'People have been coming in all week looking for something to wear to that party. You'd think the guests would be shopping at Bergdorf, but everyone seems to want vintage Balenciaga or Chanel. Okay. Let's see. What can you afford?'

*Nothing* was the truth. But I'd gotten an advance from Steve.

I spent all my money on the perfect little black dress from the Sixties that made me look so pretty that even I relaxed. A little.

'Fabulous,' said Melinda. 'Anyhow, it hardly matters. You'll be a good ten years younger than anyone there.

Fresh blood at the vampire party.'

I called in sick (Steve was definitely not happy about it) and spent the whole day getting ready. I watched the porn clip on my laptop, the one with the guy that looked like Matthew. I came when he was doing the interview and had the prospective secretary bent over the desk. I wanted to be satisfied before I went, at least sexually. It might help me act and react with more common sense and control than I'd had so far around Matthew.

I took Lyft from Brooklyn to the Upper East Side, though by this point I *really* couldn't afford it. I'd figure something out before the credit card bill came and started accumulating massive amounts of interest. Well, maybe, just maybe, I wouldn't have to pay for a car home. Maybe I would be going home with Matthew...

Three girls—around my age, dressed sort of like me, prettier than me, with better jobs than me—stood in the lobby with clipboards. It seemed impossible that my name could be on their list. But it was. One of them took my coat and gave me a coat claim ticket.

The door was open, and everything I could see inside the apartment shone—like gold, like glass, like perfect skin and hair and teeth. There were windows everywhere, and the starry lights of the city glittered in the dark sky. I hesitated in the doorway. Just walking into that room seemed like the hardest thing I would ever have to do.

The rooms were vast, the walls covered with brocade silk and gilt and mirrors. It looked more like the reception room of a French king's palace than the living room of a former movie star and fashion model. I tried not to think about my apartment, how small it was, how dark. It hurt to picture what this place looked and felt like in the mornings when Val and Heidi Morton could hold their coffee cups and drift—slowly, leisurely—from room to sunny room.

Melinda was right; not counting the girls with the clipboards, I was the youngest woman at the party by ten or fifteen years. Many of the women were beautiful, and they looked as if they spent every spare minute and dollar on that beauty. But I had the skin, the bounce, and underneath my little black dress, pretty perfect breasts. No spending required. The men looked at me, even the ones trying not to look, even the gay ones. I felt as if I was struggling to keep my head above water, fighting for sheer survival with whatever weapons I had. The bloom of youth, good skin, good tits, whatever.

A strange man who excited and frightened me had arranged to meet me in this frightening and exciting place. And I had agreed.

There were mirrors everywhere, and they multiplied everything endless times. It was dizzying, disorienting. Even so, I saw Matthew clearly, from across the room. I fought off the weak-kneed feeling, followed by the adrenalin rush.

Matthew was leaning against a green and gold wall, sipping a glass of wine. He looked at me over the top of the glass and smiled his radiant smile. By the time I'd crossed the room, he—as if by magic—had gotten another glass of white wine, which he gave me. He kissed me lightly on the cheek. He smelled of that sandalwood and vetiver cologne he wore the first time I met him. Expensive. Delicious.

I could feel people watching us. It didn't seem to matter that I was the poorest, least famous, least powerful person in the room. I didn't know where Matthew ranked, in that group, in terms of power and money. But we had something they didn't have. The aura of sex, the promise of sex. Even the oldest and most important guests sensed it.

Matthew cupped my elbow and leaned in close to my ear. 'I'm glad you came, Isabel.'

Nothing seemed real. Not Matthew, not the wine, not the party, not the other guests trying not to watch us. I'd spent so much time imagining this. How could it be coming true?

I leaned back into him, 'Who are these people? I recognize some of them, I mean from the news and magazines, but...'

'I thought you knew. I assumed you would Google the foundation and figure out the rest. I work for Val Morton. This is a fundraiser for the Foundation. This is where Val and Heidi live.'

I couldn't stop myself from saying, 'The letter I sent you came back.'

'What letter?'

'A letter I sent to the place in Brooklyn Heights. Where we had drinks on the terrace. Let's watch the sunset. The mattress ... your apartment. Remember?'

'*Right. Well, you're not the only one who can pretend to be somebody else for a minute or two. Truth is,* that was Val's apartment. Part of my job was to keep that fact out of the papers. Because when there was all that trouble, the PR was that he wasn't building it for himself—but I assumed you would figure that out. That's hilarious, really.'

'I just assumed it was yours...' I was trying to remember if he'd actually said anything to suggest that it *was* his apartment.

'What made you think that?'

'Didn't you say that you were moving and didn't want to take your old mattress with you?' I was getting my stories mixed up—when was Matthew playing The Customer and when was Matthew just being the real Matthew?

'I was,' he said. 'And I didn't. But that wasn't the same mattress. I bought that one for Val and Heidi. That was *their* apartment. Did I not make that clear?'

Something still didn't add up. He must have gotten my card with the picture of the melon if he'd sent me back a card with a picture of the world. And yet he was refusing to answer, or choosing to ignore, my question about it. Was he just messing with my head? I didn't want to think that was true, but I couldn't help it. I didn't like the slippage, the questions that suddenly rose in my mind about what was real and what wasn't, what was true and what was a lie. For a moment everything seemed like a mind game in a thriller ... and then I calmed down. After that it just seemed quirky and interesting. Funny.

No wonder he didn't want to have sex on someone else's mattress.

'It's crazy how two people can have a complete misunderstanding. Isn't it, Isabel?'

I loved how he said my name. I hadn't misunderstood what had happened on the mattress at the store, nor the feeling of his hand on my back beneath my T-shirt as we'd looked at someone else's bed in someone else's apartment.

'Let me introduce you,' he said, and steered me over to Val Morton, who was surrounded by a group of older men with good haircuts and much younger wives.

For some reason they shifted to make room for Matthew and me.

'Val Morton,' said Matthew, 'I'd like you to meet my friend, Isabel Archer.'

Val Morton smiled his famous smile and looked me up and down.

'Beautiful name,' he said.' Is that your real name? Wait a second. Don't tell me. *Portrait of a Lady*. Early Nicole Kidman. Malkovich was amazing.'

'My mom's a big Henry James fan,' I said.

'See?' he said. 'Didn't I call it? Let's give me some credit.'

His friends made admiring gestures and noises.

'You're sure it's not a stage name?' he said. 'You're an actress, right?'

*Failed* actress, I thought. Shit. Was it that obvious?

'I can always tell. I spent the best years of my life in the industry. There's something about how you hold yourself, how you study the world, I can watch you figuring out what other people are feeling. Figuring out what you can steal. Or should I say *borrow*?'

'That's my real name. And thank you,' I said.

'She's perfect,' Val Morton told Matthew.

Then he turned to me and said, 'Nice to meet you, Jessica.'

'Isabel. Nice to meet you too.'

Morton's attention drifted back to the men in his group. Matthew led me away.

'Perfect for what?' I said.

'Huh?'

'He told you I was perfect. As if he had something in mind. Perfect for what?'

'Perfect,' said Matthew. 'You're perfect. How many different things does perfect mean?'

A waiter put a full wine glass in each of our hands, and I drank mine in a few gulps.

It was happening. I was here with him. I would try to be what he wanted, if I could figure out what that was. He didn't seem to expect me to say much as he took me around to groups of partygoers and introduced me mostly to young men, all of whom seemed to work for Val. I smiled. Nice to meet you. None of them was as handsome or as hot as Matthew. We navigated around the circles surrounding the actors and politicians and socialites whose faces were so famous that even I recognized them.

Glasses of wine kept appearing in Matthew's hand. He kept passing them to me, and I kept drinking. It helped fuzz out the rest of the room, which was fuzzy to begin with, and it brought him—only him—into focus. After a while he was the only thing I could see.

'Should we leave?' he said. Together? He'd said *we*. I could hardly keep my voice steady as I said, 'Sure!' That high little squeak didn't even sound like me.

'Good,' he said. 'Let's blow this clam shack.'

'I need to go to the bathroom,' I said.

'Brilliant. So do I. I'll show you where it is. This place is a maze.'

There was a powder room downstairs off the living room. Matthew tried the doorknob.

'Occupied,' someone yelled.

'Okay. Follow me.'

He knew his way around the maze, taking me through one of the closed doors at the end of the corridor and down another short hall where three steps led up to the private wing. How did he seem so comfortable in his boss's private space?

He was holding my hand now, friendly but neutral, the way you'd hold a child's hand, crossing the street.

'Guess how many bathrooms this place has,' he said.

'Five?' I said.

'Double it,' he said.

'Why does anyone need ten bathrooms?' The question didn't interest him. I was sorry I asked.

'I'll show you the best one,' he said. 'The craziest one. As long as we're here, what the hell?'

I should have known that in order to reach the 'best' bathroom, we would have to experience the full pageantry of Morton and Heidi's bedroom. I don't know what it was supposed to be. A Renaissance Venetian Vegas palace French bordello with all the modern conveniences. A billionaire's sex cave. We paused in the doorway, just as we had in what had turned out to be the Mortons' Brooklyn Heights apartment. We seemed to spend a lot of our time looking at other people's bedrooms.

Again, I wondered how he knew so much about his boss's bedroom and private bathroom? Had he come here with Heidi? Or with Morton? Did they give him orders from bed?

He said, 'Managing both apartments, that is, managing the people who manage both apartments, is part of my job. Not the most exciting part, but the buck stops here. And the two of them can be monsters. If Morton runs out of toilet paper, he's capable of firing every employee down the food chain starting with me.'

I didn't want to imagine Morton and Heidi in that beautiful bed. But I wouldn't have minded lying down. I felt tired and hot and drunk.

But first, right ... the bathroom.

The bathroom was as large as my entire apartment, a gold-fauceted, marble-tiled, dazzlingly white Roman bath. The toilet, the bathtub, and the steam shower each had its own separate room.

Matthew showed me to the room with the toilet. I was startled when he followed me in and locked the door behind us. But I was so tipsy, it seemed to make a kind of sense.

I should have been alarmed, or maybe embarrassed. But it all seemed like fun. Matthew wasn't going to rape me in Val Morton's bathroom. If I asked him to open the door, he would. But I didn't ask, I didn't want to.

He stood with his back to the door. Across from the white marble toilet and the bidet was a white marble sink, and behind it, a mirrored wall. Did Morton like watching himself on the toilet? Matthew had said that people could get fired if Val ran out of toilet paper. I tried not to think about that.

Matthew said, 'Go ahead. Pee. You first.'

'Okay,' I said. The wine made it easier, but I wasn't so drunk that I didn't know what I was doing. I lifted the hem of my little black dress, pulled down the black lace and red ribbon underpants that had cost half a week's salary, and sat on the toilet. I closed my eyes and waited for what seemed like forever till I heard the trickle beneath me.

'You next,' I said.

I started to pull my underwear up.

'I'm good,' he said. 'I can wait.'

I made a move to get up.

'Don't put your underwear back on. Take them off and give them to me.'

I did it. I wasn't embarrassed. I'd never done anything like that. I was becoming someone else. Definitely not one of the characters I'd played on any of my online dating adventures. And definitely not me.

He folded my underwear with one hand and put it in his pocket.

He said, 'Now lift your skirt over your waist. Lean over the sink.'

He came around behind me. He kissed the back of my neck. He took his time.

Finally he said, 'You were really bad down there at that party. You liked the way those old men looked at you, didn't you?'

Did I? I couldn't think.

He ran his hand up my thigh and pulled his hand away. He gently slapped my ass.

I'd never done anything like this. I put my head down and moaned.

I was learning too slowly. I didn't get it. If I showed him that something gave me pleasure, he would stop. He stopped.

He backed away, closed the lid of the toilet seat, and sat down.

'Come here,' he said. 'Sit on my lap. No. Here. Pick your dress up more.'

I sat on his lap, both of us facing the mirror. The cloth of his suit felt great against my ass and my bare thighs. He held me by both hips, shifted me and held me just over the hard-on I could feel inside his pants. I reached down and touched it through his pants. It felt good, it felt like a triumph.

'Spread your legs,' he said.

I did. After all, I'd already spread my legs for him, at the store. At least we were in private here, behind a locked door.

'Lean back,' he said.

I arched my back and let my shoulders rock back against his chest.

'Now touch yourself,' he said.

We both watched me in the mirror. After a while I closed my eyes.

'Keep your eyes open and don't you dare come,' he said.

'I couldn't if I wanted to,' I said, though that was only half true.

'Good,' he said.

I played with myself for a while. It felt great. We were both breathing harder.

'Want to see something cool?' he whispered in my ear. I could hear him grinning.

'Yes,' I breathed.

'What'd you say?'

'Yes,' I repeated.

He grabbed the remote that was on a low table beside the toilet. He hit a button, and the mirror in front of us dissolved and turned into a screen the size of the entire wall. On the screen was projected a film of people in a room. No, wait. It was a live camera.

It was the party downstairs. I saw the guests I'd met; even more people had come. I picked out Val and Heidi, and the famous faces. They didn't know we were watching. They certainly didn't know what we were doing as we watched.

I tried to shut my legs, but Matthew's hand was there. My legs pressed tight against his hand, which felt so good I didn't want to talk and spoil it.

I'd stopped toughing myself, but I still felt on the edge of coming, with Matthew's hand inching its way up around my thigh. Finally I said, 'So does Val Morton come up here and take a shit without leaving the party?'

Matthew laughed. 'I don't know what he does here. I don't want to know. I don't ask. When he showed me around his place, he showed me how the camera works. He thought it was funny. There was no one downstairs at the time.'

Matthew pulled me back against his chest.

'Unzip my fly.'

I was shaking, but I did it. I helped him lower the zipper and get his dick out. He was so hard. The skin was soft as velvet. He put his finger inside me.

'Touch me,' he said. I did.

After a while he shifted so that his dick was between my thighs.

'I've got a condom in my purse.' I was shocked by my own boldness. I sat very still, awaiting his response.

He said, 'What's the rush? Let's take it slow. Get to know each other. We've got all the time in the world.' We sat like that for a few minutes, his dick between my legs, pressing up against me, his finger stroking gently inside me while the party guests sipped their drinks and chatted, never knowing we were watching them—or what we were doing.

I bit down on my lower lip to keep from coming. He felt so good. Slow, hypnotized by pleasure, we were still fondling each other when he said, 'We should go. It's probably okay that we're here. Val would think it's funny, too. But you never know what's going to cause a major incident.'

Carrie Blake

I jumped up off his lap and pulled down my dress. The last thing I wanted was a major incident. And I didn't know if I wanted a famous movie star thinking this was funny.

'Please don't tell anyone.'

'Of course not,' Matthew said.

As we were leaving, he said, 'Wait a second.'

I leaned against the door and watched him piss in the toilet. Then we straightened ourselves up and did one last check in the mirror.

'One more thing,' he said. 'Open the medicine cabinet. That one, on the wall.'

'Really?' I said.

He said, 'That fat amber colored bottle of pink pills. Take it. Put it in your purse.'

'I couldn't.'

'You could. Val and Heidi have more. They have plenty. They don't leave the house without them. You'll thank me.'

'What are they? The pills?'

'Happiness in a bottle,' he said. 'My gift to you. One a day. Don't overdo it.'

We returned to the party, and we walked through the crowd, arm in arm.

I thought: I still hardly know anything about him. We haven't had actual sex. But for the moment I felt comfortable, almost as if we'd been lovers for years.

Anyone who saw us would have thought we were a couple.

I gave him my claim ticket, and he retrieved my coat from the clipboard girls. I didn't make eye contact with any of them. The doorman opened the door. Matthew and I went outside. He let me go first, very gallant and cool for a guy who'd just fingered me in the host's bathroom and made me steal his drugs.

The night was cold and clear. Matthew hailed a cab and put me in it and gave the driver what I could tell would be more than enough money for me to get back to Greenpoint, tip included.

'I'm sorry. I can't leave, after all. I have to stick around till the end. It's my job.' He kissed me on the forehead. 'Weird job, huh?'

Only later would I learn just how weird Matthew's job was.

I would have stayed to the end of the party with him. But he hadn't asked. Had he kicked me out of Val Morton's apartment? Or had he protected me from something I wasn't ready to experience?

# Matthew

Val Morton's new superstar cardiologist talked him down to one cigar a week, and because Val Morton saw his cigar as a sociable thing, and because Heidi was involved with her charities and he didn't like to drink alone, he'd text me to come see him, and he would ply me with brandy and light up a cigar and talk about his favorite subjects.

One of those subjects was how he'd always wanted to direct. He didn't care where or how, film or TV or theater, a music video for fuck's sake, he wanted to be the one deciding the narrative, making decisions that weren't just about money. I always wanted to ask why, with his private fortune, he couldn't just find a project he liked and finance it himself. But I didn't say that, because I knew that what Val really meant was that he wanted someone, preferably someone important in Hollywood or on the New York stage, to *ask* him to direct. I thought: Everyone wants something—something they can't and don't have.

One night—clearly Val had started drinking some time before I arrived—he again got onto the subject of directing.

He said, 'For now the best I can do is to stage little dramas involving real people. Call them performance pieces, reality TV without the TV, I don't give a shit what you call them. That's partly where you come in, dude, facilitating and so forth...'

Once again, I knew what he meant. He was directing the little real-life drama starring Isabel and me.

When Val Morton met Isabel at his party, he agreed that she would be perfect to do—and be—what we needed, though he still hadn't told me exactly what that was.

It was my idea, not his, to play around with her in Val's bathroom. Val had gotten more insistent about the fact that he wanted me to wait a while before I actually fucked her, and I was willing to go along. A little waiting never failed to heat things up. I felt bad for Isabel, but I was working for Val. Anyway, she wasn't getting hurt. Neither of us were. We were having fun. I would have liked to fuck her, but I was being paid to act out whatever story my boss was spinning.

Whatever play he was directing.

By the end of that party at Val's, I still had a hard-on from the stuff we'd done in the bathroom. But as we were leaving, Val signaled me to get rid of her and stick around. I was sorry to have to put her in a cab.

After all the guests had gone home, and Heidi had gone to bed, Val called me into his study, a kind of glass atrium built onto the roof, like a Victorian conservatory, again over the objections of the Landmarks Commission, and in this case of his own co-op board.

He sat at his desk, J. P. Morgan's actual desk, and I stood before him.

'Sit down,' he said. 'Make yourself comfortable.'

I sat down.

'Well, do you have it?' He held out his hand.

I reached into my jacket pocket for Isabel's underwear. That was something we'd discussed. That I'd bring them to him, somehow, soon, either tonight or later.

I could feel myself getting hard thinking about how hot Isabel had looked in the black lace underwear, how I'd asked her to take them off, and about how her ass looked as she bent over the sink.

I gave the crumpled black lace and red ribbons to Val. He pressed it to his face and inhaled. Then he put it in his pocket.

It was definitely a weird moment. I told myself, hey, all over the world, smart, capable people are collecting tolls, picking up garbage, working at Starbucks. If they're lucky. Toiling away in diamond mines if they're not. So what was my job description here, exactly? I was seducing a beautiful woman and making her do what I said for some mysterious reason of my boss's that would be revealed in time.

I knew I should keep quiet. But I asked Val, 'What are you going to do with those?'

'With what?'

He was determined to make me say it.

'With Isabel's underwear.'

'I'm giving them to Heidi. And she's going to wear them. As is. I like thinking about it. Don't you?'

I didn't know if I did or not. 'What does Heidi have to say about that?'

Even as I said it, I thought: There goes my job. Getting my boss a girl's underwear and being encouraged to picture it on my boss's beautiful wife.

But Val wasn't bothered in the least.

He said, 'Trust me, my wife is fine with it. Heidi is a very nice, very *understanding* person. Thank you for everything, Matthew.'

'You're more than welcome,' I said.

'You know what?' said Val. 'Why don't we go shooting?'

'What?'

'Just target practice. There's this place in the Flatiron. In the basement. You can get pretty much any kind of weapon you want, and just pump bullets into the targets. If you call in advance, and text them a photo, they'll blow up the photos into targets that look like anyone you want. Your enemy, your business rival, your ex-wife. You can shoot at them all day long. As long as you're willing to pay. My treat. It would be a gas. What do you say, Matthew? Are we on?'

Even in his inebriated state, Val could tell that I was upset.

'I don't think so,' I said. 'I don't really like guns. They're not my thing.' I thought about my brother, about the blood in the car, about the fact that Ansel hadn't talked to me for so many years. And all because of a gun. Once I had a brother, now I didn't. And he was still alive, a few hours away, living his life, and probably still blaming me for something that was never my fault...

'Got it,' Val said. 'Point taken.' And I knew I'd said too much, that I'd given Val some information about myself that—too late—I wished he didn't have.

'Then that's that,' Val said.

It seemed that our meeting was over. I got up to leave.

'Oh, and by the way,' Val said. 'About the pills...'

I tensed.

'Enjoy them. She'll love them. And so will you.'

Had he already noticed that the pills were gone? Had he meant me to take them? Did he know that we were in his bathroom and what we'd done there? Often, I had no idea how Val knew what he knew, what his sources of information were.

And just as often, it scared me.

# Isabel

One Sunday afternoon, I was drinking at Cielito Lindo, with Luke and Marcy. It took me three mojitos before I had the courage to say, 'Here's a weird question. Have you ever had a relationship with a guy who didn't want to have sex, or maybe he did, or for some reason he wanted to hold off and do everything else first, or instead or ... I don't know.'

'All the time,' said Marcy. 'Happens to me all the time. In my experience, guys never want to have sex.'

'Never,' said Luke. 'Never happened to me. The guys I meet want to have sex all the time.'

'Your "relationship" sounds like high school!' said Marcy. 'Sick.'

'Is he gay?' asked Luke.

'No,' I said.

'Are you sure he's not gay?' said Marcy.

'Maybe he's a space alien,' said Luke.

'Maybe he is,' I said. 'That's the likeliest explanation.'

That was all I would say. Matthew was my secret life, the real life beneath my pretend life of not acting, of hanging out with Marcy and Luke, of working at Doctor Sleep.

I looked up the pills on the internet. Euphorazil. I couldn't believe I hadn't heard about them till now. What a sheltered life I'd been living. The drug was still controversial. It had been discovered as an off-label side effect of a mild analgesic prescribed for dental patients. It produced a feeling of happiness and wellbeing that lasted up to six hours. Early studies showed that it could cause dependence but not, strictly speaking, addiction.

I first took it by myself on a Saturday morning. I went and sat on a bench in McCarren Park. I liked everybody and everything: the stroller moms, the baseball players, the designer dogs. It all seemed sweet and interesting and funny. Then I went home. I have never so loved scrubbing the grills on the stove top and cleaning out the refrigerator. I watched the news, no problem there. Every disaster the newscasters mentioned seemed like something that could be solved. Matthew would ask me to marry him and I would quit my job at Doctor Sleep and Val Morton—our kindly, beneficent godfather—would get me lots of acting roles and I would prove that I was really and truly talented.

I knew better than to take the pills too often. Why

waste something so good on a day sitting around Doctor Sleep?

But I sometimes took one when I found myself obsessing about Matthew. Why hadn't he called? Why hadn't he gotten in touch with me? Why was his number blocked when he did call or text? I'd take a happiness pill (that's how I started to think about them) and I'd again start to think that somehow, some way, everything would work out.

One of the things I liked about Matthew was that he was a secret rebel. Or at least that's what I believed. Underneath the super-organized, intensely focused, buttoned-up guy who helped keep Val Morton's complicated life on track, was a bad boy who did crazy things just for the fun and the buzz.

One Sunday afternoon he called. Did I want to go for a drive? I did. He said he would pick me up in half an hour. He told me to wait for him outside my house.

It was a bright October day, cool and crisp in the shade, warm in the sun. I stared at every car that passed. I wondered what kind of car Matthew drove. I hadn't even known he owned a car.

There was so much I didn't know about him.

He pulled up in a little red Miyata, sporty but not too crazy. His driving was expert, skillful, fast but never scary.

We drove to Coney Island. We parked and went to

Nathan's and ate delicious hot dogs. We walked on the Boardwalk. We rode through the dark-house Cave of Evil. All through the ride, his hand rested on me, in between my legs.

Everything seemed funny. When he called he'd told me to take a happiness pill. He said that he'd taken one too. Cotton candy was the most hilarious thing ever invented. If you saw us you would have thought we were a normal couple falling in love on a third or maybe fourth date. He drove fast along the Belt Parkway to the Carousel in Dumbo, and we sat in the park, watching kids on the merry-go-round.

We got back in the car and started driving without any direction.

'Aren't we going in the opposite direction from where we want to be?' I said.

'I like to drive,' he said. 'Which means that every direction is the right direction. Anyway, I have a plan.'

Something about the drive—or maybe it was the pill—made him open up a little. He said he'd made mistakes as a kid. One mistake, to be exact. For which he was still paying. Working for Val Morton was better than any job he ever expected to get.

I'd known there must have been something in his past. I wanted to ask what the 'mistake' was, but I couldn't. I couldn't make myself ask. What was I afraid of? Or maybe I was just shy. Instead I told him about how I'd grown up in Iowa. I told him how my dad was killed in a car wreck when I was four, and how my mom had worked as a waitress to support us and put herself through college.

'A diner,' said Matthew. 'Perfect.'

'It was a real old-fashioned kind of diner,' I said. 'A beautiful vintage museum piece. Though everybody in my town just thought it was a diner.'

'A happy childhood,' Matthew said. 'But boring, am I right?'

'Having no dad and no money made it a little less boring.' I hadn't meant to sound bitter, but I did. Why couldn't I keep my mouth shut? Men don't like bitter girls.

'My condolences,' Matthew said. 'Having my father was probably worse than not having a father.'

Again, I wanted to ask why. Why was your dad so bad? But again, I couldn't.

A long silence fell. Finally Matthew said, 'Isabel, you know I've had fun with you these past few times we've met, right?'

'Yeah? Me too,' I replied. I wasn't sure where this was going. Was he confessing to something else or getting ready to break things off? I tried to look as neutral as possible.

'I can't stop thinking about how turned on I was pretending to be your customer,' Matthew went on, 'and how fucking hot you were, playing along with me.'

'I know,' I said. 'It was *really* hot.' Really? Was that the best I could come up with?

'I've been thinking about your career, too. Your dreams of being an actress... Is there any role you wouldn't play?' Matthew kept his eyes on the road, both hands on the wheel. Now I had no idea where this conversation was going.

'Honestly, I'd take anything these days.' And that much was true. I really would.

'I was hoping you'd say that. So I've been thinking.' He turned quickly to me, then turned back to the road, letting his hands glide up and down the steering wheel as we took the next turn.

'Working for Val has made me more curious about acting. And weirdly enough, Val's working on acquiring some space for an immersive theater project. He wants to do something that "feeds his soul again."' At this, Matthew took one hand off the wheel to hook air quotes around 'soul' before continuing. 'I know it's a long shot, but even though my current gig working for Val is interesting, I don't want to be his errand boy forever. And meeting you has made me realize how cool it would be to act, or even direct. I'm kind of hoping Val can get me into the first project in the space.'

I said, 'Wow, that sounds pretty amazing. I've never done immersive theater work. But I've always wanted to.'

He smiled, like he was waiting for me to say that, too. 'I think you'd be amazing. I'll admit—after we met that first time, I decided to go back and do my research on the 'real' Isabel Archer. I found a video of you performing Lady Macbeth, and I watched it over and over again. You were so good. And it totally turned me on.'

I tried to turn my face out the window so he couldn't see me smile and blush. I remembered that production. I *was* good. It felt incredible to hear that kind of praise again.

'Isabel, what if we kept our own role-playing games going, and used them like acting exercises? Would you play any role *I* gave you?'

I was skeptical. Or at least I should have been. Was he serious? But that part of my brain that lights up with other people's feeling was clouded over by my total desire to say 'yes' to whatever Matthew wanted. There was also the impossible dream of going back to acting. And here was this super-hot guy who not only wanted to (hopefully) sleep with me, but also wanted to *act* with me? I started to dream of our life in theater and film together. It was enough to distract me from that nagging intuition I was supposed to have. It would be for my career, I promised myself. I couldn't work in that mattress store forever.

'Yes,' I said, laughing. 'Yes, I would.'

Matthew looked away from the road for a long moment and stared directly into my eyes. 'Perfect,' he said. He took his hand off the wheel and ran his hand up to the top of my thigh, pulling my dress up along with it, his pinky finger slipping just under the hem of it.

We kept driving like that for a while. My whole body was buzzing.

'Are you hungry, Isabel? Can I cook you lunch?'

'Yes,' I said. 'I would love that.'

Now we had a plan and zipped across Brooklyn to the All Foods megastore in Gowanus.

The store was jammed, but we deftly threaded our way through the aisles. Matthew filled his basket with potatoes, asparagus, broccoli, rabe. It was a pleasure to watch him pick vegetables—the freshest, the greenest, the firmest. He knew what he was doing, but he didn't make a big deal about how knowledgeable he was.

'What about the protein?' I said.

'That will take care of itself. Don't you trust me, Isabel?' There was a funny tone in his voice, almost ... offended. If I hadn't taken the happiness pill, I might have been more worried about having said the wrong thing.

'Of course I do!' I said. What were we talking about? Meat or fish or chicken?

Maybe he meant he already had something at home. I stopped thinking about it. I trusted him ... at least enough to make dinner. He was going to cook for me.

As we waited in one of the checkout lines for our number to come up on the board, he knelt and stayed like that for a few moments, crouched near the floor. Then I felt something being pushed up under my skirt. Instinctively, I reached down to take it. It felt like a piece of meat, wrapped well, but still a piece of meat. I wanted to jump back, shrink away—but he was looking up at me, smiling.

'Grab it,' he said, looking up at me. 'Hold it.'

Then he stood up and whispered. 'The baby is due in March. Hold your belly. Right. Cradle it. Good. Like that. I handed it to you down below where the CCTV cameras could see us, down in a sea of legs. Just pretend it's our unborn child...'

'I don't know,' I said. Was this our first role-playing game? It seemed crazy to me, dangerous—and all for no logical reason. Why should I risk getting stopped and arrested for something that Matthew could so easily afford? I imagined phoning my mom from jail and telling her what had happened. Mom, I've got some bad news. I just got busted for shoplifting a steak. But if that was the only phone call I was allowed to make ... Mom didn't know any lawyers in New York. Would Matthew deal with it, or would he leave me to face it alone?

I summoned up all my mind-reading powers to figure out what he was thinking, but I drew a total blank. Maybe it was the pill, clouding my perception.

'Don't worry,' Matthew said. 'The guy who owns All Foods is a friend of Val's, or he owes Val a favor or something. Anyway, nothing's going to happen. Didn't you say you'd play any role for me?'

I stood in line beside Matthew, watching the numbers come up on the board that would send us to the right cashier. I prayed we'd get a young guy who wouldn't care or even notice if a female customer—me—was pregnant. But ... just our luck ... we got a motherly middle-aged Latina woman with curly, tightly cropped blond hair who looked at my belly before she looked at my face—or our groceries.

'When's the baby due, Mami?' she said.

I thought fast. 'Three more months,' I said.

'Girl or boy?' she said. 'Or don't we know?' I wondered if people asked pregnant women these nosy questions all the time, or if it was just because my baby was really a steak. Did the cashier suspect something?

'We don't want to know,' I said. 'We want to be surprised.'

That seemed to satisfy her.

'As long as it's healthy,' she said.

'That's right,' I said.

By now my heart was pounding as she rang up our order.

'Good luck with the baby,' she said. 'Congratulations.'

'Thanks,' I said.

A block from the market, Matthew opened the shopping bag and put it down on the sidewalk. 'Kneel over the bag,' he said. 'Put the steak in. Quick. Before anyone sees.'

I let the steak fall into the bag. Now that we'd gotten

away with it, the pill kicked in again, and it all seemed totally hilarious.

'Rib eye,' said Matthew. 'Aged. The absolute very best.'

I wondered why Matthew, who had enough money, would need to shoplift a steak—even the very best.

He said, 'All Foods is a big rich corporation which pays its workers less than minimum wage. No benefits. And they've got shitty hiring practice. They can treat us to a steak.'

'Brilliant,' I said. I'd never shoplifted, not even when I was a teenager and everybody shoplifted. I should have done this long ago! Maybe it was the taste of performance, or maybe I was still feeling the effects of the pill.

Happiness, pure and simple.

Matthew's real apartment was on the 23rd floor in a high-rise deco building on the Upper West Side. His living room window gave way onto a small terrace that over-looked Central Park, and I stood at the window, looking down at the red and orange trees against the still-green lawns.

Every piece of furniture—mid-century modern—was perfect, and every object—African baskets, Provencal plat-ters, glass vases—had been chosen with thought and care.

Matthew watched me look around.

'I can't take full credit,' he said. 'I got a little help from Val's designer, Charisse.'

'She did a great job,' I said.

'She always does,' said Matthew.

We went out onto the terrace. Matthew brought a bottle of red wine and two glasses, and he poured ours full. Then he went back into the apartment. He was gone for so long that I began to get uneasy.

He returned with the steak on a plate, peppered and salted. He turned on the gas grill and placed the steak on the rack.

'Are you cold?' he said. 'You're shivering.' He gave me his jacket, though I hadn't been cold, just nervous. Then he disappeared again.

'Want any help?' I called weakly, though I was sure he didn't.

'Keep an eye on the steak,' he said.

At the perfect moment, he came and got the steak and slipped it back on the platter.

Inside, the table was beautifully set with flowers, china and glassware, and bowls of lightly steamed vegetables. He sliced and served the steak in sandwiches on fat rolls with all sorts of salsas and pickles. It was delicious and messy. Embarrassingly messy. I must have looked like a vampire, I had so much steak blood on my face.

The only thing missing was a napkin. But I didn't ask for one. This was a man who forgot nothing. If he'd omitted to put out a napkin, he must have had a reason.

After a while he said, as if he'd read my mind, 'I love

watching the meat juices drip down your chin. I stopped being embarrassed, or almost.

'Want to play vampire?' he said.

'Sure,' I said.

He came around the table and licked the blood off my chin.

'Delicious,' he said, and we both fell about laughing.

I drank a great deal of wine.

Finally, I said, 'Is *this* your real apartment?'

He laughed and held up his hand in an 'I swear' gesture. 'My name's on the lease.'

Just beyond him, in a far corner of the living room, was a grand piano.

'Who plays?' I said.

'I do,' he said.

'Would you—?'

'No,' he said.

I said, 'Okay. Should we talk about *your* mattress? Want me to try it out? See if it's comfy?' I'd drunk *way* more than I realized. Way more than I should have.

Bad move. I knew it at once. I'd crossed a line. The wrong line.

He cleared his throat and said, 'Maybe we should call it a night. We both have to work tomorrow. Val's got a lot going on. This is a conversation we should continue some other time.'

'Fine,' I said.

I hadn't even finished my sandwich.

He took me down on the elevator and put me in a cab. He told the cab to take me to Greenpoint and gave the driver a wad of bills. The city swam outside the taxi window, as if it were a fishbowl, and I was looking at the fish—the pedestrians, the cars—from outside.

What did it mean that, every time I saw him, I wound up feeling as if I'd ruined things forever? As if I would never see him again.

A bad sign. Again, I seemed to hear my mother's voice.

A bad sign, she repeated.

Two days passed, then three. By then, I'd pretty much convinced myself that my torrid little love affair was over. Even Steve sensed it, and he began standing too close to me again. Once, he crawled practically up my back and whispered in my ear, 'Anything wrong?'

'Nothing's wrong!' I hissed. But something was very wrong, and I couldn't pretend that it wasn't.

A few days later, just after noon, a red Miyata double-parked outside the front window. Matthew rushed inside the store.

'Excuse me, Sir,' he said to Steve. 'May I have your permission to take the princess in the tower out for lunch?'

Of course Steve said yes. He'd turned beet red with pleasure, delighted that Matthew had called him *Sir* and asked him for permission to do something with me—without consulting me. As if I *was* a princess, or, more likely, a slave girl in thrall to this unlikely pair of men.

I was so happy that Matthew had come back. I didn't care who he asked if he could take me to lunch. The answer was yes!

Steve followed me to the back of the store where I'd left my jacket.

'Maybe you can sell your rich boyfriend another mattress, Isabel. For his beach house. I'm sure he has a beach house ... in the Hamptons, am I right?'

'Wrong.' I said. Probably Val and Heidi did, but that wasn't what Steve was asking. How little Steve knew and how little I wanted to tell him about Matthew, Val and Heidi. Steve was obsessed with celebrities, like everybody else. He would have been impressed to learn that I'd been in the same room as the Mortons, let alone in their private bathroom. But I didn't want to give him the satisfaction, and I didn't want to suffer because of the envy that my 'famous friends' would unleash in Steve. I knew he would find some way to take it out on me.

'So ... can I go on break?' He'd already said yes to Matthew. But didn't he have to tell me? There were no customers in the store. There hadn't been all day.

'An hour,' he said. 'An hour and a half tops. After that I dock your pay. You never know when there's going to be a rush...'

'I'll be back before then.' What rush? Steve was dreaming. But I was willing to pretend his dream was real if it got me out of the store.

'See you in an hour!' I called back over my shoulder.

Matthew drove to the far west side and parked in front of ... a diner. I'd been to the place a few times when I'd first come to New York. It was open 24 hours a day. But I hadn't been there in a while, and I was amazed that it was still there, when so many other old beautiful buildings and small businesses had been knocked down to make room for condos. The kind of condo Val Morton lived in, over in Brooklyn Heights. The kind he built.

Then it hit me: a diner! I'd told Matthew how my mom used to work in a diner. And he'd brought me here because he thought I might like it, because it might bring back memories of my childhood. He'd thought of me, and he'd tried to come up with a place I'd like.

A heavy, middle-aged waitress with shoulder-length hair dyed a flat, dull ebony stalked over to our table. Her puffy eyelids were a deep red, and she had a large wart on the tip of her nose. She looked like a witch in a fairy tale. She slammed two stained menus down on the greasy table top.

She was gone before I could say, 'Coffee?'

'What are we in the mood for?' asked Matthew. 'I'm dying for a burger.'

Suddenly, I was too, though it had only been a few days

since I'd had all that steak at Matthew's. That was more meat than I usually ate in six months. But a burger sounded divine.

Matthew signaled the waitress, but she purposely ignored him. I said, 'I didn't know you could get away from work in the middle of the day.'

'Val and Heidi are taking a "nap."' He hooked quotes around nap. 'They kick everybody out of the apartment, because I think Heidi is a screamer. I think having anyone within earshot cramps her style.'

I blushed. I remembered myself sitting on Matthew's lap, half naked, moaning as I felt his fingers touching me and I watched the party going on in Val's apartment. I wondered how Matthew knew that about Heidi, if he'd heard her himself, or if Val had told him. And I remembered how familiar Matthew had seemed with the layout of Val and Heidi's private living quarters.

At least ten minutes—minutes that seemed much longer—passed before the waitress slowly and grumpily made her way back to our table. It seemed weird to me that a man as powerful and take-charge as Matthew should be at this waitress's mercy, but there we were. I told myself: He remembers that my mom was a waitress. He's on his best behavior ... for me.

'What'll it be?' the waitress asked.

'Two burgers deluxe,' said Matthew. 'And two coffees. Milk on the side.'

The waitress pointed mockingly at the cream pitcher on the table. 'Is that far enough on the side for you?'

'Sorry,' said Matthew. 'I didn't see it.'

I waited for her to ask how we wanted our burgers cooked, but she didn't.

I said, 'Can I have mine medium rare?'

She glared at me. 'I've got news for you, honey. There's no such thing as medium rare. There's medium. And there's rare. And then there are spoiled brats like you, who want everything just so, who think they can have everything exactly the way they want it. Medium but not too medium, rare but not too rare. I'm always surprised when these little bitches don't bring in paint chips to show me exactly how pink they want it. So what I'll it be? Medium or rare?'

Had the waitress just called me a little bitch? Could I have heard her wrong?

I looked to Matthew for direction, but his handsome face, was blank, impassive—directionless for me.

'Then I'll have mine medium,' I said.

'Mine too,' said Matthew.

'Whatever,' the waitress said.

'Well!' said Matthew when she left. 'Someone got up on the wrong side of the bed this morning!'

'It's a hard job,' I said. I wanted him to think of me as someone who didn't argue with waitresses, who appreciated working people, who was always kind. Who was nice.

Meanwhile, I was thinking of all the things my mom used to tell me about customers who didn't say thank you, didn't tip, didn't clean up after their messy kids ... and that was in our little town, where everyone said thank you and cleaned up after their families and tipped ... okay, at least 10 per cent.

When our burgers came, they were cold, charred crispy black—and hard as rocks. The rolls were dry and stale and tasted slightly of mildew.

Once again, I looked at Matthew. Help! I couldn't imagine that anyone sent food back in a place like this. And frankly, I was too intimidated by the waitress...

Matthew took a bite, smiled, shook his head and kept eating.

'I've had worse,' he said.

'Me too, I guess,' I said.

We finished our meal in silence. Finally Matthew held up his hand.

Check, please.

The waitress took her time getting back to our table.

'Cash only,' she said. 'The computer's down.'

'This *is* embarrassing,' Matthew said. 'I don't have cash, I never—'

'Don't worry,' I said. 'I have plenty.'

Actually, I had a little. If the bill came to more than thirty dollars, we were screwed.

'This one's on me,' I said, hoping for the best as I picked up the check.

The total came to twenty-six dollars. 'Let's see,' I said. 'With the tip that's...'

'No tip,' Matthew said. 'Not one penny.'

'Seriously?'

'Are we supposed to reward her for the way she behaved? For the service?'

'I always tip,' I said. 'Even if the service is bad. You never know what kind of day someone's having, or what their boss said, or if someone's sick at home—' It was the first time I'd ever contradicted Matthew, and we were both acutely aware of that.

Matthew rolled his eyes. 'Not my problem,' he said.

'My mom was a waitress,' I said. 'I guess that's why I always tip. Even when...'

'I know,' said Matthew. 'I know about your mom. You told me. That's why I took you to this shithole.' That flash of anger—I'd never seen it that intense before. I sat very still, afraid to move or say a word.

I looked around. The waitress was nowhere to be seen.

'Wait,' Matthew said. 'I've got a better idea. Put your money back. In your purse. That's right.'

I did what I was told. I'd learned to listen when Matthew said that he had an idea.

'Come on.' He grabbed my hand and helped me out of the booth, and he pulled me out of the diner. Matthew started the Miyata, and we'd taken off before the waitress could have possibly known that we'd left without paying.

'This is terrible,' I said. 'This is really bad. I've never done this before. I've never stiffed a waitress. Our bill is going to come out of her paycheck. Matthew, let's go back, we can't do this.'

Matthew cut across two lanes of traffic, pulled to the curb and slammed on the brakes. 'But what if we pretended to be the kind of people who could do this? Look. You want to go back, go back,' he said. 'Pay her the money we owe her. Only don't imagine that I'm still going to be here waiting for you when you get back.'

I stayed in my seat, paralyzed. She'd been awful to us. She'd basically called me a bitch. Still ... I believed there was a special circle of hell reserved for people who left without paying their bill. Well, I told myself, at least I'll be burning there with Matthew.

He started the car up again.

'That was a test,' he said.

'A test of whom?' I shouted over the engine. 'Of what?'

'Of you,' he said. 'I wanted to see how really and truly bad you could be—what kinds of roles you could play.'

'Did I pass or fail?' I shouted.

'You passed. Or failed. Depending.'

Suddenly, it made sense to me. Or at least a kind of twisted sense. Stealing the steak from All Foods had been nothing. Kid stuff. Robin Hood stuff. That was a rich corporation. Stealing from them didn't count. It was almost righteous. But taking the money from a waitress, no matter how nasty she'd been, no matter how unpleasant—that was something else. That was bad. I was the nice girl. Miss Compassion. I didn't do things like this. I could imagine all too well how the waitress was feeling, knowing that her paycheck, for which she was working hard, was going to be smaller at the end of the day. And all because of a spoiled, privileged couple—us—that she'd despised on sight. I hated myself for it. And despite everything, I liked thinking of Matthew and me as (in the waitress's eyes) a couple. What kinds of roles did Matthew want me to play?

'Come on,' Matthew shouted. 'And anyway. Serves her right!'

He'd asked me to do something I knew was bad—and I did it. I'd gone along. I passed the test—a new and different sort of challenge.

Suddenly I had the definite feeling that he was going to ask me to do even worse things in the future. And I would say yes, I knew I would.

I would do whatever he asked.

I called my mom, for a reality check, and to remind me of who I was.

She said, 'Izzy—' (she hardly ever called me *Izzy* unless she was worried about me) '—Izzy, are you sure you're all right? I don't know ... I'm hearing something in your voice...'

'I'm fine,' I said. I wanted to tell her the truth. But how could I confess to her, what I'd done to a waitress?

Something had changed inside me. All that niceness, that compassion—where had it gone? It was no longer so easy for me to tell what someone was thinking or feeling. Or maybe I no longer cared.

In a way, a weight—the weight of all that niceness and empathy—had been lifted from me. But another weight—the burden of how passive and unfeeling I could be—had been placed squarely on my shoulders. Where would the role-playing end, and the real me begin?

I couldn't get the waitress out of my mind. And maybe that was why, a few nights after our lunch at the diner, a strange thing happened.

Or maybe it didn't happen. Maybe I imagined it. I'd always had a really strong grasp of reality before, but now I couldn't tell...

It was late. I was tired. I was home alone, watching TV.

A commercial came on, for a car insurance company. That daffy girl in all their commercials was trying to sell insurance to a tough old woman who was giving her a hard time. What if the car broke down? What if her grandchild got hurt? What if someone ran into the car on the busy corner where her stupid son-in-law always parked? The stupid son-in-law was standing right beside her, grinning stupidly.

The dyed black hair, the wart on her nose. The small, witchy red eyes. I'd seen her somewhere before.

It took me a minute.

The waitress. It was definitely the waitress.

By the time I figured that out, the commercial was over.

It was late. I was tired. I'd been obsessing.

It wasn't the same woman. It couldn't have been. Unless she'd quit her job at the diner to work as an actress ... or unless she worked at the diner to supplement what she earned as an actress ... or unless ... she'd been discovered in the diner, like Lana Turner ... or else ... it seemed to me that there was at least one other possibility, but I was too tired and confused to figure out what it was.

For the next few nights, I watched for that ad, but I never saw it again.

# Matthew

I was pretty proud of the scheme I had worked up for my little actress. Val had the time of his life when I told him about Isabel and the waitress and the steak. I knew he was dealing with stressful conflicts to do with his building company, and with some kind of investigation concerning his Long Island City project. It was a good idea, in every way, to distract and amuse him. And sex, or even a story about sex, is always good for that.

So I began to tell him more and more about what Isabel and I were doing—about this new storyline for our hookups—or lack of hookups. Of course there was no 'immersive theater project' space. And I had no interest in any sort of acting career, but I knew Isabel would need a reason to do all the bad things I wanted her to do, and would do anything I told her if it was in the name of her career. *Our* careers.

I was attracted to Isabel. I liked her. I liked being with her. I told myself that whatever my boss wanted me to do in order to put her in my power was not so much mind control or witchcraft as ... foreplay. The real thing, an actual relationship, might still lie ahead of us. Meanwhile I liked being paid to have this friendship/romance/love affair/extended sex game.

I told Val a lot, but not everything that we did. I didn't tell him I'd cooked her dinner. I didn't tell him I'd licked the steak blood off her face.

Every so often he'd do his Don Corleone imitation. There will come a time when I will ask you for a favor.

And I'd say, 'Not a favor, Val. My job. That's what it's always been. Work.'

If I had a normal life, I could have married a girl like Isabel and had kids. I could have gotten tired of her and started fucking my secretary. Like my dad did. But I didn't want to live like my dad. Maybe the best idea I ever had was to steal the neighbor's car and, accidentally, his gun. It took me off the straight and narrow path to ever becoming like my dad.

Once more I was glad to have gotten here. I was good with this life. I'd take it.

Val liked me to be creative. He enjoyed these little real-life dramas that I told him about. He gave me leeway and a substantial budget. He loved hearing that it took me a mouse click and a phone call to hire a character actress I'd seen in a car-insurance commercial to pretend to be a waitress, and another three hundred bucks to pay the diner to let her pretend to work that shift.

The idea came into my head the minute Isabel said that her mom had sent herself to school working part-time as a waitress. One of my friends had a mom who'd been a waitress, and every time when we went out for dinner he told us how the worst sin in the world was under tipping, how it was worse than rape or murder, and he guilted everyone into leaving more than twenty per cent.

Stiffing a waitress would be hard for Isabel, I knew. But I could get her to do it. In fact, the actress was well paid, so I guess you could say that it was Isabel who was getting stiffed.

I respected how hard she held out against leaving the diner without paying, though finally she gave in, and she did what I said. I felt only slightly disloyal when I told Val about it.

Maybe it had something to do with Isabel, but my working relationship with Val seemed to have evolved into a strange sort of friendship. Now most of our meetings were not at Val's midtown office but at his Upper East Side apartment. We sat in his private study beside the massive fireplace that Val's decorator Charisse had bought and imported (perhaps illegally, but no one asked) from a French chateau. The fire was always burning.

I knew that Val had been facing roadblocks and obstacles in his plan for developing more high-rise condos in

Long Island City, buildings like the one in which they had their Brooklyn Heights apartment. The way Val saw it, the way he told it, certain self-important assholes in the city council and assorted limp-dick old enemies in the state senate and a few moronic idiot do-gooders in the EPA were holding things up because they were stupid, old-fashioned, and fucking blind to the fucking future. Val never doubted that he would win; he always won. But these struggles were a source of annoyance and anxiety to him. He didn't like to lose—and what he liked even less was the prospect of losing the money he'd invested in these projects so far.

He enjoyed hearing about my affair—or whatever it was—with Isabel. It took his mind off real estate.

Meanwhile he'd developed some new favorite topics, one of which was revenge. He said that revenge made the world go round, that almost everything good that had been written for the stage or the screen had revenge as its major subject. It was, he said, the most basic human impulse.

Another topic he liked to expound on was how screwed up the government was, and how he could have changed and improved things if he hadn't been thrown out of office for refusing to incarcerate himself and his wife in Albany, that shithole up the Hudson. He'd known he could govern the state from New York City, and he could have, if he hadn't been made the whipping boy for how much upstate New York hates and fears the city.

'After 9/11,' he said, 'everyone loved everyone else for a while, and then they broke up again, with the city people thinking all the country folks were fat, and the upstate voters believing that city folks were rich and pale and helpless and thought deer and rabbits were cute because they'd never hit one in their car or had one destroy their garden.'

From time to time he would say things—drop hints— that made me realize that his interest in me having control over a pretty young woman wasn't sexual, but ... professional. I thought maybe he had some idea that he could use us as a weapon against his enemies. An instrument of power or revenge. But how would that work, exactly? I waited to find out.

I'd gotten more comfortable with my boss, but not comfortable enough to ask. Every so often he would do his Don Corleone, puffing out his cheeks and mumbling like Brando. Some day I'm going to call on you, at some time in the future I will ask you for a favor...

If I thought about the future, it was to wonder when and where I would find someone I could tell about this time in my life when I worked for Val Morton, about making a woman fall in love with me, about breaking down her moral sense and undermining her conscience in case I needed her to do something immoral—something deeply wrong—all for the sake of careers.

# Isabel

The last few times I'd been with Matthew—the shop-lifting, the episode with the waitress—had been all about the theater of petty crime, not sex. I wondered if this was how it was going to be from now on. A bad boy and his girlfriend. Emphasis on the *friend*.

Those doubts and questions disappeared on the day he called early Sunday morning and asked me to meet him at noon, in downtown Brooklyn.

By then the fall was turning into winter. Fortunately the day was warm, because again I'd stayed awake most of the night wondering how I could dress warmly and still seem sexy—and available. It was warm enough for me to wear a short dress under an oversize leather jacket which I borrowed from Luke and which Luke was getting too skinny to wear. It projected the message I wanted to send. The jacket was a tough shell, but the skirt could be lifted by the slightest breeze.

I took one of the happy pills. I knew Matthew liked

me better when I was in a good mood, and I didn't want anything to spoil it.

Matthew was waiting for me at the top of the stairs outside the Municipal Building exit from the Borough Hall station. It wasn't possible that he'd known what train I'd be on, not unless he'd had me followed. I thought things like that to scare myself, but with someone like Matthew, working for someone like Val Morton ... who knew? Probably it was just lucky that he was standing at the top of the subway stairs.

Seen from below he looked even taller and more long-legged, and when he reached out and took my hand, as if to help me up the last few steps, I felt lightheaded, and I was glad for his help. He was wearing jeans and an elegant long-sleeved, pale blue cotton shirt. Had we been friends or lovers, I would have reached over and touched the soft fabric. But every word, every gesture, every touch we exchanged was so confusing and unclear, so open to misinterpretation, though I had no idea what the correct interpretation might be.

He kissed me lightly on one cheek. Another friendly peck.

Okay. I could be friendly too. 'So are we just going to hang out? Or have you got plans?' I tried to sound in control. My voice shook. I was too eager. Where did all my skills go? Why couldn't I play the cool girl I wanted to be for Matthew? Whatever. I couldn't unsay it now.

Matthew said, 'Our day's wide open. But I need to ask you a favor. If you wouldn't mind coming with me, I need to check out Val and Heidi's apartment. They're in Paris for the weekend. And Heidi always thinks she's left every appliance on. The minute she boards the plane, she texts me to make sure the coffee pot's off, even though it turns itself off automatically, and everyone knows that. And I have to go there myself. No one else is good enough to check the knobs and faucets.

'That's fine,' I said. 'You don't have to talk me into seeing that amazing view again.'

'Good,' said Matthew. 'I promise. It will just take a minute.'

He took my hand, and we walked down Montague Street towards the water. Hardly anyone was out on the street but neighborhood residents walking their dogs and buying the Sunday paper. We passed a few couples, and I stared at them, as if I somehow could figure out what they were seeing when they looked at *us*. An ordinary couple out for a Sunday stroll—or lovers whose entire affair had been furtive, inconclusive encounters in a mattress store and an Upper East Side bathroom.

Val Morton's massive high-rise looked a little less ... overwhelming this time, maybe now that I knew that Matthew didn't live there. Or maybe I had gotten used to it. You could get used to things, fast. Walking into the building with Matthew was very different from entering it alone, as I had on that evening that already seemed like years ago. When I thought that Matthew lived here, and when I didn't even know his name. I knew so much more about him now ... or did I?

Matthew waved at the doormen, and they waved back. Good morning, Sir. They knew him. The second set of security guards also waved us through, also smiling, though one of them did seem to me to have a slightly shady leer on his face, and I wondered if Matthew had often taken girls here when Val and Heidi were gone. Well, he'd taken me here and nothing had happened, just as nothing would probably happen now. Maybe he simply wasn't attracted to me. Stranger things had happened.

Matthew let us in with his key. No one came out to offer me a drink. No one was around.

'It's just us,' Matthew said, unnecessarily. Did he sound nervous too? Was he scared of being alone with me? Of having sex with me? He was so self-assured, that didn't seem possible, and yet ... I'd been with guys who couldn't get it up, and they always made such a big deal of it. They always seemed so crushed. Once a guy I was dating tried to blame his being impotent on me, but one good thing about having any sexual experience at all is that you're not going to fall for that.

'Can I get you something to drink?' Matthew asked. 'I don't know what's here ... I'll have to stock the pantry before they come back on Tuesday, but for now...'

'I'm fine,' I said. Well, that was a lie. I was anything but fine. 'It's a little early for alcohol.'

'Wait for me here,' Matthew said. 'I'll check the kitchen. Heidi wants me to personally touch every knob on the stove.'

I wandered around the living room, looking at the art. It *was* a real de Kooning, a real Diebenkorn, a real Mark Rothko. Bands of deep color and a wash of California light announced to those in the know—even me, I guess— that Val and Heidi had a great deal of money.

Matthew joined me in such a short time that I wondered how carefully he could have scrutinized the appliances. But he probably knew that Val and the maid and the cook and the rest of the staff made sure that everything was off and the apartment was not going to burn down or fill with carbon monoxide.

'Let's check out the bedroom,' he said. 'Let's see how that *feng shui* is working...'

He took my hand and led me down the hall lined with Greek and Egyptian sculptures. He opened the door, and this time he crossed the threshold and drew me in after him.

The room was almost unrecognizable from the first (and last) time I'd been here. Then it had been as sleek and modern as the rest of the apartment, but during the intervening time—weeks? months? a lifetime?—Heidi or the famous decorator Charisse or maybe both women together had transformed the room into the bedchamber of a Venetian Doge, the love nest where a Borgia would take his teenaged mistress. The room was corny but sexy. The walls were covered in blue-green brocade, the bed in forest-green velvet. The bed was raised and canopied, with tassels hanging from the edges. The heavy curtains were drawn. A few stripes of bright light came in where the curtains didn't meet—and fell across the bed. The décor should have been over the top, in bad taste, but the truth was I wanted to lie down on the bed and pull Matthew down with me. I wanted to have sex with him. *Right here, right now.*

I tried to stay calm. I thought: This is Val and Heidi's bedroom. They sleep here. They have sex in that beautiful bed. That should have sobered me, or turned me off, but it only excited me more.

'Are you sure they're gone?' was all I could say.

'They landed in Paris this morning,' said Matthew. 'I got a text from Heidi. That's why we're here, remember? Making sure that the oven's off.'

Was *that* why we were here? Was that the only reason? What exactly did Matthew need to check out in their *bedroom*?

'Lie down,' he said. 'Try out the bed. I want to see you lying on it.'

He switched on the soft, muted bedside lamp.

I touched the mattress and tried to think about how

far it had traveled from Doctor Sleep, and of all the changes it had already seen during its brief life in Val and Heidi's bedroom. But I didn't want to think about Steve's store, nor about the fact that I was not only trespassing in Val and Heidi's bedroom but about to lie down on their bed.

I lay down across the bed, with my feet facing the door. I couldn't bring myself to lay my head on Val and Heidi's pillows.

'Relax,' Matthew said. 'Like the last time. In the store.' He was still standing.

It thrilled me that Matthew and I had a history. Maybe it wasn't a 'normal' relationship, but...

He undid the top buttons of his shirt as he watched me try to get comfortable. I lay on my back, then my side. I waited for him to tell me what to do. But I could tell that this was going to be different. This was a private, darkened, sexy bedroom, not the selling floor of a mattress store in full view of the street and with Steve about to return from lunch any moment. Anything could happen here.

Anything or nothing.

It was up to Matthew. The thought made me go warm all over.

'You look flushed. You're turning pink,' Matthew said. 'Are you okay? Do you want some water?'

'I'm fine, I...'

He sat on the bed, then leaned over and kissed me on

my neck and shoulders. He was amazingly sure and graceful, it was like watching a cat climb a building. Or maybe like watching a cat *burglar* climb a building. We made out for a while. He'd never kissed me before, except for those friendly cheek pecks. Never *really* kissed me. So few men knew how to kiss—but he did. He really did.

After a while he pulled away from me and slid down the bed, down my body. He lifted my skirt and pulled down my underwear and parted my legs.

'Hang on, wait a second,' he said.

He went into the bathroom and came back with a towel almost as large as a table cloth and as soft as the softest skin. He half-picked me up and spread it out under me.

'No point getting stains on you-know-who's bedspread,' he said.

It didn't seem finicky, it wasn't a buzz kill. It made him seem like a guy who enjoyed taking risks but who never forgot that he had a job. And that too was a turn-on.

He lay down again, alongside me, and waited, resting on one elbow, just staring at the space between my legs. Then he brought his head closer and began to lick me, teasingly, playfully. I tried to stay cool but within minutes I was thrusting my hips forward to pull his tongue in deeper. But whenever I pushed, he pulled away. There was nothing to do but lie back and let him take control. I felt his chest against the inside of my thighs, the cool cotton of his shirt. His glossy hair tickled my stomach.

I relaxed into the pleasure, the excitement of feeling what he wanted to do to me. The deep warmth of it. How could someone know exactly how to make someone else feel so good? It was as if he knew me, knew what my body wanted and needed.

Every so often I'd open my eyes and watch the top of his beautiful head moving between my legs. Then I'd close my eyes again so nothing could distract me from the pure sensation. With both hands he gently pulled my legs further apart.

He hadn't even unbuckled his belt. Fine. We were taking it slow. We had all the time in the world. No rush.

I heard myself moan.

Suddenly I had the weirdest feeling, a prickling on my skin, an intimation of danger. The sense of another presence. That sudden, serious *uh-oh* sliced through everything else. I can't explain what it felt like. Those warnings have no words. All I can say is, I knew that something was wrong. Deeply wrong.

Heidi was right. Something was about to catch fire. The rooms were filling with carbon monoxide.

I opened my eyes and raised my head, just slightly. Matthew was grabbing my hips and didn't notice that I was suddenly alert.

The door across the room at the foot of the bed was slightly open.

I saw someone standing in the doorway, watching us.

*It was Val Morton.*

He'd opened the door so quietly that Matthew hadn't heard. I didn't hear it either. But ... I'd sensed it. I'd felt it on my skin. Like a chill. The kind of warning chill you're supposed to feel in the presence of the devil.

Val was smiling a cold, reptilian grin. Our eyes met. He didn't seem at all upset to find us on his bed. I wanted to scream, but I didn't. I wanted to jump up and shout, but I didn't. I wanted to say, Matthew, stop! Your boss is watching you go down on me, on his bed. I should have done all of that. I should have screamed and jumped up and shouted and made Matthew see what I saw.

Later, I was sorry. Later, I wondered if Matthew had set this up. I didn't think so. But people were always surprising you. And how well did I know him, really? People were always misreading and misunderstanding other people.

I decided not to think that Matthew was involved. I convinced myself that he wasn't. Best case: some awful, embarrassing misunderstanding. Worst case: Val had somehow planned this, tricked Matthew somehow. But how would Val know to just pop in on his bedroom at this very moment? Maybe he had just come home, maybe he'd never gone away. Maybe Matthew had gotten it wrong. Maybe Val had changed his mind and come home at the last minute. Maybe he'd just pretended to leave. But why would a person do that?

It might have been awkward, really awkward, if I'd made

a scene at that moment. But ultimately it would have spared me so much trouble, so much sorrow, humiliation and pain. It would have prevented—or at least helped—everything that happened later.

Instead, I lay there, having consensual sex with one man and being molested by another man's eyes. I don't know why I didn't react. I was ashamed. Embarrassed. Intimidated. Or just passive. And I told myself that maybe I was so high on sex that I was imagining things.

Maybe it was the happiness pill. Or maybe I was just being … nice.

Matthew took one hand off my hip and pushed it up the back of my skirt until it was resting against my ass. I squirmed against it. Could Val see this? Surely he couldn't. Could he? Knowing that Val was there made me stiff and self-conscious, and at the same time made everything hotter. Another reason to feel ashamed, embarrassed—and turned on.

I picked my head up and looked again.

The door was shut. Val Morton was gone.

I lay back. I made myself forget about everything except what Matthew was doing. I would deal with all that later. I was not going to waste this moment worrying about what I had just seen.

Through the fog of warmth and pleasure, I heard Matthew say something.

'What?'

He raised his head and stared at me. I'd seen some guys

look pretty stupid, looking up from between my legs, but Matthew looked at once aroused and totally self-possessed.

'You're beautiful,' he said. 'I love this. And I can tell you do too. But I'm not going to let you come.'

'Whatever,' I said. 'Some other time.'

'We've got time,' he said. 'All the time in the world.'

It was crazy, how happy that made me.

Matthew stood up and straightened his clothes, tucked in his shirt. He went into the bathroom. I heard the water running. He came back, drying his hands on a towel.

He helped me up, and as I struggled back into my underwear and pulled down my skirt, he took the towel off the bed and threw it, along with his hand towel, in a pull-out hamper that slid, surprisingly, from the brocade-covered wall. How did he know it was there?

'Best of twenty-first century meets best of seventeenth,' he said. Was he repeating something he'd heard from Val Morton?

Val was the last guy in the world I wanted to think about right now. I wanted to say something about what I'd seen, but I didn't. It seemed like the wrong moment, but maybe it wasn't.

Matthew looked into my eyes with an expression that someone who didn't know better might think was love. Or at least affection.

He burst out laughing. Had he taken one of the happiness pills, too?

'Are you hungry?' he said. 'Let's go. I've made reservations.'

Matthew had chosen a funny little place, on the border of Brooklyn Heights and Dumbo. It was called Pierre and Menard's. It wasn't much from the outside, a dimly lit place, a couple of steps down from the sidewalk.

But to go from the street to the restaurant was like going from Sunday afternoon in Brooklyn Heights, 2016, to Saturday night, 1952, like being whisked back to a historic place in old New York, half night club, half French bistro.

'What *is* this place?' I said.

'It's not a theme park,' said Matthew. 'It's been here forever. Actually survived. Old school French. But not bogus. Your cream sauce. Your snails. Your duck a l'orange.'

It was like a food museum, staffed by the waiters who all seemed to be a hundred years old. They weren't actors, like Luke and Marcy, working as waiters. They were waiters. Our waiter was actually named Gaston. Matthew seemed to know him. Gaston said, 'How is Mr Morton and the *fantastique* Heidi.'

'They're in Paris right now.' Matthew was proud to be in the know about a famous person.

Did Val Morton have an identical twin? How could he be in Paris and, half an hour ago, at his bedroom door, spying on me and Matthew?

Matthew said, 'Are you okay?'

'I'm fine, why?'

'You looked ... upset for a minute.'

'I'm not upset,' I said. 'So how did you find this place?'

'It's Val's favorite,' said Matthew. 'He's been coming here for decades. Even when he lived in LA, he would come here every time he visited New York. And when he was supposed to be in Albany ... well ... he practically lived here.'

I studied Matthew's face for ... what? I told myself he couldn't have talked so comfortably about his boss if he and his boss had conspired to put on a sex show in Val's bed. He would have looked a little guilty. A little sheepish. He wasn't a total psycho. Or was he? I let him go down on me on his boss's bed, but I wasn't comfortable enough to bring up the question of who his boss *really* was.

Matthew wasn't crazy, just maybe odd. And there was no denying the fact that with all its ups and downs, all its stresses and obsessions, life was a thousand times more exciting and interesting since I'd met him than it was before.

I decided that I needed to warn Matthew about who his boss really was. A voyeur and a weirdo. It wasn't going to be easy. But even if we were just friends with benefits, or whatever we were, I couldn't let it go. I owed it to myself—and to Matthew.

It was still early lunch, the place was mostly empty.

Matthew and I had lots of room around our table. No one would overhear anything we said.

Matthew asked Gaston to bring us a bottle of white wine, something fresh and light. I drank a glass and felt better. I could handle this, somehow.

Maybe I would begin this way... 'How was work, this week?'

Matthew said, 'To tell you the truth, I'm glad that Val and Heidi are out of the country.'

He really believed that they were gone. In a way, that was good news. The bad news was that I was going to have to tell him something that he would have real trouble believing.

'Why?' I said.

'Mushroom omelets?' said Matthew. 'They're really delicious here.'

'Perfect,' I said.

Matthew ordered two omelets. Gaston thanked him and practically backed away.

This was not going to be like the diner. Matthew would not stiff the waiter here for the tip or the check.

I wasn't about to let it go. 'Why are you glad they're gone?'

'I don't know what's up with Val,' he said. 'Something ... I don't know. I think he did a serious amount of coke in his youth, but he hasn't for years ... I don't know. He's been ranting. Going on and on about how he could have been president, how he could have saved the country if those bastards hadn't gone after him for not wanting to live in that shithole Albany. They were never going to live in Albany, where nothing ever happens. Every day he'd gone into his office in Tribeca, where the rain was being made.

'He drinks and chews on his cigar and paces back and forth in front of the fire in his fireplace, supposedly talking to me. But really I'm just there so he can talk to himself and not think he's going crazy.'

More good news—if Matthew had doubts about his boss, it might make it easier for me to tell him what I saw in Val's bedroom.

'That can't be all that much fun for you,' I said.

Another mistake.

'You know what?' he said. 'It is. It is fun. I'm sitting there drinking the very best top-drawer brandy and I'm getting paid to watch a movie star act like a maniac. My friends' jobs are shit compared to this. They're constantly nervous about this guy's promotion and that guy's new deal, but all I have to do is sit there and pretend to listen and check the gas knobs on the stove.

'Bottom line: I like the guy. And Heidi's not my problem. She's Val's problem. She hardly even speaks to me. I hardly even know her.'

I was glad to see my omelet arrive.

'Thank you,' I said.

'My pleasure,' said Gaston.

Food loosened things up a little bit. Matthew was right. Our omelets were delicious.

I still knew I shouldn't mention it. But a little volcano inside me started burbling up, spitting out words.

'Matthew, I have something to tell you. Something weird. Back in that room ... when we were in bed ... on the bed ... Val's bed ... when you were...' I didn't have to say it. 'There was this moment when I looked up ... I looked up and ... I saw Val Morton standing in the doorway. Watching us.'

Matthew shook his head and smiled. 'In your dreams,' he said. 'Not possible.'

'It happened,' I said. 'He was there.'

'Really? How long was he there for?'

'Not long. Two minutes maybe. It seemed longer. He smiled at me.'

'And I didn't hear? I didn't—'

'He was silent. Your back was to him.' I blushed.

'It didn't happen,' Matthew said. 'It didn't happen. First thing, I didn't hear. Second, you didn't say anything when he was there. You didn't mention it, for Christ's sake! Third thing, my man is in Paris.'

'But ... I didn't want you to stop.' I sounded whiny and pathetic.

Matthew gave me a *you-must-be-joking* half smile. The smile faded when he realized that I wasn't joking.

He looked shocked, truly shocked. He couldn't understand why I would be making this up, or why I would be lying.

He said, 'Heidi texted me from the plane.' He took out his phone and scrolled through the texts. 'Taking off for Paris."

No way could I make him believe me, especially when his doubt rocked my own certainty about what I'd seen. Had I hallucinated about Val Morton?

I knew I'd seen what I'd seen.

Neither of us said a word until we'd finished our entrees. The silence was excruciating.

Over coffee, he said, and not in a friendly way, 'To clarify things. That wasn't Val you saw. If you saw anyone.'

'Probably not,' I said. 'You're right. I'm sorry.'

'Don't apologize,' he said. 'People make mistakes.'

# Matthew

I was sorry to find out that Isabel was crazy. I've had a lot of crazy girlfriends. Maybe I attract a certain type. Women who want to fix me but need major repair themselves. It was always surprising how long it took sometimes to figure out that a woman was nuts. I tallied them up in my mind. The beautiful successful real estate mega-lawyer who on weekends morphed into a suicidal pill freak. The actress who had her razor blades flown in from a small Tokyo artisan because they inflicted the least obvious cuts that drew the most blood. The tree huggers, the New Agers, the frigid, the freaks. The journalist with the countless food allergies, more of which revealed themselves on each successive date.

I'd gotten used to it. Each time I found out I was dating a crazy person, it came as less of a shock, though it had started to make me tired. And sad. Isabel imagining that Val was watching us when I was giving her head hardly even registered on the scale of the female craziness I'd seen.

Even so, I was disappointed. Maybe because, despite

everything I'd learned, I'd let myself have some hope for Isabel. Even some affection...

Val liked a good story, with lots of twists and surprises. He liked playing around, he liked being what he called *creative*, playing director, staging little dramas, hearing me talk about the sexual games I was playing with Isabel.

But I believed that he and I had a straightforward and honest relationship. For him to say that he was going to Paris and then not go would have been impossibly—unbelievably—out of character. And why would he have done that—bought tickets, made reservations, had me arrange for transportation to and from the airport? He could have said he wanted to watch me give Isabel head on his bed—and I probably would have agreed.

For Christ's sake, he could have filmed it. There were surveillance cameras everywhere. There was no need for him to show up, no need for him to pretend to be in a place he wasn't. He could jerk off to the porn of me and Isabel on his bed. He liked his little games and plays, but he wasn't a liar.

Not with me.

On Tuesday afternoon he phoned me to say that he was home and to thank me for having gone round to his apartment to indulge Heidi's neurosis.

Val said, 'When you don't come from very much, like Heidi, you're always afraid it's going to be taken away.'

Very casually, I asked, 'So how was Paris?'

'Fabulous,' Val said. 'We ate at this restaurant Heidi knew about from her modeling days. It had gotten better with time, which never happens. They served the kind of fussy food I don't usually like, but it was totally fucking delicious.'

I said, 'Where is it? Not that I'd know.'

'In the sixth,' Val said, 'Right on the Seine. We had the most blissful walk back to the hotel, and then, with a bottle of champagne in each of us, a perfect night in our fantastically beautiful suite.'

'Congratulations,' I said. He didn't sound like a guy who'd stayed home to spy on me and Isabel.

Why would Isabel invent that? Did she really imagine she'd seen him? Or was she yanking my chain, adding her own details to our little script. Maybe she was trying to find out how I really felt about Val, to see if she could find a way of separating me from him, the way women love to do? There was no other explanation, except that she was insane.

It was disappointing. What made it all the more annoying was that I was really starting to like Isabel. She was trusting and innocent, but she wasn't stupid, not at all. I liked her laugh, I liked how graceful she was. I liked her bright spirit.

I liked getting paid to have edgy sex with her and to string her out and make her fall in love with me whether she wanted to or not.

But making a crazy girl fall in love with you wasn't all that much fun. Ultimately you had to decide if you *wanted* the crazy girl in love with you. And mostly that was the last thing you wanted, unless you were crazy yourself. Which I'm not.

# Isabel

It's terrible, not being believed. It takes you back to being a kid, when none of the adults think that you know what you're talking about, and you have less than zero input. When I was little I used to say I could remember the car accident that killed my father, and everyone thought I was lying, because I'd been home with my mom.

It was hard, not being believed by a guy with whom I'd been ... intimate, you could say.

For days after the incident in Val Morton's bedroom, I sleepwalked through my daily life. I showed up at Doctor Sleep looking so haggard that customers couldn't imagine why anyone would ask someone who looked like me how to get a good night's sleep. I went home to Greenpoint and ordered out for Thai food and watched TV and fell asleep. I slept for an hour, two hours, then woke up and stayed awake, replaying what had happened.

Matthew didn't call me. Would he ever call me again? I had insulted his boss or him—or both of them. I'd called one, or both of them, liars.

If only I could have told my story to just one other person. I wished I could have heard how it sounded, how unlikely or sleazy or simply embarrassing. I wished I could tell it until I got bored, until it started to sound funny. This guy and I were fooling around on his movie-star boss's bed and I looked up and saw the boss watching us from the doorway. But it was my secret, and like all secrets, the longer I hid it, the more it hurt.

No one knew. No one could help me. I'd gotten into something deeper than I could get out of, something messier than I could handle. Any sensible person would have advised me to stop seeing Matthew, and I didn't want to hear it. I didn't want to stop.

My mother kept calling. Sometimes I didn't return her calls and texts because I felt so awful about lying to her every time I reassured her that really, I was all right.

Once she asked me if I was dating anyone. *Dating* didn't seem like the exact right word for what was happening with me and Matthew, so I didn't feel quite so bad about telling her no, I wasn't dating anyone.

I felt so unhappy and desperate that I decided to tell Luke and Marcy about the romance I wrecked because I told the guy that his boss was a voyeur. I had to tell someone, anyone. If they judged me or made me feel ashamed or bad about myself, it meant they'd never really been my friends in the first place.

Sitting with them at Cielito Lindo, I waited patiently as they complained about all the untalented actors who were becoming rich and famous, all the juicy roles they should have gotten but which had gone to others.

I was so withdrawn and silent that finally Marcy said, 'Isabel, what's wrong?'

And I told them. I left out a lot of the story. The most intimate details—especially the part where I told Matthew I'd play any role he gave me—and that it was all leading up to some incredible opportunity in some amazing new theater. But I told them about what Matthew and I did in Val's bathroom and about shoplifting the steak and cheating the mean diner waitress—and about Val watching us from the doorway. It was better if they thought I was doing it all for the sex, rather than understand it also had something to do with my own frustrations as an actress, too.

When I'd finished my story, I was in tears.

Luke said, 'Okay, I get it. Something totally unpleasant happened. And I'm not sure about this guy. But what I'm hearing here is that the sex was amazing.'

'It's all been amazing,' I said.

Marcy fetched another round of mojitos from the bar. All three of us gulped our drinks, even though Marcy was working and wasn't supposed to be drinking at all. I was glad they hadn't jumped up and run away from me in horror and disgust. I had no idea what they were thinking.

Marcy said, 'That was bullshit about the stiffing the waitress. I don't care how shitty she was.'

'I know,' I said. 'I was really sorry.'

Marcy said, 'You know this guy is crazy right?'

'Is he? I don't know.'

Luke said, 'Do you think he's lying? Do you think that he and the boss planned that pervy thing in the boss's bedroom?'

'I don't,' I said. 'I don't think so. I believe him. But he doesn't believe me.'

'This is wild,' said Luke. 'But the truth is, I'm so glad that something this bizarre and exciting is happening to you. I was afraid you'd given up and resigned yourself to selling mattresses forever.' *If only he knew the extent of it all.*

We watched the restaurant filling up with customers who had actual money to spend. Time was running out, and Marcy and Luke hadn't said or done one single helpful thing.

Marcy said, 'You know what? I want to meet this guy. Do you think you could arrange that?'

'Me too,' said Luke. 'I'm dying to meet the dude.'

I couldn't imagine Matthew agreeing to anything remotely like that—the new boyfriend being vetted by the girlfriend's pals. For one thing, he wasn't my boyfriend in any regular sense of the word. For another, I couldn't even imagine asking him. But it would have been a fantastically useful reality check. What did my friends think about him? I wanted to know. I wanted it to happen.

Matthew didn't call. *He didn't call*. I was in a state of grief and at the same time in a rage at myself for even caring. How had I let this happen to me? I didn't have to put up with it. My mom had raised me to be a strong, independent woman and in a matter of weeks I'd become this sketchy guy's love slave.

One Monday, after work, I drank so much white wine that I managed to convince myself that I had nothing to lose. I went to Matthew's apartment.

The doorman looked dubious, but he called up, and Matthew told him to let me up.

Matthew opened the door halfway, but he didn't invite me in. Why hadn't he just told the doorman to say he wasn't home? Did he want to torture me?

'Isabel,' he said, his face lit up by a purely friendly smile. 'How are you?'

It was encouraging that he didn't shut the door in my face. I tried to look around and past him to see if anyone was in the apartment, but he blocked the door. *Was* someone there?

'Fine,' I said. 'Listen ... would you like to ... can you meet me and a couple of my friends for a drink on Sunday afternoon, like around four?' I gave him the address of Cielito Lindo. 'That would be lovely,' Matthew took his phone out of his pocket and typed in the address and time. 'See you then. Oh, wait, wait a second. I'd be glad to. But ... I have two conditions.'

He was keeping his voice low. Now I was sure there was someone in the apartment. Another woman, I was certain.

He ticked his conditions off on his fingers. 'One: You sit beside me. To the left of me. In a booth. Two: You wear a short skirt and don't wear underwear.'

I said, 'That's three conditions. But okay. Agreed. My friend Marcy's place has booths.' Ceilito Lindo would be quiet if we met up early enough, and it would be cheaper to drink where Marcy worked, in case there was any question about who was paying the check.

I couldn't deal with his conditions yet. I'd think about that later, when I wasn't afraid of being sexually turned on by them as I stood in the corridor outside his apartment.

'See you then,' Matthew said.

Somehow I managed to make my way home. That night, I lay awake, thinking about his conditions. I thought about what I wanted him to do to me. I wanted his hand up my skirt while he talked to my friends. The idea got me so hot that I masturbated. I came, and fell asleep.

I tried not to think about the upcoming meeting when

I was at work. Steve had been keeping his distance lately, as if he knew that I might be about to explode into a million tiny pieces, and he didn't want to scrape the exploded fragments of me off the walls of his store. But the minute I got to my apartment in the evenings, I fell into a sort of haze with only a few recognizable objects materializing out of the fog.

His hand. A table. My body.

Maybe because I'd imagined it so often, and in such detail, it was as if it had already happened when it finally did. In a way, the most shocking thing was how casual it seemed.

I wore a short white skirt and stockings that came up to my thighs. Matthew and I met outside the restaurant, and went in. I'd told Marcy to stake us out a booth in the back, as far from other tables as possible.

When I introduced Matthew to Luke and Marcy, I could see, from the looks on their faces, that they were both thinking more or less the same thing. Somehow I'd failed to communicate how drop-dead handsome Matthew was. And I could watch the fact of his beauty working on them, persuading them that what I'd told them—all about the strange and risky things he'd gotten me to do—couldn't have been as bad as they'd thought. And the bottom line was, they could understand exactly why I would have done whatever this gorgeous guy told me to do.

I'd never seen Luke and Marcy nervous before, but they

were now. They made anxious small talk. The winter had been mild so far. Yes, Cielito Lindo was the perfect place to come for a quiet drink in the afternoon. It was too quiet, actually. There were a lot of uncomfortable silences that Marcy—bless her—jumped in to fill, asking Matthew if he'd seen this or that new film, none of which he'd seen. It was all very awkward. But these kinds of meetings—the new boyfriend vettings—are always awkward. The guy is on trial, the friends are on trial. Wariness and suspicion is the name of the game.

After some time I felt Matthew's hand move up under my skirt and come to rest on the top of my thigh, grazing my pubic hair with his knuckles when I moved, which I couldn't help doing. It should have made me more nervous, but oddly, it calmed me down. It seemed to make him more relaxed, too.

His left hand stayed under the table while he drank mojitos and slowly but steadily began to charm my friends.

'So how did you three meet?' he asked.

'In drama class,' said Luke.

Matthew turned to me. 'How come you never mentioned that you'd taken an acting class?' Matthew was performing well—of course he knew I had taken acting classes before.

I smiled, turned my chin down and looked up at him. 'You never asked,' I said. I loved this. Holding the secret of our game in between us turned me on. I became more aware of the heat of his hand on my thigh.

Conversation died again. Luke and Marcy were uneasy about this question. I guess because I'd surrendered (or so they thought) and they hadn't—and they feared that they might too, some day.

Matthew stroked me under the table. It felt so good. At least I had that: his hand on my thigh.

Suddenly, an unwelcome memory wormed its way into my consciousness. I thought of that high school guidance counselor, Mr Chambers, stroking my thigh as he administered that bogus compassion test. But that was nothing like this. That was molestation. That was taking advantage of a girl too young and afraid to protest. And this ... I was a woman now, and I wanted this to happen. This was what *consensual* meant.

'So you're actors?' he said, directing his question at Luke and Marcy and now in my general direction.

They adored being called actors!

'Yes!' they said, in unison.

'Cool,' Matthew said. 'I work for an actor.'

'Which one?' Marcy said. 'Anyone we would have heard of?' I could have kissed her for that! Of course she knew that Matthew worked for Val Morton. I'd told them all about it. But I didn't want Matthew thinking about how much we'd talked about him behind his back, and Marcy, bless her again, understood that. We were all playing the best versions of ourselves.

'I work for Val Morton,' said Matthew.

'Doing what?' Marcy asked.

I wished she hadn't asked that. I certainly never had.

'I'm something like an assistant,' Matthew said. 'But it's much more than that. I'm like ... his second in command. His ... right hand.'

He gave my thigh a gentle squeeze with *his* hand, and I bit my lip to keep from moaning.

'I'm like The Godfather's *consigliere*,' Matthew said.

'No way!' Luke said. 'You're kidding!'

I loved my friends. I really did.

'It's the truth,' said Matthew. While he stroked me under the table, in the half light of the back booth that Marcy had chosen for its privacy, I tried to concentrate on the conversation, to keep my eyes open and watch his impersonation of a normal guy who'd lucked into a great job, working for an actor.

'What's he like?' said Luke.

'Who?' Matthew said dreamily, and it occurred to me that he too was distracted by what was happening under the table.

Matthew leaned toward Luke and Marcy. Pressing the heel of his hand ever so lightly against the lips of my vagina, he said, 'Actually, you might like the guy. He tells terrific stories about starting out in Hollywood, living with five other actors in a crappy apartment, and about all the humiliating roles he had to take on his way to stardom.'

It was exactly the story that Luke and Marcy wanted to hear.

'So what happened?' Marcy said. 'What was Val Morton's big break? How did *he* get lucky?'

'You can't say *luck* around Val,' said Matthew. 'That's a forbidden word. Totally taboo. He claims not to believe in luck, and I've heard a million times how luck had nothing to do with anything that happened to him. It was all about *taking control*. He and his roommates *took control* and formed a little company that performed the classics in a loft in downtown LA, where *nobody* went in those days. This was decades before gentrification. But people started coming to see them, first other actors, then industry people, and almost all the actors in the troupe went on to become big stars.'

'I'm pretty sure I've heard about that group,' said Luke.

'I'm sure you have,' said Matthew, shifting his weight so he could lean closer to me. His hand slipped back and cradled my ass. If some guy just *did* that, stuck his hand up my skirt basically right in front of my friends at a restaurant, it would have been horrifying. Unbearable. It would be like rape. That's what it was like when Mr Chambers groped me in the cubicle off the gym.

But I'd sat where Matthew told me to sit. I'd worn what he told me to wear. I didn't want him to take his hand away.

'You guys are so lucky to be friends,' Matthew said. 'To

have each other's backs. Isabel's an amazing person, as I'm sure you both know. One of the things I like about her is her imagination.'

Marcy and Luke beamed at me and Matthew. Not only was Matthew a nice guy, but he was the kind of nice guy who actually complimented a girl in public. I thought I might faint from pure joy. No one had ever praised me for imagination before.

But suddenly I began to wonder what he had meant. Was he referring to the fact that he still believed I'd imagined Val Morton watching us from his bedroom door? I'd tried to put that incident out of my mind, but now it struck me that it still loomed large in Matthew's.

My imagination. *Had* that all been in my imagination? How I wished I'd taken one of those happiness pills this evening so I could relax. Matthew had said they weren't addictive, but now I began to wonder about that too.

Later that night, I called Luke, and the next morning, Marcy. Both of them said, 'He's way cool and sort of ... dangerous. *I'd* fuck him in a heartbeat.' I guess they'd agreed on that after Matthew and I left. To have sex, was probably what they assumed.

But we didn't have sex, no matter what they imagined we were going off to do. We kissed goodbye and went our separate ways.

They'd both used the word *dangerous*, so they must have agreed on that too. I asked myself how they'd reached that conclusion—surely not from anything he'd done or said that evening. So maybe they were factoring in all the things I'd told them before.

Anyhow, the consensus was that Matthew was maybe dangerous, but still definitely boyfriend material. Fuckable, anyway.

Or as it turned out, more than that. Marcy and Luke had found Matthew ... *inspirational*, you could say.

The week after they met Matthew, Luke and Marcy told me they'd stopped waiting for stupid casting directors to recognize their talent. They'd decided to start their own theater group with all their unemployed actor friends. They would stage classic plays, like Val Morton had, and they'd try to get them seen in small neighborhood venues.

I was hurt they didn't ask me to join their group. I guess they thought I'd really given up. *Forever.* I told myself: I don't need them. I have Matthew. My roles are more exciting than theirs. More ... dangerous.

For a while it was hard for me to be around Luke and Marcy, because all they could talk about was how they'd decided to stage a gender-neutral performance of *King Lear*. An under-funded high school on the Lower East Side had agreed to let them put it on for one performance only, in their auditorium. The teachers would encourage the students and their families to come. Tickets would be sold to the public for five dollars apiece, and the school would get the proceeds.

They asked me to ask Matthew to come to the show. Maybe they were hoping that Matthew would tell Val Morton about it, and that Val would be so moved—they were doing just what he'd done when he was starting out—that he'd want to see the play too.

I knew *that* wasn't going to happen. I could just imagine Val and Heidi getting out of their limo going into some smelly high school auditorium on Essex Street.

One night, Matthew asked me to meet him for a drink in a bar near Doctor Sleep. He seemed irritable, edgy, and I sensed that it had something to do with Val.

Finally after a few drinks he loosened up, just a little. He said, 'Val Morton keeps trying to get me to come to this shooting range with him. And I just can't. I don't want to. It's not my thing. I can't do it. And every time I say no, I get the feeling that he respects me less. That he thinks I'm a wimp. That real men know how to shoot, so I must not be a real man.'

'I don't blame you,' I said. 'I hate guns too. They scare the hell out of me.' I was aware of how banal, how totally stupid I sounded. But it was the truth, and I hadn't known what else to say.

Matthew shot me an angry look. He didn't want me to suggest that he was in any way like me, that we agreed on the subject of guns. He didn't want to be in the same club with a weak silly girl who was afraid of firearms.

I was so flustered and upset that I did the completely wrong thing. I chose the completely wrong moment to ask Matthew if he wanted to come to watch my friends, the ones he'd met, put on King Lear on the Lower East Side.

What is wrong with you? I thought. Why would you even say that?

I cringed and stared so hard at the table that I was startled when I finally glanced up and saw him looking at me with a smile that seemed ... affectionate, you could say. I was even more shocked when Matthew agreed to come to the show.

'Hey, they're your friends,' he said. 'We need to support them.'

Only now did it occur to me. I'd asked for Luke and Marcy's sake, but I didn't want him there. It would be humiliating, writhing in embarrassment beside him while Luke and Marcy and their friends destroyed Shakespeare.

I immediately started listing reasons why he wouldn't want to go. 'They've hardly had any time to rehearse and they've got weird ideas, the male roles are being played by women and vice versa, that kind of thing, and—'

Matthew said, 'A girl King Lear? I already love it.'

Relax, I told myself. Matthew was doing something that I wanted him to do. He was doing something for me. It should be making me happy. But what made me happiest was that he'd said *we*. We need to support them.

It was embarrassing, how much that *we* made my whole life seem brighter.

# Matthew

People are so easy. You hardly even have to try. It takes about a half a second to figure out what they want to hear, and another half second to tell them what they want to hear, and boom! One second, they're eating out of your hand.

It was important to Isabel that I meet her friends. I think she was beginning to have doubts about me ... you'd have to be a lot crazier than Isabel not to have doubts about some of the things I asked her to do. And I think she wanted her friends to look me over and reassure her that I wasn't some psycho killer waiting for the right moment to tie her up and throw her in the trunk of my car and stash her in a barn somewhere in Sullivan County.

It helped that her friends were actors. Or anyway wanted to be actors. Self-identified as actors. Or whatever.

I knew this was going to be easy. I *could* have been a psycho killer. But a psycho killer who worked for Val Morton ... that was a different story. Maybe the strange new boyfriend wasn't as sick as they'd thought, when Isabel told them about me. Maybe I wasn't sick at all. Maybe I was the nicest guy they'd ever met.

Isabel's friends were pleasant enough. The guy—Luke—needed to gain about twenty pounds and bulk up and stop doing bad shit to his hair. And if the girl—Marcy—wasn't careful, she'd wind up as a waitress who'd wanted to be something else. The good news and the bad news was that their desperation reminded me of myself before I went to work for Val. When I thought nothing good would ever happen and all my opportunities would come to nothing. That I was going to wind up as a broke elderly guy working in a fried chicken joint.

Marcy and Luke were easy. Their eyes glistened. Their breath quickened. They were practically falling off their chairs as I told them how Val and his friends had *taken control* and transformed themselves from nobodies into famous actors.

I was saying all this and at the same time feeling Isabel under the table in the sweet little Mexican place where Marcy worked and they hung out. What I was doing with Isabel was way more fun and involving than the conversation, but that too was sort of fun. Total multitasking.

The truth was, I had no idea how Val got from nobody to star. But they wanted to hear the story so badly, I made it up on the spot. If they found out I was lying, I could say that it was part of the myth that Val created about himself. As far as I knew, it was true. Maybe Val would have liked the story. It was about him about taking control. Anyway, they were never going to check it out with Val.

I wished I hadn't said that about Isabel's imagination. But I couldn't help it. I still hadn't gotten over how she'd imagined Val watching me do her from the doorway of his room. It was her wishful thinking, I guess. Her insisting on it had kind of spoiled things for me. I thought: Okay, she's fucking crazy. I've gotten involved with yet another crazy girl.

But so what, if this crazy girl was going to help me do whatever weird thing Val wanted. He still hadn't made that clear. In time, he said. In time.

He said, we have all the time in the world.

Anyhow, dealing with Isabel and her friends was a walk in the park compared to what Val had been putting me through lately. He'd been in a horrible mood. We were hearing rumors that some of his business practices might be investigated by the city agencies in charge of building safety. In the prototype condo he'd built in Prospect Heights, a counter top had come off in the new owner's hands, and the owner was suing. The contractor had gone home to Romania. And the authorities were looking into that too.

Val never took his problems and worries out on me— he was always reasonably polite and appreciative of whatever he asked me to do. But he'd been drinking more, and it seemed to me that his incipient coke problem was getting worse. More and more often, he'd summon me at some absurd hour of the night. He'd rant and rave about the people who'd screwed with him in the past, the wrongs he'd never forgotten, the bullshit he'd never forget, and all the ways in which he hoped and planned to make sure certain people pay. So many new names were added to his list of enemies past and present, I could no longer keep track of who exactly they were.

Two of his kids had started to worry. They'd called into the office. But it seemed Heidi had handled it. I was glad they weren't my job.

What made everything more difficult was that he always assumed I knew the backstory to whatever he was talking about, that I had been following each new development and had memorized the names and sins of everyone who'd ever crossed him. Sometimes it seemed he knew I was there, sometimes he didn't ... but it never mattered, never affected the speed and tone of his rants.

Every so often he'd stop cold, as if remembering something, or maybe remembering that I was there, and he'd say, 'That girl. That perfect little girl of yours. What's happening with her?'

'She's fine,' I'd say. 'I'm still seeing her.'

'Good,' He said. 'Keep seeing her. Let me know when you think she's ready.'

'Ready?'

'Ready to do *anything*. To go for it. Cross a line.'

What line? I wondered.

'Not yet,' I said. 'We're not quite there.'

That's when I'd remember that Isabel was in Val Morton's sights.

Was I protecting Isabel? Myself? I had a bad feeling about what Val wanted me to get her ready *for*. In a way, I liked having Isabel at my beck and call, watching her fall in love with me. Charming her friends. Still ... I knew that it was somehow hooked up to one of Val's schemes, his plans, his revenge fantasies ... and I wasn't sure I liked it.

I tried to drink a fraction of what Val drank. But one night when I was tired, and he'd kept refilling my brandy glass, a silence fell that I felt I needed to fill. I was feeling a little looser than usual, more expansive. Less on my guard.

I said, 'I met a couple of Isabel's friends. When I mentioned your name, Val, you would have thought I was acquainted with God. Their eyes lit up. They worship you. They wanted to know all about you.'

Maybe that was why I was saying it, I thought, even as the words came out of my mouth. How flattering to Val, whose vanity was always in need of some fluffing. Val could get self-pitying when he was drunk. The world had forgotten him, moved on. He was old. And when I'd point out that he was currently involved in several high profile real estate deals, he would say, Oh yeah. That's right. The world was out to get him.

A group of young actors who worshiped him. That would plump his ego.

'What did you tell them?' Val asked.

'How brilliant you are,' I said. 'And just my mentioning your name got them so fired up, they're trying to put on a play because they think it will make them more like you.'

'What play?' Val asked.

'*King Lear*,' I said.

'Good God. I played Lear in my twenties,' Val said. 'How fucking dumb was that? I didn't even know what the play was about. I couldn't have known. I had no fucking idea. Now I get it. But the fucking worst part is, now that I finally understand the play, no one is asking me to play Lear.'

'They're doing it in a high school auditorium,' I said, just for something to say.

'I'm on it,' said Val. 'Get me and Heidi tickets.'

One night, the doorman called up and said I had a visitor. I was afraid that it might be Isabel again, who'd had the bad manners to appear on my doorstep not that long before.

Isabel's timing had been terrible. It couldn't have been worse. That same night an old girlfriend—the crazy shrink with the food allergies—had phoned and come to visit. As long as I didn't have to have dinner with her, I was glad enough to fuck her. That was all the shrink wanted too, so we were agreed. I could work off some of the sexual tension that had been building up from my encounters with crazy Isabel. The shrink and I split a bottle of champagne and then a bottle of wine (at least she wasn't allergic to alcohol), and we were making out on the couch, which was probably why I didn't have the brains to tell my doorman to tell Isabel I wasn't home.

I met her in the doorway. Of course I agreed to have drinks with her friends. I would have agreed to anything to get her out of there. The sexual stuff popped into my head, as it always seemed to with Isabel.

But now I was alone in my apartment, and cold sober, and when the doorman rang, I asked him to find out my visitor's name.

After a silence, he came back on.

'Heidi,' he said.

Heidi? Not only had Heidi never been to my apartment, she'd never even seemed to register the fact of my existence. I was shocked that she knew where I lived.

'Heidi!' I greeted her at the door. 'What an unexpected pleasure.'

'Please,' Heidi said, and swirled past me, looking as bored and distant as she always did in my presence. She was wearing a deep red fur coat over a short black dress and high boots. A cloud of musky perfume surrounded her and spread out to fill my apartment. She sprawled on the sofa, her tall thin frame and long legs stretched diagonally across the cushions.

'Can I get you a drink?'

'Club soda on the rocks, with lime if you have it.'

'I do,' I said.

I retreated to the kitchen, where I took as long as seemed reasonable, pouring the soda, adding ice cubes, slicing the lime. What was Heidi doing here? Did Val know? Had he sent her?

I didn't have to wait long for an answer.

'Val doesn't know I'm here,' she said, accepting the drink. 'Nor do I want him to know. But I wanted to talk to you...' She sipped her drink and let a silence fall. Her phone buzzed, she took it out of her purse, checked it, and silenced it.

'That was him,' she said. 'If I'm away from him for an hour, he calls. That's why I'm here. I might as well be honest with you. I'm worried about him. He's drinking too much, and I have no idea what substances he's taking. I tried to make him take a Euphorazil, just to chill him out, but he won't touch it. Nor will he touch me, to be brutally honest. He hasn't fucked me for weeks. And he's obsessing. Constantly. Talking about all the people who have screwed him or are planning to screw him. I can't tell anymore, how much of it is real.'

'I know,' I said. 'I've heard him. It's troubling.'

'You're goddamn right, it's *troubling*.' Heidi made the word sound like an idiotic understatement. But still, why was she here? What did she want me to do about it? I was surprised—shocked, really—that she seemed to be genuinely worried about Val. Somehow I'd always assumed that he was her meal ticket, her credit card—and not much more. I don't know why it had never occurred to me that she might actually care about him.

'He likes you,' she says. 'And he doesn't like many people. So you need to do something. Or pretend to do something. Something that will amuse him. Maybe with that little girl you brought to our party... Do something weird. Be creative. Maybe something sexy. Something you can tell him about. Something that will take his mind off himself and his problems, if only for a little while.'

'Like what?' I said. And now I *did* sound idiotic.

'You tell me,' she said. 'If I knew I wouldn't be here. I wouldn't be asking you. Like I said, be creative.'

Heidi put down her drink. She sat up very straight. She crossed and uncrossed her extremely long and shapely legs—the legs that were so famous during her modeling career. Then she let her knees fall apart so I could see up her skirt.

I could see her underwear—black lace with red ribbons stitched through it. Something about it looked vaguely familiar ... I'd seen it before.

The underwear I'd taken off Isabel in the bathroom at Val and Heidi's.

Why was Heidi wearing them? Or something like them? What was she trying to say? That Val told her everything I told him about what I'd done with Isabel?

Was she trying to seduce me? She was hot and beautiful, but she was also my boss's wife.

Heidi snapped her knees together. That answered that. She got up and put her fur coat on.

'Please,' she said. 'Just be creative.'

And with that, she was gone, leaving a cloud of perfume in her wake.

After she left, I sat there, thinking. Nothing is harder than being creative when someone tells you to. It would have to be something to do with Isabel, something I could tell Val about, something that would amuse him.

Something sexy and fun.

# Isabel

One blustery November day, I realized suddenly that I was going to go crazy if I had to spend one more minute at Doctor Sleep. When lunchtime came, I told Steve I had an errand to do—it was crucial, a matter of life and death, I implied—that might take up to an hour.

Steve was obviously annoyed. Perhaps he was planning to go see his dominatrix. But even he could see I was standing on the ledge, and so he said, 'Sure, fine, okay, just get back as soon as you can.'

When I left he was picking up the phone, maybe to reschedule whatever appointment he had to be tied up and burned with candle wax or whatever.

The fact was, I had no reason that I had to go out, nothing to do, no money to do it with. I went to the nearest coffee shop, ordered a coffee, and sat on an uncomfortable stool at the counter. I'd downloaded onto my phone a book about Shakespeare's plays. I used to read them, but I'd hardly read anything since I met Matthew. Thinking about him constantly had made me so distractible and distracted, I could no longer read. I'd forget one sentence even before I'd finished the next. It was like having dementia.

Now I wanted to read King Lear, because Matthew and I would be going to see Luke and Marcy in the play, in just a few days. I wanted to have something to say. I was *so* looking forward to going to the play—to doing something normal, something a normal couple might do—with him.

As if we were girlfriend and boyfriend.

It was terribly cold and windy, and I might have hurried back to the store, where at least it was warm. But I still couldn't bear returning to the silence and boredom of Doctor Sleep. I walked more and more slowly as I got closer to the store—and then I stopped dead in my tracks. Stopped cold.

Steve was standing near the window. And he was talking to ... Matthew!

Ordinarily, I would have been so excited, I would have run inside. But something held me back. My nose was red, I was shivering, I looked totally unattractive. But it wasn't just that. Something about the way Steve and Matthew stood—close together, conspiratorial, huddled together, looking at something that Matthew was holding—made me paranoid. I was certain that they were talking about me. Plotting something ... to do with me.

It was completely ridiculous, but I couldn't get rid of the thought.

I walked very slowly around the block, shivering all the while, and by the time I got back Matthew was gone.

Steve leered at me as I took off my coat.

'Your rich boyfriend was here,' he said. 'He left a little present for you.' He handed me a small black box tied with a thin red ribbon.

'You're blushing,' said Steve. 'It must be something exciting. Expensive. Can I see?'

'Absolutely not,' I said. 'Didn't you say you wanted to go out after I got back?'

'I guess so,' said Steve reluctantly, consoled, I assumed, by the prospect of whips and chains and restraints. But who was I to mock Steve for his sex life? What about all the ... *unusual* things I'd been doing with Matthew?

As soon as Steve was safely gone, I ripped off the wrapping paper. Inside the box, nestled on a pillow of purple silk, was what looked like a little bright-pink plastic bullet, or maybe a skinny egg, with a thin leather cord attached. Underneath the little bullet-egg was a note:

Dear Isabel,

I want you to put this up inside you, the night we go to see your friends' play. It shouldn't be uncomfortable. Try it out if you want, so you get used to it.

Oh, and take a happiness pill.
Love,
Matthew

*Dear*, it said. *Love*, it was signed.

I knew I would do anything he wanted to hear him *say* those words instead of just scribble them in a set of weird exciting instructions.

That evening, when I got home, I slipped the vibrator up inside me. I didn't feel it, any more than I felt a tampon. (I was so glad I didn't have my period, which would have made everything impossible, really). I walked around with the thing inside me, and after a little while, it felt perfectly fine. It felt good. I wondered if Matthew was thinking about me wearing it, if he was looking forward to the night of the play.

Matthew met me outside the theater. He gave me a quick little hug hello and whispered, 'Are you wearing it?'

I nodded. I couldn't speak. I was conscious of the little egg inside me, and of all the strangers around us who had no idea... It was so private. So intimate, so secret. It was something that only we knew about, something that connected us in this special intimate way.

'Is it comfortable?' he asked.

I nodded again, lying this time.

'Good,' he said. 'That makes me happy.'

I was so happy—overjoyed, really—to make him happy. The theater was already full: neighborhood people, young actors, friends of Marcy and Luke, a smattering of high school kids. The presence of the teenagers made me feel a little weird, a little dirty about having something inside me. I told myself they would never know. There was no way they could suspect.

As cool as they thought they were, they were still too innocent. *Like I used to be.*

Marcy and Luke and their friends had decided against costumes or sets; anyway, they'd been in too much of a hurry to get any of that together. But they did have an artist-friend to create a slide show, so when the play began in Lear's castle, we watched a sort of montage: stone walls, Stonehenge, a hall hung with banners with a throne at the far end.

Because the play was gender neutral, Marcy was playing King Lear. It took some getting used to, and the sight of Marcy in bushy eyebrows and a long beard took my mind off the fact that I had something inside me. I cringed, waiting for someone to laugh, but no one did. I looked over at Matthew to see how he was reacting, and as if in response to my look, I felt the faintest buzz inside me.

It was a vibrator. Remote control. Of course I'd known what it was—and I hadn't let myself think too much about it. Matthew had the control in his pocket.

There was something so sacrilegious about watching

Shakespeare and waiting for the next buzz between my legs. But it was exciting and weird and fun. I told myself that Shakespeare, with his bawdy humor and dirty puns, would have approved. But in the midst of his greatest tragedy?

I looked over at Matthew again. He was watching the stage.

Luke was playing Cordelia. And when she refused to be false and follow her wicked sisters in their phony avowals of love for their father, I found myself forgetting that Luke was a boy playing a girl and that Marcy was a woman playing an old man. I began to lose myself in the play.

The buzzing inside me started again, slightly faster and more intense. For a moment I was afraid that someone around us might hear. But it was totally silent. I was the only one who knew—only me and Matthew. He wouldn't look at me, but his hand was deep in his jacket pocket, and I knew he was thinking about when to make the pleasure start again.

I wanted to watch the play, and I wanted the vibrator to buzz inside me. I wanted to do both things at once. The happiness pill was kicking in. I felt almost delirious. Ecstatic. I should have been embarrassed to have this happen in public. But it just felt totally great. I did my best to concentrate on the production—Marcy was surprisingly convincing as the elderly king—but every time I got into the play, I'd feel the vibrating pulse between my legs. It was almost as if Matthew knew, and was making sure my attention stayed focused on him, on what he was doing. He was competing with Shakespeare and winning. The buzzing got faster, then slower. A feeling of warmth spread from between my legs all the way down to my toes and up into my shoulders. I arched my back against the seat, trying to escape it and to intensify the feeling, all at once. Now *this* was immersive theater.

Marcy and Luke had told me that they'd scheduled in two intermissions, because they expected the audience to include a number of teenagers who couldn't be expected to sit still for very long. When the lights came up at the end of act two, I was embarrassed to look around. I imagined everyone was looking at me, that they knew what I had inside me and what I'd been feeling during the performance.

People *did* seem to be looking at me—or at least looking in my direction. In fact so much attention focused on my part of the auditorium (fifth row center) that I had to fight the impulse to get up and run out of the theater. They knew! But I would be leaving Matthew, giving up that feeling inside me. And how would I explain my hasty exit to Luke and Marcy? How would I apologize for deserting my friends? I couldn't leave.

I turned around in my seat, and immediately I understood what the fuss was about. People were staring, but not at me. Sitting directly behind me and Matthew were ... Val and Heidi Morton. I could sense the celebrity sighting thrill going through the auditorium.

What were they doing here? Matthew must have told them. But why had they come to see an amateur production?

The moment I turned around, I locked eyes with Val Morton. I thought back to that day I caught him spying on Matthew and me in his bed. He smiled at me, the same lizard smile he'd had that day. He knew, and I knew. So all that hadn't been in my imagination, no matter what Matthew tried to make me believe.

How much did Val Morton know now? Did he know about the vibrator inside me?

Matthew didn't seem at all surprised to see the famous couple. Of course their being there had been his doing.

'Val,' he said. 'Heidi. Great to see you. You remember Isabel, don't you?'

'Certainly,' said Val. Certainly, I thought. Heidi nodded, pretending. Though maybe she knew something. There was the slightest flicker of ... something in her perfectly made up hazel eyes.

'How are you enjoying the play?' Matthew asked.

'Interesting,' said Val. 'I always like to see what young actors are up to these days. The gender thing was a little hard to wrap my head around for the first few scenes. But after a while you stop noticing, right? After all, the poetry is still the poetry, it's still fucking gorgeous no matter who's saying it. Right?'

'Absolutely,' said Matthew.

'Your friends have some talent,' Val said to me. 'I'm surprised you're not on stage with them. You would have made a stunning Cordelia. So why...?'

I'd almost completely forgotten about what Val could do for me. Was he still buying the space for that new immersive theater project Matthew told me about all those months ago? I had pushed that possibility so far back in my memory, I wondered if I ever believed it to be true.

But why wasn't I Cordelia? Because I wasn't invited, that's why. Because I was too busy playing some sort of sexual theater with Matthew. But I couldn't say any of that out loud without seeming angry or crazy and making everyone uncomfortable.

'Thanks,' I said. 'But I think they were determined to have a guy play Cordelia.'

'Kids,' Val said. 'Go figure.'

As everyone chuckled politely, I looked at Matthew, as if I could read the answer to my questions in his face. But his expression was impassive as he listened to Val, who was saying something about other Lears he'd seen during his years on stage and in film.

And then ... the buzzing inside me began again. Was this Matthew's idea of a joke? Of fun? Of humiliation? To make the vibrator pulse so thrillingly as we were chatting with his boss? It should have been awful, but it was great. I wanted to laugh out loud.

'Excuse me,' I said, and got up and stepped over (and on) some feet as I made my way out of the row. The buzzing stopped when I moved out of range. I went to the ladies' room and stood in line for a while. I pulled the leather cord and took the little pink bullet out when I peed. I sat on the toilet, deciding what to do next. I could have put the vibrator in my pocket and returned to the theater to watch the show without the distraction or the pleasure. Or...

I pushed it back up inside me and returned to my seat.

Matthew smiled at me. I could tell that he knew what I had done. I don't know how he knew, but he did. I guess he could read it on my face.

He was the mind reader now. It was as if I'd slowly but surely transferred that gift to him.

'That's my girl,' he said.

*His girl.*

The lights flickered and went down, then the spotlight came up again on the heath. The video projector flashed slides of threatening dark clouds. Lightning flickered on the screen, a low rumble of thunder sounded.

I knew what was going to happen—on the stage and inside me. I was conscious of Val Morton sitting behind me, watching the back of my head even as he watched the stage. Once more, I was going to have sex with Val looking on. Was my whole romance with Matthew just another play staged for Val's entertainment only? Was Val a wicked puppeteer, pulling everyone's strings?

The storm onstage grew more intense—as did the throbbing inside me. The buzzing got faster, harder. I wanted it to stop, and I wanted it to go on forever. I writhed in my seat, not with embarrassment, as I'd imagined, but with physical pleasure, trying to escape the feeling and at the same time to make it get stronger. As King Lear raged against the storm, another raged inside me. I was just about to come, almost there, almost…

The buzzing stopped. I felt nothing for several scenes. Would it never start again? I felt myself becoming irritable, almost angry. How could Matthew do this, leave me here feeling like this?

The vibrator started up again during the scene in which Gloucester is blinded. The sensation was sudden, hot, strong. Almost painfully powerful. I felt my orgasm building. When they put out Gloucester's eyes, the actress playing Gloucester screamed. The audience screamed.

I came. An electric jolt shot through me. Matthew put his hand over my mouth. Wild with pleasure, out of control, unaware of my surroundings, I screamed into Matthew's hand. I noticed that my cheeks were wet. Tears were running down my face.

When the lights came up before the final act, I turned around. Val and Heidi were gone. Somehow I couldn't help thinking that they'd stayed around till I came, then left. But how could they know? My scream was no louder than anyone else's. I sat in my seat, deeply shaken and still trembling all over, through the second intermission.

'How was that?' said Matthew. 'Good?'

I nodded. I couldn't speak.

The last act began. I heard sniffling and sobs around me when Cordelia died. I was crying too. They were crying for Cordelia and King Lear, as was I.

But I was also crying for myself, for the person I used to be and the person I had become. Just a few months before, if you'd asked me which of the three sisters I identified with, I would have said, without hesitation, Cordelia. Honest, straightforward, sensitive, loving. But I'd turned into one of her sisters: lustful, greedy, rapacious, willing to do whatever it took to get what I wanted. Whatever it took to have that feeling.

After the play, we went back stage to tell Luke and Marcy how much we'd loved the production.

'Look at you, Isabel,' said Marcy. 'Your mascara is all streaked.'

'I was crying,' I told her. 'The play made me cry. It was totally amazing.'

They invited us to the after party in a bar around the corner. I thanked them and said I was tired. Luke looked at me strangely. He'd never heard me say I was too tired to party. But I did feel exhausted, drained not only from the force of my orgasm, and the tension that had built to it, but from the guilt I felt. I'd been disloyal and disrespectful to my friends, who'd been trying so hard to create something, to make art. What I was doing with Matthew wasn't art, not in the way I'd been telling myself it might be. I could have refused at any point. Matthew wouldn't have forced me. But I'd wanted it. I'd loved it.

Matthew took me home in a taxi. I knew that he wasn't going to come up to my apartment, but that was fine with me. I didn't need him to see the squalor in which I lived.

As the cab drove over the Williamsburg Bridge, Matthew put out his hand.

I knew what he wanted. He didn't have to ask. Hoping that the cabdriver wasn't watching too closely in the mirror, I reached under my skirt and pulled out the leather string attached to the vibrator. I dropped it into Matthew's hand, and he put it into his pocket.

'Thank you,' he said.

'Thank *you*,' I said.


The next morning, I got two calls before I'd even gotten out of bed. First Marcy.

'Val Morton was at our play!' said Marcy, practically yelling into the phone. That's how excited she was.

'I know that,' I said.

'Do you think he liked it?' she asked.

'I'm sure he loved it,' I said. 'Everyone did. Listen, I'll talk to you later. I've got to take this. It's Luke.'

'It's all you,' said Luke. 'You're the one who got him there. You creep around like a quiet little mouse who doesn't see anything and doesn't make a peep, but you've got this life that's full of celebrities who will show up if you just say the word. It was because of you that Val and Heidi Morton came to our play. They would never have known about it otherwise. And your boyfriend is an angel for telling him. Don't think we don't appreciate it. That's some boyfriend you've got, Isabel. Who cares if he fucks you or not as long as he can get Val Morton to come to our play.'

I didn't know what to say to that.

'Sorry,' said Luke. 'I guess that was a little out of line. I'm just trying to tell you how grateful we are.'

Once more, I thought: Oh, if only you knew. But I just kept saying that it had nothing to do with me, it was all Matthew's doing.

For the next two weeks, Marcy and Luke couldn't stop talking about the fact that Val had come to their play. I think they expected something to come out of it. They'd be discovered, the way Val was. Or anyhow, the way Matthew *told* them Val was. Val and Heidi would rave about the play to all their famous friends, and their friends would tell the right casting directors, who would naturally tell the right directors.

None of that ever happened, of course. And Marcy and Luke went back to complaining about the bad auditions and the unfair casting directors. Not that anything much was happening. Everyone had already gone on break for the holidays. They'd try again in the New Year. Despite everything, they were hopeful. They had to be. What was the alternative?

Meanwhile, I understood that Matthew was their new hero. No matter what happened in our relationship, no matter how he made me unsettled and uneasy, no matter if he raised doubts and questions that worried me, Luke and Marcy—my only friends—were the last people I could ask for answers or advice. No matter what, they would want me to keep seeing Matthew. They would tell me about his good points.

I knew way more about his good points than they did. And despite everything, I wanted to keep seeing him, too.

# Matthew

Two nights after the play, Val summoned me to his home. His study was thick with cigar smoke, and he was well (as far as I could tell) into his third or fourth brandy. The TV was on loud, he held the remote in one hand and was switching rapidly from channel to channel, without staying on any channel long enough to actually watch anything.

He turned off the TV when he saw me. 'Heidi wants to go somewhere. I can't remember where the fuck ... some private island in Croatia. Or the villa in Jamaica where Ian Fleming wrote all his James Bond books. Croatia, Jamaica. Who gives a fuck? Not me. I don't want to go anywhere. It's a bad time for me to leave, what with everything going on. The mess in Long Island City.

'Some truly massive shit that could hit the fan at any given moment. And do we think Heidi cares deeply? Heidi does not care. My wife is getting restless. She keeps saying it would be good for me to get away. Chill. Don't you hate that word *chill*? Chill is for oysters, for white wine. Not human beings. We're warm-blooded for a reason. To stay awake and alert. What would really be good for me would be to have the city council and the mayor and the whole damn city and especially the fucking EPA finally get the fuck off my ass and let me do what's best for me and, whether they know it or not, the city. But that's not going to happen, so I have to pretend to give a shit while Heidi flips through pictures of expensive vacation paradises where I don't want to go.'

'I've heard Croatia is cool,' I said carefully. 'Not that I've ever been there.'

'Cool,' Val spat into the fireplace. 'The fucking grave is cool. But listen, hey, how bullshit was that play? Have you ever seen anything worse in your life? You get to a certain point in your career, you've seen some lousy Shakespeare, you think you've seen all the bad Shakespeare you're ever going to see, but that production should have won a prize for sheer unadulterated badness. The kid playing Cordelia was flopping around the stage like a dying rainbow trout, and that girl who was supposed to be Lear—she looked like a toddler in a Santa Claus suit at the kindergarten Christmas pageant.'

I must have flinched, because Val said, 'Oh, have I offended you? Sorry, I forgot. Those were your girlfriend's pals.'

'She's *not* my girlfriend,' I said.

'Now you sound like a twelve-year-old,' said Val. 'And who gives a fuck if she is or she isn't your girlfriend?'

'How did you get Heidi to go?' I said.

'That was the easiest part. Heidi thought it might be a goof. She thinks every goddamn stupid thing is going to cheer me up. If she says *chill* one more time ... anyhow I like supporting young actors. It's good for the soul. And I especially like keeping the little lady happy. How did your girlfriend enjoy the play?'

I took a deep breath. Should I tell Val? Why not? Heidi had instructed me to lift his spirits. She'd told me to be creative. And what I'd done with Isabel at the play had been pretty creative. Isabel would never need to know that Val knew—unless of course she got it into her head that he was spying on her again. And I would have to deny everything.

'My girlfriend wasn't thinking,' I said. 'Or anyway, she certainly wasn't thinking about the play.'

I felt a little bit bad for Isabel, but something had bothered me at the show. When she turned around and saw Val there, the look she gave me said, 'See, I was right about him watching us in his bedroom.' I knew that was bullshit. It reminded me how crazy she was. She was fun. She was loose. She was pliable. But I didn't owe her a thing.

'What do you mean?' said Val.

I told him about the vibrator.

Val burst into gales of laughter. He laughed so loud

and so long that I realized it was the first time I'd heard him laugh in a very long while. His laugh was so raucous that Heidi looked in.

When she saw Val laughing, she gave me a thumbs up sign. She didn't know what he was laughing about, but she gave me credit. I'd done what she'd told me to do. I'd been creative.

'Guess what?' Val said. 'Matthew had a remote control vibrator up his girlfriend's snatch during that awful King Lear, and he kept giving her little jolts all during the play.'

'Fabulous!' said Heidi. 'Did you make her come during the storm on the heath?'

'Too obvious,' said Val. 'He made her wait for the blinding of Gloucester.'

'I adore it,' said Heidi. 'Let's get one, Val. I can't tell you how many boring events would get a whole lot more interesting. All those gala benefit dinners and...'

'Consider it done,' said Val. 'Order us one,' he told me.

'Tomorrow morning pronto,' I said. 'Any color preference? Black? Hot pink? Lavender?'

'Black,' said Heidi. 'Definitely.'

'Okay, you got it.'

'My God,' said Val. 'You know what? Next time, you should take her to see *Romeo and Juliet*, and make her put it up her ass.'

Heidi winked at me. I could tell that Val didn't know about her visit.

I had a vision of Isabel, so real it was as if I saw her. She was standing on an ice floe that had broken off from a glacier. She waved at me as I watched her getting swept further to sea.

I was sorry for her, sorry that I was turning a good person into a not so good person. And using her real dreams of becoming an actress to do it. But she wasn't all there. Like so many women, she was nuts. My boss and his wife were laughing for the first time in months. They couldn't begin to say how much I'd amused them, what a good job I was doing. How creative I was being. For the first time, I felt like the director instead of another one of Val's actors on stage.

No one got hurt. We all had fun. Isabel most of all.

# Isabel

I'd never spent Christmas apart from my mother, and I wasn't going to start this year. I needed to be with her more than ever before, even more than when I was a fatherless kid and she was a lifelong widow. I needed her to remind me of who I was, where I'd come from, of what I believed in. I needed someone who knew me as the nice Midwestern girl, the compassionate one, the thoughtful one. The person who knew what others were feeling. Someone who knew me when I *was* that person.

In the back of my mind, I think I believed that if I could just spend a few days at home with my mother, all the dirty things I'd done with Matthew would somehow be undone, wiped clean from my record. I would never have cheated a waitress or shoplifted a steak or let him ... do *that* to me while I watched the Shakespeare play.

After I'd spent some time with Mom, I would turn a new leaf. I could start over—clean and fresh, pure and new. Maybe Matthew and I would have some kind of relationship, but this time I would stick up for myself. I would make sure he knew who I was, what my limits were, what kind of principles I had, what I did and didn't do. The only problem was, I'd wanted to do everything he'd told me to do. But maybe if I hung out with Mom and reminded myself of who I was, the slate with which I would begin again would have something different written on it.

Two weeks before Christmas he texted me to say he wanted to meet after work. I steeled myself for some complicated game, but it turned out that he just wanted to have a quiet conversation in that bar near Doctor Sleep.

There were lights strung across all the streets and wound round the trees and branches, neon stars shining over the avenues. Holiday shoppers passed by the window of the bar, laughing and carrying bags and packages. I never expected Matthew to be moved by the Christmas spirit.

But when I saw him from the door to the bar, he looked strangely, unusually dejected, and it crossed my mind that maybe he was actually a human being who like so many other human beings, got sad around Christmas. As a child I always had, without a dad when all the other kids had dads, but for years now I'd liked it, relaxing and hanging out with my mom and getting high on sickly sweet eggnog.

Matthew was drinking scotch, though he usually stuck to white wine. I ordered an Irish coffee, to get into the spirit of the season. He reached across the table and wiped the whipped cream from my upper lip with his thumb. I started to get excited—that was how Pavlovian things had become. All he had to do was touch me.

'I wish this crap were over,' he said. 'In my opinion, December 26th is the happiest day of the year. My dad felt the same way. That was the only good thing about him. One year we came downstairs the day after Christmas and we found him taking down the Christmas tree and throwing it in the trash. My mom cried, but I was happy. That's what kind of family I had.'

I waited a moment, not wanting to follow this story of dysfunction with an expression of family love and loyalty. Then I said, 'I'm going home to see my mom in Iowa. Just for a few days.'

I could tell he didn't like it. He would never say he would miss me or he would be lonely, but his mouth tightened in a way that I had come to recognize: a sign of disapproval. Usually he made that expression when I responded too quickly to something sexual, but this was different. This wasn't a game. *This was real.*

'Lucky you,' he said.

'What are *you* doing for the holidays?' I asked.

'Nothing,' he said. 'Taking a break. Val and Heidi are going to St Bart's, so after I've checked the gas burners and lights in their various apartments, I'm pretty much on my own.'

'What about your family?' I said. I knew that his parents were dead, but that was all I knew.

'What family?' he said. 'My brother hasn't spoken to me for years.'

It was totally weird that I hadn't even known he'd had a brother. That was how little I knew about him. That was how little I'd asked.

'You have a brother?'

'Yeah.'

'What's his name?'

'Ansel.'

'Where does he live?'

'Long Island.'

'What does he do?'

'He's an architect.'

'And why won't he speak to you?'

'He hates me,' Matthew said.

It was the most intimate and revealing thing he'd ever told me about himself. And even though it was a bad thing, I couldn't help feeling exultant.

'My God,' I said. 'Why? What happened?'

'There was an accident,' he said.

'What kind of accident?'

'An accident,' he said.

'Was he hurt?'

'Barely.'

'Is he okay now?'

'He's fine. He made more of it than it was. I was the one who took the hit.'

Matthew ordered another scotch. A double. And drank it in two swallows.

The discussion was over, for him. He wasn't saying one more word about his brother, or his family. Or Christmas. The look on his face was so ... troubled ... so sad ... I was shocked by how much it upset me. Underneath, I was still the compassionate person I'd always been. I could feel what he was feeling, and it was dark, dark and lonely... Some new (or maybe old) impulse moved me, and I was shocked again, this time to hear, coming from inside me, the voice of the sweet, nice, generous human being I was before I met Matthew.

That automatic, instinctive, self-sabotaging voice said, 'Then why don't you come home with me? To Iowa.'

'Iowa? What?' Matthew waved over the waitress and ordered another round. 'What did you say?'

'Come home with me.' I was sorry as soon as I'd said it. Would he think I was trying to move our 'relation-ship' to 'the next level?' I suppose the invitation to meet your parents was one step before a couple began to talk about getting engaged. But as I kept reminding myself, we weren't a couple. We didn't have a relationship in any traditional sense, so what would 'the next level' be? Doing something hotter and dirtier than what we'd done? I blushed, just thinking what that might mean.

In fact, I couldn't imagine. But I felt sure that Matthew could.

'I have to warn you,' I said. 'My mom's very old-fashioned. My dad died years ago and in some ways she's never quite made the transition into the modern world. We'd have to sleep in separate rooms.' What was I talking about? Matthew and I had never slept in the same room here in New York, where there was no one to stop us.

Matthew smiled, a rare event.

'I can do old-fashioned,' he said.

* * *

When I told my mom, on the phone, that I was bringing a friend, she said, 'Boyfriend or girlfriend?'

'A man,' I said. 'A friend.'

'Boyfriend or friend friend?' she asked.

'I'm not sleeping with him if that's what you're asking,' I said.

Strictly speaking, it was true. I thought of Bill Clinton and Monica Lewinsky, of the scandal that erupted when I was in grade school, and of how our parents and teachers tried—unsuccessfully—to shield us from the details of what the whole mess was about.

I did not have sex with that man.

'Actually, that's not what I'm asking,' said my mother. 'But thanks for telling me, anyway. Oh ... and listen. I have some good news. Some really good news. But I want to wait till you get here to tell you.'

'Tell me now,' I said. 'Mom, please.'

'No,' she insisted. 'I want it to be a surprise. I want you to...'

She caught herself.

I don't know why I was suddenly sure that she had been about to say: *I want you to meet him*? It was an intuition I got. But it was a fairly strong one. I knew what she was thinking. What she'd been about to say.

Had Mom finally met someone after all these years? That would be so great, for her to have someone to grow old with! I pictured a sweet old guy, balding, with a ring of gray hair and bushy eyebrows, a widower, maybe a professor who taught in the department where she worked.

I could wait to meet him until I got home, if that was what my mother wanted.

I still thought of Iowa as home. Would I ever feel that about New York?

Matthew, Mom's new ... whatever. It wasn't what I'd had in mind: a calm, relaxed time to catch up with Mom, a chance to tell her some—though obviously not all—of what was happening and to ask for her advice.

Matthew's presence would make everything more awkward and tense. I didn't want to have to feel self-conscious, to worry about what he thought of my childhood home, my life. My mom. Of how and where I grew up and the person I was before he met me. I didn't want to think or worry about what Mom was thinking of him.

But still, I trusted Mom's judgment more than anyone's in the world. She would look at Matthew and understand who he was. She would know what I saw in him. And since I didn't know what I saw in him, except for the crazy sex, which she didn't have to know about, maybe she could tell me. She might also be able to figure out how he felt about me. Nothing she said would stop my obsession with him, my craving to see him, to be with him. But it might help me cope with the craziness of this relationship that was so unlike anything else I knew or imagined. Ever.

'What does your friend do?' asked Mom.

Unrealistically, I'd hoped against hope that the subject of Val Morton would never come up. I knew that Mom would ask, as she just had, what Matthew did, and I would have to tell her that Matthew worked for Valentine Morton. The next best thing would be if the conversation stopped there. Mom had seen a lot of Val Morton's films, she was sort of a fan. She would like it that Matthew worked for him. And that, I hoped, would be that.

Among the things I could never tell her, and didn't even want her suspecting, was that Val had seen me—not once but twice—in sexual situations. I didn't want to her to figure out, with her laser intuition, how much Matthew was telling Val about what he did with me.

That was something I didn't know myself.

I didn't want to know.

# Matthew

You may think you know who you are. You may imagine that you know what you think and what you'll do and not do—and why. But as it turns out, you don't. If I were being tortured, with a cattle prod pointed at my head or my genitals, and my torturer said, 'Why did you say you wanted to go home to Iowa with Isabel for Christmas? She doesn't even really want you,' I couldn't have explained it. I didn't understand it myself.

Maybe it was the scotch—scotches—I'd had before Isabel got to the bar where I'd asked her to meet me. I didn't even know exactly why I'd asked her to meet me in the bar. Maybe it was something about Val, something new and weird and hard to pinpoint or explain about how he'd changed, how he'd started talking to me, dealing with me. He'd begun to seem ... guarded, as if he didn't quite trust me, or as if he was secretly thinking of moving on, hiring another guy he found more interesting, more fun. Maybe he'd found out that Heidi had come to see me and flashed me with Isabel's underwear.

Or maybe I said yes to Isabel just because I was bored and lonely. I had nothing to do, nothing planned for the holidays. My friends had moved steadily further into their own lives, further away from mine. The group bromance was almost over. They had girlfriends to spend Christmas Eve with, families to party with, to open presents, and drink eggnog, and feel sick from all the heavy cream and rum and eggs, and fall into bed with. What was I going to do? Order out for Chinese food? Go running in the cold empty park? Buy myself something special and get it wrapped so I could open it all by myself Christmas morning? Bring out the violins, I know, but still...

Anything seemed better.

Even Iowa, with Isabel.

I was getting ... attached to her. I'd mostly put that whole incident—her hallucinating that Val was watching us in his bedroom—out of my mind. Or almost out of my mind.

I was almost always glad to see her. She was brave, in her crazy way. Always up for anything. And she was in love with me, also in her own crazy way. If she was crazy, a couple of days with her mom in her childhood home might help me understand just how insane she was. Or why. Or not.

I'd never been to the Midwest. Isabel said that her mom was an excellent cook. It would be a strange low-key, low-level adventure. Very low key. Low level. Not St. Bart's. But something different, nonetheless.

I came up with dozens of explanations, and still I couldn't explain why I'd said I wanted to go, why I'd actually bought my ticket. I'd arrive two days after Isabel to give her time to hang with her mom.

I bought her a silver wire bracelet from Tiffany's. Snobbish, maybe, but I knew the little blue box from Tiffany's would impress the folks in Iowa. The bracelet was very plain, very simple. No one in their right minds would mistake it for piece of jewelry that a guy would give a girl to whom he was planning to get engaged. It was more like something a boss would give his secretary for staying late and not complaining. Isabel wasn't the type to check on the Tiffany's website where you could sort the jewelry from lowest price to highest. The bracelet came up first.

But also there was this: I could imagine how pretty the bracelet would look on Isabel's slim pale wrist.

I asked Charisse, Val's decorator, about what I should get the Iowa mom, a little something for the home, pretty, not too personal, neutral. Charisse ordered, from the Museum of Modern Art, a set of place mats woven from a high-tech silvery mesh with a geometric design: little rectangles that gleamed in variant shades of silver. The shopping bag said MOMA and fit neatly into my carry-on.

I went through all the motions, as if I were a regular

guy going to visit his regular girlfriend's mother on a regular Christmas. But I wasn't that guy. And Isabel wasn't that girl. This wasn't that Christmas.

This was nothing like that.

Val Morton was in St Barts. Were he and Heidi talking about me? What were they saying?

Would Val mind if I charged the Foundation for a business class ticket? Probably not if I did some sex thing with Isabel and told Val about it.

I didn't care. I charged the ticket. A business expense.

Flying business was another reason I didn't want to travel with Isabel, who would fly coach. That would be awkward. On a short flight to Iowa, the seats in business were only a few inches wider, a few degrees softer and deeper than in coach. But it was worth it to have the flight attendant come around before take-off with champagne and orange juice.

The flight attendant was young and reasonably hot. But I controlled myself. It was Christmas. I wasn't a total bastard. Not totally.

I took a glass of champagne in each hand.

'Someone's having a merry Christmas,' the pretty flight attendant said.

'If it kills me,' I said.

'I'd drink to that,' said the flight attendant. 'If I wasn't working.'

# Isabel

Something had changed. My mother looked different. For years I'd been after her to do something with her hair, which had slowly turned into a hank of graying straw that she wore in a tight knot at the back of her neck. I teased her about shopping where kindergarten teachers shopped, wherever that was.

She used to say she'd check back with me in the future when I was her age and I was trying to find something that looked reasonably decent and comfortable and didn't call too much attention to all the problem spots that weren't problems when she was my age.

At the airport I was looking for a gray-haired lady in a puffy jacket and a long skirt and boots, maybe the Peruvian knit hat she'd gotten one Christmas from her book club. So it took me a moment to recognize the rather pretty, rather stylish woman with blow-dried, blondish hair, a long navy coat with a hood, and bright red gloves. Maybe if we'd Skyped, I would have had a clue, but Mom hated Skype (she said she didn't like how she looked on the screen) so we always communicated old school, on the phone. And sometimes we texted.

'Mom, you look amazing!' I said, as we threw our arms around each other and squeezed. How happy I was to see her! How great it was to hug!

'So do you, sweetheart,' she said, though actually I'd seen her brow cloud slightly when she'd first spotted me in the arrivals hall of our small, old-fashioned airport. Had I too changed in some way she'd picked up on her faultless mom radar? Changed in a less positive, less healthy way? What did she see that I didn't?

At least the airport hadn't changed: one magazine stand, one local café advertising breakfast all day, and their specialty, chicken fried steak. How unbelievable that a place like that could still be here—or anywhere!

I looked through the café window at the waitress serving coffee. Mom waved at her, and the waitress waved back. They'd known each other for years, for decades, really— ever since Mom used to work there, I recalled now. The airport café was the first place I remember my mom working. Guilt washed over me, and I forced myself not to think about Matthew and I leaving the diner without paying the bill. Stop it, I told myself. New York is far from Iowa, in every way. New York is dangerous, just like Mom thinks, but not in the way she thinks.

Anyway, I was here now. I was safe, here with her.

'Your hair,' I said. 'Your coat ... really. You look great.'

My mother blushed. 'I told you I had good news.'

She'd definitely met someone. My suspicions were correct.

'Okay, who is he? When do I get to meet him?'

Whatever Mom was, she wasn't coy. 'Christmas afternoon. He's coming for lunch. By then your friend will have been here a couple of days, I'll have a chance to get to know him. And before your friend comes, you and I will have the time to hang out and have fun and catch up.'

'I love you, Mom,' I said.

'Let's go home. Let's get started. We probably have enough to say so we could blab away nonstop till your Matthew gets here.'

*My* Matthew? Oh, if she only knew. But I didn't want her to know. Let her think he *was* mine.

She was right about one thing; we started talking in the car going home, and we didn't stop. I told her all about Steve. I made the whole thing sound funnier than it was, and as I told my mother about it, and she cracked up over my descriptions of Steve's medical décor and the white surgical jackets we wore, I began to think, maybe it *was* that funny. Maybe I just hadn't seen the humor. I'd taken everything too seriously. I could start over, with a better attitude this time. Enjoy the joke, laugh, and move on.

When I told my mom about all the awful auditions, and the way the casting directors didn't even try to hide their boredom and lack of interest, she was genuinely shocked that people could be so rude. Seeing it through her eyes, it almost stopped seeming personal and started to seem like a rude thing that rude people did. It was the custom of another society, far from the one I'd grown up in. I'd spent my early years in, and had just returned to, a place where people constantly put themselves out to make other people feel *better*.

My mother was beloved in the English department where she worked, and though the professors often feuded with one another, no one feuded with Mom. Somehow she managed to tell me about the intrigues, the conspiracies and betrayals without being gossipy or mean, but just in a tone of wonder: look what people will get themselves into. Look how stupid smart people can act.

We pulled up in front of the pale gray, two-bedroom ranch-style house I loved more than any place in the world. How could I have forgotten how deeply and passionately I loved it?

I hesitated on the porch, where the junk of the house had always collected until we could bring ourselves to throw things out. Now the porch had been swept and straightened for the first time I could remember. Had my mom moved in with this guy? Would the house be different—a house for the two of them, with no more room for me? You heard those stories all the time: someone goes home to find that Mom has turned their old bedroom into a sewing room, or sometimes into the room of their new step-sibling.

I was so thrilled that the house was exactly the way I remembered—the gently worn hooked rugs, the round oak table, the carved, high-backed Victorian chairs. The comfy couches worn lumpy and soft by decades of reading and hanging out.

I looked at the framed photo of my handsome dad, and of my young mom and dad together. One of the photos of my father had, I knew, been taken a few weeks before he was killed in the car wreck. He was standing, waving, leaning against the blue Dodge Minivan in which he would die.

The living room was the same, only neater. Had Mom cleaned up for me ... and Matthew? Or was it always this tidy, these days? Did it have something to do with the mystery person I was going to meet on Christmas day?

'I think I'll go to my room,' I said. 'See you in a few minutes.'

Nothing in my room had changed. All my old high school books were on my bookshelf, including the marked-up copies of the plays I'd been in. My stuffed animals, my signed photo of Elvis Costello, dumb sulfide snapshots of me and my friends in various holiday places. How young and happy we were! Most of the girls were in college or married. In my present insecure state, I knew that I wouldn't have the strength to bring myself to look them up.

I turned out the light and lay down on the bed, and it was gone, all gone, the humiliating auditions, the dull afternoons at Doctor Sleep, the hours and days of waiting for Matthew to call. I lingered on the edge of sleep. I felt like a child again, warm and safe. I thought about Matthew, about sex with him, and it did nothing for me at all. He had no control over me here. I was the person I used to be, the strong independent girl I was before I met him.

There was one more thing I wanted to check, one thing that said *home* to me. I got up and went to the bathroom and pulled back the shower curtain, almost violently, as if I was planning to surprise an intruder hiding in the tub. But actually I was looking for the decals of cute little animal babies that my mom had pasted on the wall so long ago. The stickers had somehow managed to remain there, only slightly peeling, despite the years of hot water and steam.

For a year or so, when I was little, I'd developed a strange fear of the water. I never wanted to take a bath and would only very reluctantly agree to shower.

So my mom came up with a plan. She went out and bought all these decals—silly cartoons of ducks and bunnies and monkeys. Each time I took a shower, she pasted another one to the tile walls until there was hardly any space that wasn't covered by one of the images.

I was suddenly afraid that in mom's clean-up program, she'd done something about the semi-sloppy menagerie that lined the shower stall. But there they were, the merry little ducks and carrot-eating bunnies and monkeys gobbling bananas, the leftover remnants of my childhood that I knew—or I hoped—would never change.

Another thing that hadn't changed was how easy it was to talk to my mom. To a stranger watching, our conversation would have seemed like a super-fast ping pong game, the ball whipping back and forth as we talked about books we'd read, music we'd heard, films we'd wanted to see; with Mom living in our little town, and me having to pay the price of movie tickets in New York, neither of us had seen most of the films we'd heard about. There was no one else I could talk this way to, this comfortably and with the same ease: not Marcy or Luke, certainly not Matthew, obviously not Steve. Mom and I talked about politics: national, local, global.

*Then she asked me about Matthew.*

I told her that I'd met Matthew when he'd come into the store to buy a mattress. I was afraid to say much more than that for fear that I'd blush and give something away. But I made it sound totally normal. After all, single New York women were always dating men they met at work...

As I told her, she was cooking one of my favorite meals—eggplant parmesan—and I sat at the kitchen table, talking to her, being her sous-chef, cutting and slicing the ingredients as I had so often in the past.

'Did he?' asked my mother.

'Did he what?' I put down the knife. I didn't trust myself, my hand was trembling so hard.

'Did he buy a mattress?'

'Yes,' I said. 'An expensive one.'

'Then we like him already,' my mother said, laughing.

'I don't know,' I said. 'I do like him ... but I keep having these doubts. I can't wait for you to meet him. I'm dying to know what you think.'

'I might be the last person you should ask. I'm prejudiced. I'm your mom.' She turned away from the stove, gently took the knife from me, put it down on the table, and pressed the back of her hand to my cheek.

'You feel a little feverish,' she said. 'Are you okay?'

'I'm fine,' I said. 'Really.'

'You're my only daughter,' she said. 'I'll never love anyone like I love you.'

Was Mom simply telling me how much I meant to her? Or was she warning me not to get jealous when I met the man who had inspired her to buy new clothes and fix up her hair and make the house look ... presentable?

We would both have to try to open our hearts wide enough to admit the man who had won the other's ... what? The man who had made each of us want the other to like him.

I was hoping to take Mom's car by myself to the airport to meet Matthew, so I would have some time to debrief him, to prepare him for whatever lay ahead, to gauge what kind of mood he was in. Maybe, if he was in the mood, we could take a few minutes to pull off the road and drive up to the bluff where high school kids go to make out. I'd spent so much time there fending off boys who wanted to have sex, and now I would be driving a man there expressly to have it.

I was obsessed with where and how I could find ways to do something sexual with Matthew. But he had always been the one who decided what we'd do—and when. That decision was never up to me in New York. But he would be a stranger here, I thought. Maybe it was my turn to direct.

Anyway Mom's insurance had lapsed, and when she renewed her policy, she'd accidentally (she claimed) or on purpose (I suspected) dropped me as an insured driver. Why would she want to pay good money to include a daughter who had moved away and was never there?

So there we were, the two of us. My mother and I. At the airport. Like some kind of welcoming committee, you could say. Poor Matthew.

But 'poor Matthew' looked very confident, handsome and assured as he appeared in the arrivals area, wearing a forest green jacket with lots of pockets and a large leather bag slung over his shoulder. In fact, he appeared so fresh and unrumpled, so untouched by travel that I thought: Of course. He flew business class. No wonder he'd been so eager for us to travel separately. It would have been awkward, him in business, me riding back in coach.

I stood very close to my mother, and when Matthew waved at me, and I waved back, and she realized who he was, I could feel her change, the way a woman changes—standing ever so slightly straighter, pulling in her stomach in, lifting her chin—when she is, or when she is about to be, in the presence of an extremely handsome man. Even Mom—alone now for all these years—was obviously affected. I felt her eyes on me, watching closely as I stood on tiptoe to kiss Matthew on the cheek.

'Mom,' I said. 'This is Matthew. Matthew, my mom. Glenda.'

Mom held out her hand, a little stiffly, I thought. Matthew shook her hand, then bent down to kiss her on the cheek  pretty much the same mild, neutral peck I'd given him. Mom was flustered, but I could tell that she was pleased.

'Glenda. The good witch of the east,' said Matthew. 'I guess you've heard that one before.'

'The good witch of the Midwest,' said my mom, which is what she always said when she didn't want to embarrass the person who'd said something she'd heard a million times.

He put his arm around me, and we exchanged two more chaste little kisses. Maybe Mom thought we were toning things down, acting cool because she was present.

But actually that was the way we always greeted each other in public, and sometimes in private, too.

I watched Matthew look at Mom. There was no way for him to know that this reasonably stylish woman was the same person as the loveable frump I'd pictured in my mind all the time I'd been away. He must have thought Mom had always looked that way. How little he knew about me, really!

On the drive home from the airport, I rode in back and let Matthew ride shotgun. The cornfields began just a few miles from the airport, and I watched him look at the bare, rolling landscape, already covered with snow.

'It's beautiful,' he said. Did he mean it?

'We think so,' said Mom. 'It's not for everybody's taste. I know it doesn't have all the lights and glitter and excitement that you and Isabel enjoy and probably take for granted in the big city. But we love it. It's home.'

*You and Isabel*. Mom thought we were a couple. How I wished we were. I longed to lean forward and rumple Matthew's hair or squeeze his shoulder or make any of the countless small gestures that a woman would have done to reassure her boyfriend, riding beside the mother he was just meeting. But I couldn't do any of that. We weren't a couple, in any traditional sense. That wasn't how we treated each other. And thoughtful loving gestures of affection and support weren't what we did.

'It's very soothing,' said Matthew. 'Peaceful. All that bright lights, big city stuff can wear you down after a while.'

'I suppose it can,' my mother said. 'Though I suppose it's still quite new for Isabel.'

Stop it, I thought. Stop it, Mom. She meant well, as always, but she was talking about me as if I were still a little girl.

The conversation died. Mom drove (always in the slow lane) along the interstate, and the snow-covered fields rolled on and on beside us.

'It's almost like the ocean,' Matthew said.

I couldn't believe how hard he was trying.

'So they say,' said Mom.

After another silence, Mom said, 'Won't your parents miss you for the holidays?'

What was *wrong* with her? I'd told her that Matthew's parents were dead. I remember how sympathetically she'd clicked her tongue. *Poor boy, an orphan, tsk tsk*. But Mom must have been so distracted that she'd forgotten what I'd said.

I purposely hadn't mentioned the fact that Matthew had a brother he never spoke to. That would have raised too many questions to which I had no answers.

I'd been curious about Matthew's brother Ansel ever since he first mentioned him. But every time I even got near the subject, Matthew got so obviously tense that I dropped it.

'We're not much for family celebrations,' Matthew said.

At least Mom knew better than to ask if he had siblings. They were *both* trying so hard. After all, they had nothing in common except me.

I watched the back of Matthew's head and shoulders, searching for his reaction as we pulled into the driveway besides my beloved gray home.

'What a lovely little house,' he said.

I shot him a quick look at that *little*, but Mom didn't seem to notice.

'Home sweet home,' said Mom.

There was an awkward stall at the door. Matthew stepped back to let Mom enter the house first, and because I was daydreaming, not paying I attention, I kind of crashed into Matthew's back as he stood on the doorstep. Even that tiny physical contact with him—accidental, casual, brief, fully clothed, wearing our winter coats— made me feel that familiar warmth, and I remembered all of it. I felt as if we were naked.

Once more I told myself it was important not to think about the things I'd done with Matthew: starting with that day in Doctor Sleep, then locked in Val's bathroom, then in Val's bedroom in Brooklyn Heights. Sitting next to him at *King Lear*. The moment these memories entered my mind, I made an effort to push them away. But even so, I kept being struck by how much of our sex had had some weird connection to Val Morton. Was I being paranoid? Only now did I realize how much I mistrusted and feared Val. As soon as I thought about him, the sexual buzz I got from Matthew subsided, at least slightly, and I felt simultaneously anxious and controlled.

Why was I afraid of Val? He'd never done anything but watch. He was Matthew's boss. He'd been good to him.

'Let me show you your room,' Mom told Matthew.

Thank you, Mom, I thought. I sank into one of the living room couches, weak with gratitude and bad nerves. I didn't want to have to show Matthew to his room, at the other end of the house from mine, along the corridor that went past my mom's room. Mom used the spare room as her study, but it had a comfortable single bed. We wouldn't be having sex there, I was sure of that. But when had we ever had sex like normal people in a normal bed?

I was afraid of finding myself standing in another doorway with Matthew and looking at another bed. It would remind us, or anyway it would remind me, of so much that had happened.

I still had no idea what Matthew was thinking of my mom, of our house. Not that I ever really knew what was going on in his mind. The one person who was opaque to me was the one I most wanted to understand.

To sneak into each other's room, one of us would have had to cross the living room and pass right by mom's door. I made a mental note to tell Matthew that she was a very light sleeper. If we wanted each other, we'd better wait till she was out of the house. That is, if Matthew wanted me. It had always been his call.

When I'd left my mother's house, I was an innocent girl, a nice girl. And I'd come home as a sex maniac who could think of nothing else. But being a sex maniac didn't seem nearly so bad as being so passive and weak that I could only wait meekly for some sort of sign from Matthew. I didn't like that about myself, and I knew that Mom wouldn't have liked it if she knew. She'd raised me on *Free to Be You and Me* and *A League of Their Own*. And when I got older, *Thelma and Louise*. She'd always told me that I could be as strong and powerful and self-determined as any of the boys in my class. *Don't let them bully you or push you around. Stand up for yourself. Be proud you're a woman.*

What was I afraid of?

Of losing Matthew, I guess. Of never having sex with him again.

Or anyway, that was what I feared then.

I didn't know what I had to fear, what the real dangers were.

After Matthew had showered, Mom started dinner. Steak and potatoes, a real Iowa meal, she said, as she poured us glasses of surprisingly good red wine. Mom must have gone all out, I thought, and then I remembered that on Christmas morning we were going to meet her new boyfriend. Or anyway, the person who'd persuaded her to clean up her act.

Mom motioned for Matthew to take a seat at the kitchen table. It was very pleasant with the light shining down on us as I peeled potatoes and Matthew sipped wine and Mom sautéed onions at the stove.

The very first thing Mom said was, 'I hear you work for Val Morton.'

'For the moment,' said Matthew.

For the moment? Was his job in serious danger? He'd told me that Val had been acting strange, but he didn't seem all that worried. Had Matthew decided to leave and try something else? Had he been offered another job?

Why hadn't he told me? But I'd often seen it in the past; Mom had the ability to make people talk about themselves. To say things they might not ordinarily say. Like me, she was intuitive. I must have inherited it from her.

'For the moment?' said Mom.

'You never know,' Matthew said.

'Do you like your job?' said Mom.

Matthew nodded. 'It's stressful but mostly fun, and it's definitely got its perks. I mean, it's how I met Isabel. Basically, thanks to Val Morton. Meeting Isabel is the best thing that's happened to me in my job.'

I'd thought that Mom was too smart to be won over by something that corny, but I could tell his talking so sweetly and flatteringly about me had worked. I should have been happy to hear such kind words from Matthew, but again I felt scared. What did Val have to do with our meeting? How much had they planned together? How much did Matthew tell him? Why hadn't Val told the truth about watching us from the doorway? All those troubling questions returned.

'How did you two meet?' said Mom, though I distinctly remember telling her a version of that story. I intentionally left out the bit about my early online dating forays. I prayed Matthew could intuit that much from the way I looked at him.

'I was buying a mattress for my boss and his wife.' He didn't skip a beat.

I got up from the table and went to the refrigerator. I wasn't looking for anything in particular, but I wanted some cold air. I guess I could have stepped outside, but I didn't want to miss a word of Mom and Matthew's conversation.

Mom said, 'I guess that's the kind of thing that can only happen in the city.'

'And only if you're lucky,' said Matthew.

Mom turned from the stove and beamed at me: what a nice guy I'd brought home.

Matthew rented a car. Mom was off from work for vacation but even so, Matthew said he didn't want to impose any more than he already was. He ended up with a little red Ford Mustang, the sportiest they had in the airport in central Iowa, and on those cold, crisp, clear Iowa afternoons, we'd take drives. There wasn't much to show him, there weren't many places to go. But I did take him to the Amish colony not far from our town, and we had a delicious lunch, all you can eat, the table piled high with meat and potatoes, homemade preserves and pickles. As he drove home, we were both groaning and laughing about how full our stomachs were.

At first I'd thought he'd rented the car so we could have sex someplace beside my house, some risky furtive groping by the side of the highway. But clearly he didn't want to do that. Once, when I reached over and ran one finger suggestively (I hoped) down his spine, he gently pushed my hand away and said, 'Let's save that for later.'

That's what he'd been saying almost since the day I'd met him. I wondered what he was waiting for, and again the image of Val Morton popped up, uninvited, in my consciousness. Could it be that Val was telling him when he could finally have sex with me? But why would I even think that? Did I still have that instinctive knack for knowing what people were thinking and feeling? My time with Matthew had thrown that sensor so far out of kilter, I no longer trusted it, or even believed I still had it.

Meanwhile Matthew, Mom and I fell into a kind of rhythm. Late breakfast, long chats over lunch. It was almost as if we were becoming a weird little family of three, complete with a family joke: the identity of the person we were going to meet on Christmas Day. Matthew and I would tease her about it, but she wasn't talking. I decided that she and the mystery person must have made an agreement not to call each other at home. If Mom talked to him on the phone, it must have been when she went out. Sometimes I wondered if he was married. Married guys who had affairs didn't usually choose women like Mom, but maybe I was being unfair. Maybe my kindly, decent mother was just what this guy needed. Once it even crossed my mind that he didn't exist. I'd fantasize that Mom was losing it and the nonexistent boyfriend was the first indication that she was falling apart.

I turned it into a guessing game. Do I know him?

'No,' said Mom. 'I don't think so. But ... you may have met him once.'

One night Matthew asked if he could cook, and he made the steak and vegetables he'd cooked for me in his apartment. That all seemed so long ago, the afternoon I'd shoplifted the steak from All Foods and almost gotten caught by the cashier, or so I'd feared. I could almost convince myself that it hadn't actually happened, that it was part of a dream of the life that Matthew and I led in New York.

In just a few days, *this* had become our real lives: the leisurely hours we passed in this tiny house in Iowa, living almost like brother and sister, incestuous siblings with a sexual past and a weird attraction that thrummed under everything no matter how we ignored it or pretended it didn't exist.

In the evenings we'd sit with Mom between us on the couch and eat popcorn and stream movies on the big flat-screen TV, Mom's major concession to modern electronics.

Sometimes we couldn't decide on what film to watch, so we'd take turns picking. I don't know why I expected Matthew to like raunchy comedies about bachelor parties gone horribly wrong, but he surprised me. He loved old black and white movies—westerns, detective thrillers, noir crime stories, movies made before either of us was born. Matthew was always surprising me, and each surprise felt like a little tug on my heart, a little chink in the defensive, protective wall I'd been trying so hard to build up between us. We'd had sex, or a kind of sex, and yet these little discoveries—what foods he liked, what he thought of the Iowa landscape—brought us more closely together than anything he'd done with my body.

It made me feel, and it made me fear, that I might be falling in love with him. But what good was a love like that? For months we'd had sex without love and now, it seemed, we had love without sex. Each morning I put on my fanciest underwear in the hope that this would be the day he'd find a way for us to be together, that he'd touch me in that way that made me ready for anything he suggested. Anything he wanted. But his touch was friendly, affectionate. At night, I took the underwear off and put on the long flannel nightgowns that I still had in the bureau.

Mostly, I was having fun, enjoying myself. I liked being home, with Matthew and Mom. And at the same time I was waiting for something else to happen.

Together the three of us decorated the tree. I stood on the highest step of the ladder as Matthew passed me the angel to put on the top of it. His hand touched mine and lingered. He caressed my fingertips as the angel passed from one of us to the other.

I knew I hadn't been imagining the electricity that had been sparking between us ever since the day he'd arrived. *Something* was going to happen.

It happened on Christmas morning. Mom had made us promise not to open the presents without her, so we hung out in our rooms, waiting to hear the noises of Mom bustling about. I was a little self-conscious about letting Matthew see me in my old pink terry cloth robe, but I'd worn it on Christmas morning for so many years that it had become a tradition. I was afraid that Mom would be disappointed if I got dressed or wore anything else. Matthew appeared in a pair of sweatpants and a soft, much washed T-shirt; he looked handsome and rugged and hot. And Mom wore her bathrobe which was just like mine.

I was equally afraid that Matthew would see us together and make the obvious connection—in not so many years, I would be just like Mom: old, thick around the waist, no longer sexy, but still sweet, puttering around the living room, making sure that everything was just so.

What was wrong with that?

As always, Mom and I sat on the floor beside the tree to open our gifts. Matthew sat down beside us.

We took turns opening the presents. I ripped open my gift from Matthew, which—Mom and I couldn't help noticing—came in a Tiffany's box.

'Oh my God,' I said. 'It's gorgeous.'

It really was. The thin, silver, delicate bracelet was perfect! It was something I would have picked out myself—if I'd had the money. I could hardly imagine what it had cost—from Tiffany's, no less.

'Try it on,' said Matthew.

I pushed back the sleeve of my bathrobe and slipped it onto my wrist.

'Oh, it's lovely,' said Mom.

Matthew reached over and took my hand, and with Mom watching, lightly kissed my wrist just above the bracelet. It was good that I was sitting on the floor because I suddenly felt so weak with desire I might have fallen down otherwise.

'Merry Christmas to you both,' said Mom. She loved the fact that Matthew was being affectionate, and it certainly wasn't as if we were making out in front of her.

Now it was Mom's turn, and she opened her present from Matthew. Beautiful, elegant placemats, in an abstract design, with little rectangles of silver mesh. She held them up to the light, which shone dazzlingly off the silver mesh. As excited as a girl, she took them over to the dining table and laid them out. She put all eight on the table, then removed four.

For later, she said, reminding us that in just a few hours we'd been meeting the new person who had come into her life.

Mom opened the present I'd gotten her, a silk scarf in a deep burnt orange; there were cut outs in the fabric, delicate little slashes that recalled the way children made paper snowflakes and dolls.

My gifts from Mom were a five-hundred-dollar check (I didn't need to show that to Matthew) and an order receipt for a lovely, warm-looking blanket that was scheduled to arrive at my Brooklyn apartment next week.

'Sweet dreams, honey,' Mom said, and she kissed me. I put my arm around her shoulders and hugged her tightly.

'Thank you,' I said.

Mom had gotten Matthew a gorgeous pair of black leather gloves. They were made from the finest Italian leather. They fit perfectly and looked handsome on his long, strong hands.

As he tried them on, I couldn't help imagining him touching me in those gloves. I pictured the intimate places where he would fondle me, and how sweet and exciting it would feel. Right in front of Matthew and Mom, I descended into my erotic daydream until I heard Mom's voice.

'Isabel, dear? Are you okay? It looked like you left us there for a moment. And you look flushed.'

Embarrassing! I was blushing. I stole a look at Matthew, and I was sure that he knew what I'd been imagining. He winked at me to confirm it, though anyone else would just have seen it as a friendly wink to express his pleasure over the gloves he'd received.

'Beautiful gloves,' I said. 'They fit like a...'

We all laughed—a little uneasily, it seemed to me.

Finally it was time for Matthew to unwrap his present from me. Instantly I realized what a huge mistake I'd made. I'd bought his gifts before I knew that Matthew would be coming home with me, and I imagined him opening it with just the two of us there. I'd pictured us looking through the books together and ... silly me hadn't imagined that Mom would be right there watching us. At least I hadn't gotten him anything suggestive, anything that referred to the secret life we had together. Or anyway, nothing that anyone *else* could have connected with that secret life.

Wrapped together in the large package were three books. The first one Matthew took out was a copy of *King Lear*, an old edition I'd found in the Argosy bookshop, with eerie, powerful woodcuts, from the 1930s.

'*King Lear*!' my mother said. 'What a magnificent work of literature. It's one of those Shakespeare plays that ages along with you. When I was younger, I just thought it was sad. I guess I identified with Cordelia. But now that I'm older it seems almost impossibly sad...'

'Thank you,' Matthew said, smiling slyly at me. Only he and I knew... 'Isabel and I saw a performance of *King Lear*,' he explained. 'Some of her friends were in it.'

I couldn't look at him. Yes, I was giving him a handsome edition of Shakespeare, but it was also a memento of what we'd done together during the performance.

'I think Isabel mentioned that,' said Mom. 'And that's marvelous, really marvelous. From what I understand, couples nowadays only go to those sentimental dating movies, preferably starring Julia Roberts.'

'We're not a couple, Mom,' I almost said, but caught myself at the last minute.

'Sadly,' I said, 'Julia Roberts is aging out of those movies.'

'So who's the new hot young actress?' Mom chirped. Was she flirting with Matthew?

'Jennifer Lawrence,' Matthew said. 'Brie Larsen, maybe. They're cute ... but not half as cute as Isabel.'

That was really too much. He was laying it on way too thick, and I watched Mom flinch ever so slightly. Did he think she was stupid?

'Gosh.' Mom recovered quickly. 'Where did you find this guy, Isabel? What a prize! Look, Matthew, there are more books in that package. What else did Isabel get you?'

I clenched my eyes shut. All I could think about was how many detached, manipulative, basically unavailable shithead guys all over the country and probably all over the world are, on this Christmas morning, receiving copies of Pablo Neruda's *Love Poems* from their yearning, hopeless, pitiful girlfriends. Like me. You would have thought I'd gone into the cheesiest book store and said to the dopiest looking sales person, *Hey, could you recommend the corniest and most pathetic Christmas gift in the world?*

'Oh,' said Mom. 'How perfect! Do you know those poems, Matthew?'

'No,' said Matthew. 'I'm sorry to say I don't.'

Of course you don't, I thought.

'You're in for a treat,' Mom said. 'What a lovely present, Isabel. What could be nicer than giving something so powerful and beautiful to a person who will experience all that power and beauty for the first time?'

Mom beamed at me, and after a moment, so did Matthew. Was his smile even halfway genuine? Mom grabbed the book from his hands. I told myself: Watch out. Here it comes.

Mom leafed through the pages. How did she know what she was looking for? She clearly did. We'd had a copy of the book in the house for years, and only now it occurred to me that she might have gotten it from my dad. Before I was born.

Before he was killed.

"'If little by little you stop loving me,'" Mom read, "'I shall stop loving you little by little.'"

A funny chill seemed to lower the temperature in the room. I stole another look at Matthew, and it seemed to me that he looked ... scared. He glanced at me, then looked away. What was he frightened of? Was he scared of losing me? Of not having me in his life? Of the chance that his life might be that much emptier than it was before. Or was he scared that I might find out something about him that he didn't want anyone knowing?

All at once I remembered the night I'd dropped by his house to invite him to come have drinks with Luke and Marcy. I was sure that there had been a woman in his apartment. And I knew that he would be just fine without me. He would forget me in a heartbeat. So I would have to forget him too, just like Neruda wrote.

In my memory he would become the guy who made me do all those dirty secret things. It would be a funny story. A story with no one to tell it to ... I was glad that Mom stopped reading before Neruda makes it clear that the lovers will never forget each other, that they will never stop loving each other, that they will live in each other's arms and each day will be a flower. It didn't seem even remotely possible that Matthew and I were going to live in each other's arms. But you never knew. Stranger things had happened...

'There's one more book in there,' said Mom. 'And this one seems to be the big one.'

I prayed. Let the phone ring. Let a pot boil over on the stove. Let something distract my mother from what's about to happen now.

Again, I would never have picked that particular gift if I'd had the brains to realize that Mom would be watching Matthew open it. On the other hand, the presents I'd gotten him were at the far limit of what I could afford. I didn't have the money to hold on to the books, not give them to Matthew, and buy something else. Besides, what could I have gotten for a man like Matthew in the dead center of smalltown Iowa? I couldn't even have ordered something online. You can't count on timely delivery at this time of year...

I was just trying to distract *myself*. This was not about money. This was about my having given Matthew an art book of erotic drawings by Egon Schiele.

Matthew flipped through the pages. I knew what he was seeing. Bodies, penises, vaginas. women ready for sex, having sex, after sex, men and women, women and women, entwined couples, women posed in suggestive positions.

And there was Mom, looking over his shoulder.

'This is ... great,' mumbled Matthew. 'Thank you!' And no one spoke for a while.

'Schiele was a great artist,' said Mom, defusing things. How could I ever repay her?

'Thank you so much, Isabel,' Matthew said. 'These are the best presents I've ever gotten ... not counting the gloves I got from your mom.' He came over and gave me a friendly hug, so self-possessed and cool that you'd never know I'd given him a mini-library about sex. About art and love and sex, maybe. But sex, nonetheless.

'Who wants more coffee?' Mom hurried off to the kitchen before we could offer to help, or before we had to say anything else about the Schiele drawings.

Matthew held the book open and showed me a drawing of a woman in dark stockings spreading her legs. He turned the page, and there was a young man masturbating, his pants pushed down to his hips. A woman with her head cradled in another woman's lap. Two women, twisted together, dozing. Another on her knees, raising her ass.

He looked steadily at me over the top of the book. He watched me looking at it.

We could hear Mom moving around in the kitchen. The refrigerator door opened and shut. Cups clattered on a tray. Any minute she would be back. Matthew closed the book.

He said, 'I've got a plan for the new year. Let's do everything in the book.'

All I could think about was the fact that he had plans for us to be together, to do things together. A plan for the new year! The prospect made me joyful.

'Hey, you kids, 'Mom said. 'Fresh hot coffee.'

I felt sick with shame and desire and at the same time, I was almost bizarrely cheerful. As if my life, or at least the promise of a life, had been given back to me.

\* \* \*

After we'd taken our presents to our rooms, and tidied up the living room, Mom announced that she'd be gone for a couple of hours. She'd forgotten to buy a few grocery items. All the stores in our little town were closed for the holiday, so she had to drive to the supermarket, two towns over. I wondered if she was planning to meet the mysterious Mr Right. Maybe she wanted to give him a little pep talk before he met her daughter and her daughter's young man from the big city.

Matthew had gone off to take a shower, and I was in the living room cleaning up the last scraps of wrapping paper, trying not to think about Matthew opening the Schiele drawings in front of Mom. A lot of awkward moments had occurred, but none quite as bad as that.

I was also trying not to think about the fact that I was finally, for the first time, alone in the house with Matthew.

I noticed that my mom had left the scarf I'd given her on the dining room table. I didn't feel slighted at all, I knew she liked my gift. In fact, her moment of carelessness sort of cheered me up. It was like a getting a little visit from the mom I used to know: more offhand, less neat and in fact quite a bit sloppier before she met the guy whom we were about to meet.

I decided to put it in her room, safely out of the way. Because it would also be not unlike Mom to walk in from shopping and put a leaky grocery bag right beside something fragile and nice. Her new scarf, for instance.

On the way, I passed the bathroom. I heard the hiss of the shower running inside...

The bathroom door opened. Matthew came out into the hall. He was naked. His skin was dry. He hadn't started his shower yet. He seemed to have been waiting until he heard me pass by.

He took my arm and pulled me into the bathroom. I let my mother's scarf slip through my fingers onto the hall carpet. I would pick it up later.

Matthew had a hard-on. I realised this would be the second time that he and I had sex in a bathroom. Why couldn't we do it in bed, like a normal couple? But I knew that I would take whatever I could get...

Soon enough, I was distracted by the steam, the thick air and the heat, and especially by the sight of Matthew's strong, smooth body, perfectly proportioned, muscular but not too muscular. How beautiful he was! He had a movie-star body, except that I knew that movie stars often used stand-ins because their real bodies weren't that great. Matthew's body was that great. The sight of it made me so hot that I almost (but not quite) forgot the weirdness of the fact that this was the first time I had ever seen him totally naked.

He slipped the robe from my shoulders, lifted my flannel nightgown over my head, and hung my robe and nightgown neatly on the hook on the back of the door.

Then he pulled me into the shower and closed the plastic curtain behind us. There was no way I could resist, and I didn't want to. I felt so warm, so taken care of. I inhaled deeply, steam filled my lungs. The water was the perfect temperature. It felt fantastic against on my skin.

'Quite a little menagerie you have here,' said Matthew, looking around at all the animal decals pasted to the tile walls.

'They're from when I was little,' I said. 'I hated taking a shower, and Mom put them up as rewards for me. And somehow most of them stayed.'

My whole body went hot with shame. Maybe it was the fact that I was standing naked under the running water with a man in the same place where I'd been so young and innocent, and where my trusting and loving mother had figured out such a sweet solution to my problems. Or maybe the heat coming off my skin was simply a response to the hot water running down over my body.

Mom was always a little cheap about bath products. Soap was soap, she said. Drug store shampoo had the same ingredients as the more expensive brands. Read the labels! But Matthew had brought his own soap. Fragrant, lemony and strong. I wondered what kind of man brought his own soap? Maybe a man planning to take a shower with a woman.

He rubbed his slippery hands all over me, sliding rapidly but seductively over my breasts, my belly, my ass. He turned me around and soaped my back; he knelt to wash my legs and feet.

I lost myself in a fog of bliss. The water ran over my back and dripped through my hair, rinsing away the soap he'd left there, touching all the places he had touched.

'Now me,' he said. 'My turn.'

I lathered my hands with his lemon soap. He leaned back against the tile wall. I began with his shoulders. In all this time I hadn't fully realized how much taller than me he was. He slumped slightly, so I didn't have to strain. I rubbed soap over his chest and hips, avoiding, for now, his penis. He thrust it toward me, but I pretended not to notice. Instead I knelt and washed his legs and calves.

Just as he'd done to me, I turned him around and ran my soapy hands all over his back and his muscular ass. His muscles tensed in response to my hand, then relaxed. I had the strangest sensation, as if he was doing to me, at the same time, what I was doing to him. He turned around and leaned back again. His hips jutted out from the wall. For a fleeting second, I thought of the young man in one of the Schiele drawings. Matthew's penis stood straight up, curving slightly in toward his chest.

He very gently pushed my shoulders till I was down to my knees. He held me tightly with both hands, so I wouldn't slip.

'Be careful, it's slippery,' he whispered thickly.

I knelt before him, and the water ran over my head and my back, and in a circle around my belly.

'Put it in your mouth,' he said, and I did. How smooth his penis was, like velvet. I'd done this with other guys, but it never felt like this. Every little thing I did with my lips and tongue got me as hot as it was getting him. His hips bucked toward me. I licked his balls and tightened my lips just under the tip of his penis.

'Put your finger up my ass,' he said.

The soap helped it go in smoothly, and he wriggled to take it in deeper.

I could tell he was going to come. I could see his toes curl, and I could almost feel the blood rushing in from wherever it was.

Then he stopped me. Pushed me away.

I stood up and faced him.

'Seriously?' I said. 'What are you saving it for?'

The water sluicing over me somehow gave me the courage to say what I could never have begun to say if we weren't in the shower. 'What's with you? Do you belong to some kind of cult? Are you some kind of religious freak? Like some male virgin who's taken a vow to save himself for marriage? Or ... does this have anything to do with your working for Val Morton? How the hell is Val going to know if you come or not?'

I could tell I'd struck a nerve. His body stiffened, but now it wasn't from desire.

'That's ridiculous,' he said. 'What makes you think that?'

'Intuition,' I said. 'I've always had a knack for knowing what people are really thinking.'

'Then it's misleading you,' he said. 'If you think there's one tiny thought in my head about Val Morton.'

'Are you in love with him?' I said. Why had I said that? I didn't even think it. And now I'd really spoiled everything forever! This was the end. We would never come back from this, I'd pushed my luck way too far. I'd be lucky if he didn't leave before my mother got home from the store.

But all Matthew did was laugh.

'Hilarious,' he said. Matthew took a deep breath and shook the water from his eyes. 'This has nothing to do with anything or anyone except how much better it is if you wait. I've waited and made women wait before. And believe me, not one of them has ever asked for her money back.'

I knew I'd heard that last line somewhere. In a movie, I thought ... but before I could place it, Matthew had turned me around, and edged me over against the slick wet wall. I pressed my face into the tiles. He soaped my back again, then knelt, and began to lick my ass.

I never thought I would like it. The idea had always sort of turned me off.

But all it took was three flicks of his tongue, and I came, sobbing into the ducks and chickadees and bunnies.

After Matthew stepped out of the shower, I stayed under the running water for a long time. I didn't like to waste water and run up Mom's heating bill but I needed to feel cleansed, purified, to wash away my guilty (and exciting) memories of what I'd just done with Matthew in this place that was almost sacred to me: the baby-animal shrine to my childhood.

By the time I got out of the shower, Matthew had left the bathroom. I dressed and found him in the living room, calmly reading the paper.

'Look,' he said. 'They report every time someone hosts a bridge game.'

'That's the news,' I said. It seemed important to make my voice sound like my normal voice. To talk about what had just happened would just be to ruin it.

We waited for Mom to return from the store or wherever she'd gone.

The door flew open, and she rushed in, clapping her hands, stamping her frozen feet, all flushed and energized by the cold.

Matthew and I watched my mother transform into a human whirlwind. Chopping, dicing, stirring, setting the table, basting the turkey. I'd seen it before, but I could tell that Matthew was impressed by the speed by which she got the bird in the oven, peeled potatoes, washed greens. We offered to help, but she wouldn't let us.

'I've got my ways,' she said. 'Isabel knows I can do practically everything except delegate authority.'

'I do know that,' I said.

I was amazed that Matthew and I could act this composed, this normal, after what we'd just done. Mom suspected nothing, or maybe she had her own private thoughts: the surprise guest who would soon be arriving.

I won't deny that I felt a little resentful of this stranger about to intrude on our domestic paradise. But I liked it that Mom had someone. And it was all for the better, it seemed. She'd not only fixed herself up and straightened up the house but her mood was buoyant. A happy person normally, she seemed happier even than normal.

Everything was ready. The table was set, delicious turkey smells filling the house.

The doorbell rang, precisely at four.

I gave myself a last-minute talking-to. Don't judge, no matter what.

Mom went to answer the door.

I looked over her shoulder at the man who was standing in the doorway.

An older guy, a few inches taller than mom. Long coat,

thick gray hair. I watched from a distance as he gallantly bent and kissed Mom on the cheek. Just like Matthew kissed me in public, I thought, but in private … I couldn't let myself think anything like that. There was no way that Mom and this guy were doing what we'd just done in the shower.

But wait. Wait a minute. I'd seen this guy somewhere before. I remembered him from somewhere. And it wasn't a pleasant memory.

'What is it?' whispered Matthew.

'I've met that guy. He's someone I used to know,' I said.

Mom came closer. 'My daughter Isabel. This is Jim Chambers.'

*Mr Chambers. Of all the guys in Iowa…*

Mom said, 'You remember Mr Chambers, don't you, Isabel? I believe he was the guidance counselor in your high school.'

'Retired,' said Mr Chambers, as if that changed everything. Did he recognize me? I couldn't tell. I couldn't tell if he remembered anything that had happened.

He was the guidance counselor who'd given us that bogus compassion test, the one who put his hand on my thigh in the cubicle off the gym. Of all the people in our town, what were the odds of his showing up as my mom's new boyfriend?

'Jim, you remember Isabel, don't you?' said Mom. 'Everyone in the school was over the moon when she'd played Emily in the senior class production of *Our Town*. You were probably at the school then, Jim...'

I loved it that Mom remembered.

'Actually no,' said Mr Chambers. 'I don't remember that. Sadly, the kids I remember were the ones who got into loads of trouble and spent lots of time in my office.' He laughed, though no one else did. 'I'm sure Isabel wasn't one of those, were you, Isabel?'

'Actually, I remember you. We had to take this weird test to see how much compassion we had. And you were the guy who gave the test. In a room beside the gym. Remember?'

Did I see the slightest flicker of anxious recognition in Mr Chambers' eyes? If so, it was only there for an instant. Immediately wiped clean. Maybe he didn't remember me, maybe he did, I honestly couldn't tell. If he did, he was very good at hiding it. Those hardcore perverts always were. That's how all those rogue priests and coaches and teachers had gotten away with it for so long.

Matthew could tell that something was very wrong. He reached out and took my hand—something he'd never done.

Mom noticed, but she thought my problem was that she'd forgotten to introduce Matthew. How could she have been so rude?

'And this is Isabel's friend, Matthew,' she said. 'Matthew, Jim. Jim Chambers.'

'Pleased to meet you. Pleased to meet you.' The two men shook hands. Matthew glanced at me. He could see that I was unnerved.

There were so many reasons I had to keep myself under control. We would get through this peacefully, for Mom's sake. Have a civilized family Christmas. And then I would have to choose the right time to tell her what I knew.

Mom relieved Mr Chambers of his dirty-old-pervert trench coat, and she showed him into the living room. We sat down, all perched on the edge of our seats.

'Well!' said Mom, over heartily. 'Who would like some Christmas cheer? Homemade eggnog, anyone?'

'That's a little rich even for my Lipitor,' said Mr Chambers. 'Do you have any of whatever you put *in* the eggnog to cheer it up?'

'Of course,' said Mom. 'Brandy. Coming up.'

'I'll take some eggnog,' said Matthew, who—unlike Mr Chambers—knew how much trouble Mom had gone to, getting the eggnog just right. Mom and I went into the kitchen to get the drinks.

'What's wrong, dear?' Mom said as soon as we were in the kitchen. 'You seem upset.'

'I'm fine,' I said. 'He seems nice enough.'

'That he is,' said Mom. 'Nice enough.'

What in the world did she see in him? But that was always a mystery, wasn't it? What people saw in each other. Maybe the guy had reformed. Repented. Did I want to ruin Mom's happiness? Happiness with a pervert. Probably Mr Chambers no longer did the kind of sleazy things he did back then. And who was I to talk, considering what Matthew and I had just done in the shower in full view of the baby animals of my childhood?

In any case, I wasn't ready to ruin what promised to be a long and difficult afternoon even before it began. If I started some kind of drama, we'd still have the rest of the day to get through. Once more I reminded myself to keep cool and tell Mom in private.

Back in the living room, we found Matthew and Mr Chambers having what seemed to be a halting and unpleasant conversation.

'No, I've never been to New York,' said Mr Chambers. 'Never wanted to go. You never know what's going to happen in a place like that. I'm not stupid. I watch the news. You never know when someone's going to drive their taxi up onto the sidewalk, or stick a knife in your back, or shoot you for beer money.'

'You're thinking of New York thirty years ago,' said Matthew, as much to reassure Mom as to correct Mr Chambers. 'The city is very safe now.'

'Statistically speaking,' I said. 'You're more likely to get killed in mass shooting in a small town like this one than in New York City.'

Matthew and Mom looked at me, slightly shocked— perhaps by the unusually strident tone in my voice.

Actually I had no idea whether what I'd just said was true or not. I just wanted to argue with Mr Chambers.

I could read the expression on his face: Who are *you* to contradict me? Who's interested in anything *you* have to say? Well, I thought, I have something to say that would interest you very much indeed.

An uncomfortable silence fell.

Take it easy, I told myself. Relax.

'So how did you two meet?' Matthew asked Mom and Mr Chambers.

Bless him, I thought. He was totally doing the right thing, taking on the burden of politeness and sociability for us all. Again I reminded myself to be careful. I was letting myself slip into a dream in which Matthew had become one of those small-town people who were good and kind and acted from all the best motives. Soon we'd be going back to New York with its rush and stress and pressures, and with the lurking presence of Val Morton doing ... I didn't know what Val was doing. Anyhow, that dream of small-town goodness was only a dream. The man sitting in front of me, the man who was presumably dating my mom, was a pervert who had groped me when I was a schoolgirl.

'Well,' said Mom. 'It's a nice story. I met Jim in the office. We met at work, like you two did.' She smiled at Matthew and me.

Not *exactly* the way we met, I certainly hoped.

'He brought around a couple of high school students he was personally mentoring, girls he was bringing to visit the faculty at the college because they were smart and talented and he wanted the professors to meet them and maybe overlook the fact that they hadn't gotten the highest grades or the strongest SAT scores. I was working that day at the front desk in the department, while the girls were chatting with one of the professors, Jim and I got to talking and...'

*Mentoring. High school girls.* Suddenly I remembered the full horror and disgust of feeling his hand creep up my thigh.

'One thing led to another,' said Mr Chambers. 'Your mother and I had a lot in common.'

'Like what?' I was screaming inside.

'Like what?' I said, more politely. But still it must have sounded odd, because Mom looked flustered.

'Mr Chambers is a widower,' she said.

*What* thing led to what other thing? What in the world did Mom mean? The town was probably full of perfectly nice widowers. Why him?

'That *is* a nice story,' Matthew said. 'Nicer than ours.'

No one asked what Matthew meant by that. What would he have said?

It didn't matter. Mr Chambers wasn't interested in us. He just had to get through this, and then we would go away.

I nodded. I couldn't speak.

Mr Chambers poured himself more brandy.

'More eggnog?' I asked Matthew.

Matthew shook his head.

'Perhaps we should switch to wine,' said Mom. 'In fact, why don't we eat? I don't want the mashed potatoes to get cold.' Poor Mom! If Mom got any more cheerful—or tense—her head was going to explode.

Matthew and I helped Mom bring in the turkey and mashed potatoes, the green beans and gravy and the bowl heaped high with cornbread stuffing. Mr Chambers just sat there, like a king being waited on by his servants. He didn't offer to help.

Matthew sat across from me, while Mom and Mr Chambers sat at the heads of the table, as if they were the mom and dad. It was sickening. I couldn't stop myself from thinking about that time I'd introduced Matthew to Marcy and Luke, and he'd felt me under the table while they made small talk. How long ago that seemed!

It occurred to me that this was my punishment for that. But why should I feel so guilty about something that had felt so good?

Mom and Mr Chambers already seem to have friends in common. Professors in Mom's department, teachers who'd come to the high schools since I'd graduated, but whom he'd kept in touch with. I poured myself some more wine, drank it, poured more. Mom shot me a warning look and slid the wine bottle away from my place, but I moved it back to where I could reach it.

'Somebody's thirsty,' Mr Chambers observed.

'Die, you pervert,' I thought.

Calm down. What Mr Chambers had done to me was nothing compared to the things that Matthew had asked me to do—and I'd done. But that was completely different. I'd *wanted* to do them with Matthew. I was older, my own person. Mr Chambers had taken advantage of me, without my consent. Just like he was probably taking advantage of all those bright deserving students he was 'mentoring' and taking to meet the college professors.

He shouldn't have taken advantage. My mother shouldn't be with someone like that.

Everything blurred out for a minute. They were talking about something ... I couldn't follow. I should have quit drinking a couple of glasses of wine ago. I felt really woozy. But Mr Chambers had kept up with me, drinking brandy, so you could say we were more than equally matched in terms of alcohol consumption.

There was a lull in the conversation.

I said slowly, 'Actually, I do remember you. I remember something else. You had your hand on my thigh the whole time you were giving me that ridiculous compassion test.'

I was sorry the moment I said it. But it was too late to take it back.

'You're dreaming,' said Mr Chambers.

'I'm not,' I said. 'Mom, believe me, I'm not. It was him. I never told you.'

My mother stared at me, slack-jawed. Matthew put down his fork.

Unlike Matthew, my mother believed me. She knew that I would never lie. Still, maybe it was possible that I had it wrong, that I'd confused him with someone else. People change over time. I really didn't feel at all well...

'Fantasizing,' said Mr Chambers. 'Pure wish fulfillment fantasy. I see it all the time. Especially with girls like yourself, young women with a history of childhood trauma.'

'*What* childhood trauma?' I said.

'Your dad,' said Mr Chambers. 'You know.'

'What about my dad?' I said. 'What do I know?'

'Your dad—my husband— died,' said Mom. 'He was very young. It was tragic. What more do you need to know?'

But that wasn't what Mr Chambers meant, and he wasn't letting me off the hook so easily.

'Glenda,' he said. 'Don't tell me your daughter doesn't know the truth.'

Now we all looked at Mom. What truth? What *about* Dad? Was there some awful secret that I was about to hear from Mr Chambers? Why didn't Mom try to protect me? Why didn't she tell him to keep his fat mouth shut?

Carrie Blake

Maybe *she* wanted me to know the truth and had never been able to tell me herself.

Mr Chambers was relentless, and after all this time I understood why people had been afraid to blow the whistle on him, to tell the authorities what he did in that cubicle off the gym. Who knew how often he did it, how many girls he touched after that? Maybe that was just the start...

'It's not every little girl who sees her father die in front of her eyes,' he said now.

'Jim.' Mom finally woke from her coma. 'Please. That's enough.'

'What do you mean?' I said.

'You were there at the accident. You were a little girl. You were, so to speak, involved. You were in the back seat yelling and screaming because you wanted something, you'd dropped something. Your dad reached back to grab for it, and lost control of the car. You and your mom were barely hurt, but your dad died before the ambulance came. Your mom put her hand over your eyes. You remembered, and then you forgot. That's how your mom tells the story.'

'Mom,' I said. 'Is that true?'

Suddenly, so many things made sense. I'd always insisted that I remembered the accident. I'd always felt sure I was sure. And Mom had always denied it. I knew Mom had just wanted to protect me. To keep me from feeling responsible—and I wasn't, not really. How could a little kid be

250

blamed for something like that? Still it seemed all too clear now: I'd been lied to, pretty much all my life.

'More or less true,' said Mom.

'Why would you tell him and not me?' I said.

'I don't know,' my mother said. 'He seemed to already know it.'

'He targeted you,' I said.

The word *targeted* did something to Matthew. He twitched, as if he'd been shot.

'This has been great fun,' said Mr Chambers, rising from the table. 'It's been wonderful to spend the holidays with a real family again. It's been three years since my wife died ... thank you all so much for your kindness and hospitality.'

And like robots, we all said: *You're welcome*.

Mr Chambers knew his way around the house. He knew where his coat was. He retrieved it from the closet. This time he shook my mother's hand (no more tender cheek pecks) and thanked her again and left.

Mom came back and sat at the table, where she and Matthew and I remained as the late afternoon passed and it was almost dark outside the windows. Mom wept, on and off. She kept apologizing to me, saying how sorry she was. But I could tell that all the pain and loss of my father's death was hitting her all over again, and I kept telling her not to worry, I understood. It was all right.

Except that it wasn't all right. Being lied to had hurt

me, damaged me in ways I couldn't completely understand yet. It had set me up for a relationship like the one I had with Matthew: always kept off balance, never knowing what to expect, never feeling secure, never being entirely sure if what he said was true or not.

It was all too much to take in. I said I wasn't feeling well. I excused myself, and left Mom and Matthew at the table. I went to my bedroom and lay down in bed and pulled the covers over my head.

# Matthew

I'd liked the mom from the start. She seemed like a person who wanted people to be happy and feel better, an unusual sort of person, practically unheard of in the crowd I moved in. Neither of my parents had been that way, so it came as something of a shock to see what it looked like: a mother who actually loved her child. The strangest part was that Isabel's mom seemed ready to love me too, just for being there with Isabel. She seemed to love me with all her heart while at the same time letting me know her daughter came first. By miles. She would kill me if I hurt Isabel and be perfectly fine with it.

Meanwhile I was surprised by how comfortable I felt. I'd been afraid of feeling like I was on trial, or on show, like an animal in the zoo, but I blended right in. I felt like a normal person going home to spend the holidays with a friend and her mom. Friends with benefits, as they say. Val Morton could have been on another planet. I would deal with him later. This was a break, a welcome break, from my normal life. This was what a holiday was supposed to mean.

No one was asking anything from me except that I be nice. I made Isabel wait for sex. I liked keeping her off balance, never knowing when something sexual would happen. And I wouldn't have done it if I hadn't been so sure that she liked it that way.

Finally, I made her come in the shower, with all those ducks and bunnies and monkeys looking down at my head pressed into her ass. Was I wrong to think she liked it? She seemed to like it fine.

The mother's boyfriend was a sleaze. Anyone could have seen that right away. Everything about him gave me the creeps. That Christmas dinner was sheer torture. I felt so sorry for Isabel's mom for even knowing a guy like that. Let alone going to all that trouble to make him a nice holiday dinner.

I kept thinking it didn't make sense that, after all these years on her own, she would start dating again, and that this slob would be the lucky guy she picked. Maybe the guy had something that was invisible to the naked eye. Some special secret charm that neither I—nor Isabel, I could tell—was able to see. Or maybe it was just her response to the fact that Isabel had finally left home—left her alone with her memories. Maybe the house was just too silent without her daughter.

I knew there was something wrong with the mom's new

boyfriend, something untrustworthy and extremely creepy. Still, I have to admit that it made me paranoid when Isabel went off on him about having groped her when she was in high school. It was all too reminiscent of her insisting that Val was standing in the doorway watching me give her head on Val and Heidi's bed. And it began to occur to me again that she might be crazy, like so many other women I'd dated. I'd begun to convince myself that she was sane, that the whole incident with Val had been some kind of weird aberration. But now I wondered again.

After Mr Chambers left, Isabel excused herself. She said she'd had too much drink. She said she wanted to lie down.

'Lie down and take a rest, dear,' her mother said. 'Matthew and I will do the dishes.'

Her mom's eyes were red from weeping. Poor woman! This certainly hadn't been the merry Christmas she'd had in mind, everyone happy and warm, gathered around the eggnog, helping themselves to turkey and mashed potatoes and gravy. The poor thing had had a lot to deal with in one day. Mr Chambers revealing the truth about Isabel's dad's accident, and Isabel blowing the whistle on Mr Chambers. No wonder most people hated Christmas with the folks. Look at what could happen!

Isabel's mom rose, and I stood to help her stack the dishes and bring them into the kitchen. I was glad we had a lot to do. It meant we didn't have to talk for a while. I didn't know how to begin to talk about everything that had happened in the last few hours.

Finally, I said, 'I feel so sorry for Isabel.'

Her mom said, 'I always meant to tell her. But I never found the right time. And it just got harder and harder. I didn't want her to feel responsible for her dad's death, and she wasn't. She was just a tiny little thing. How could she have known what would happen? She just wanted her favorite toy bunny she'd dropped on the floor of the car. And my husband was trying to help her...'

Standing over the sink, she began to weep again.

'Oh, poor everyone,' I said. 'And it must have been so awful for Isabel, hearing the truth from a guy who...'

My voice trailed off. What had I said? The guy had been Isabel's mom's boyfriend. She must have liked him, trusted him. Maybe she'd even loved him. The last thing in the world I wanted to do was make Isabel's mom feel even worse.

'Do you think that ... Isabel may have made a mistake?' I was back-pedaling like mad, saying the first thing that came into my mind and at the same time knowing that I was only making everything worse. 'Could she have remembered wrong, gotten it wrong ... maybe she was just a little jealous, maybe she, maybe it...'

Isabel's mom heard something in my voice, something I hadn't even known was there. She turned from the sink and turned to face me full on, glaring.

'My daughter would never do something like that,' she said. 'My daughter would never get something like that wrong, or say it if it wasn't true. My daughter doesn't imagine things, she doesn't lie. She's never told a lie in her life. I know that. And I will swear to it on all our lives.'

She kept on staring at me with her sad, pink-rimmed eyes. And I don't know exactly why, but I believed her completely. Of course I knew she was Isabel's mother, and wanted to see only the best in her daughter. But still I believed her.

Isabel didn't lie.

Could it be that Isabel had told the truth about Val having been there in his doorway? Why would he do something like that, mess with my mind that way? He liked staging little dramas. He said that all the time. His ambition was to direct. But I thought this was my show. Had he directed the little live-action porn film in which the older man voyeur watches a younger couple and subsequently denies it?

'My daughter never lies,' repeated Isabel's mom. 'Never has and never will. If she says Jim Chambers did that, he did. I'm sure he did. I don't understand how I could have not seen the signs, how I could have gotten him so wrong. Imagine thinking you know someone so well, and really you have no idea who that person is.'

'I can imagine.' I saw Val's face as clearly as if he were there in the kitchen with us. 'I can imagine, all too well.'

# Isabel

I woke up later that evening with a terrific headache and an even more painful sense of shame. Oh, right. I remembered now. I'd personally drunk more than a bottle of wine at dinner, and I'd insulted my mom's boyfriend. Well, he deserved it. Then the reason for it all came back to me. He told me that I'd been in the car when my dad died, that my mom had lied to me about it all those years, I guess because she didn't want me to feel responsible for what happened. Except that I *was* responsible. It didn't seem right that anyone could blame a small child for crying for something she wanted. I hadn't meant for there to be disaster. I just wanted whatever I'd dropped on the floor.

A thick fog of depression and gloom settled over me. What was I doing? How was I living? What kind of life did I have in New York, working at a failing mattress store for a pitiful boss? Having some kind of relationship with a man that involved hot sex—but not intercourse—and that was obviously going nowhere. And here was Mom living alone in our old house without me, so desperate for companionship that she had taken up with a pervert and a child molester.

It was too much to process. I knew that Mom had some sleeping pills in the bathroom. I'd seen them there the other day. Too bad I'd left the Euphorazil back in the city. I'd been too paranoid to take a drug I didn't have a prescription for on the plane. What if they caught me at security? What a wimp I was! I could really have used one of those happiness pills at that moment.

I was just pulling myself together to get up and get one of Mom's sleeping pills when I heard someone knocking on my door.

'Isabel?' It was Matthew. 'Are you awake?'

My God. Did he want to have sex now? Did he think *that* would cheer me up? For the first time since I'd met him, I really didn't want to. I wondered if seeing Mr Chambers again might have turned me off sex forever. Then I thought that maybe having sex with Matthew was just what I needed. It might be a great distraction. I would be thinking about something besides my sad life and my poor mom and her pervert boyfriend and the fact that I was responsible for my father's death.

Better yet, sex might stop me from thinking about anything at all.

I opened the door. Matthew was fully dressed. He even

had his jacket on. And he was wearing the gloves he'd gotten from Mom. All I could think of was that he'd had enough, he was leaving, tonight, right now. Driving to the airport where he'd stay until he could get on the first flight out, tomorrow morning. He'd been sickened, disgusted by what he'd witnessed at Christmas dinner. And I didn't blame him for wanting to leave. If I could have just have left, disappeared, I would have liked to, also. Except that it would have meant leaving Mom, who was probably in no shape to be alone.

'Get dressed,' he whispered. 'We're going out.'

'Going out where?' I said. Did he think we were still in New York? Everything in this town had been closed since the afternoon of Christmas Eve.

'It's a surprise,' he said. 'Does your mom have a flashlight?'

'Of course,' I said. 'This is blizzard and tornado country, remember? Everyone house has dozens of flashlights stashed in strategic places.'

'Great. I'll wait for you in the living room,' he said. 'Hurry up, okay?'

I threw on some clothes, then stopped in the kitchen to pour myself a large glass of cold water, which I drank all the way down. Almost immediately, my headache felt better.

I got the flashlight from the drawer under the sink where I knew Mom kept it. Matthew was sitting in the couch, in the dark.

'Come on,' he said. 'Let's go.'

I considered leaving Mom a note.

Out for a drive. Back soon. Don't worry.

Only now did I look at my watch. A drive at three o'clock in the morning?

Mom had always been a light sleeper, and I hoped we didn't wake her as we left. I told myself that if she got up and found that we were both gone, along with Matthew's car, she'd assume we'd gone out for a drive. Maybe neither of us could sleep, and who could blame us, after everything that had happened that day. Maybe we wanted to have a private talk. Or maybe we were planning to have sex in the back seat of the car like she probably did when she was young. Like all the kids did in our town...

I didn't want to think about that. I didn't want to think about her and my dad having sex in the car.

Maybe Matthew *was* planning to have sex by the side of the road. In the bitter cold. Maybe they'd find us frozen to death, my mouth around his penis. I'd rather think about that than about anything that happened yesterday.

We got in his car. He drove slowly out of the driveway, clearly trying to make the least amount of noise. But as soon as we got out on the street, he picked up speed. I looked over at him, his chiseled features illuminated by the dashboard lights. He was staring straight ahead at the road, concentrating hard. He looked like a man on mission.

'Where are we going?' I said.

'We're going to pay a little visit to your old friend, Mr Chambers.'

'I never want to see him again. Not after today.'

'This isn't about *seeing* him,' said Matthew. 'This is about scaring the shit out of him. This is about making him pay.'

I looked at him again. My hero! Driving out on a cold night just to avenge something that happened to me a long time ago. And, I guess, what happened more recently: Mr Chambers doing whatever he did to get close to my innocent, trusting mom. In a way, I guess, it was a little weird, Matthew wanting to punish the guy for having touched me when Matthew himself had spent so much of the time I'd known him with his hand up under my skirt. But Matthew understood. He and I had never done anything that I didn't want to do. And I hadn't wanted any of what Mr Chambers did to me.

'How do you know where he lives?' I asked.

'There's a little something called the internet,' he said. 'Even here in Iowa. It took me about three seconds to find him.'

'Got it,' I said. 'I'm in.'

'I knew you would be,' he said. 'Good girl.' His saying that made me so happy that I felt almost okay for the first time since I saw Mr Chambers walk in Mom's door.

Matthew typed an address into his GPS, and we drove though the dark streets until we reached the edge of the town, a neighborhood where the houses were far apart and bordered the snow-covered corn fields. I shivered, partly because it was really cold even with the heat in the car going full blast, and partly because the fact that Mr Chambers lived this far out in the middle of nowhere made me feel doubly alarmed and suspicious. I imagined him moving here on purpose, taking innocent girls out to his house—where no one could hear them scream.

'A perfect spot for a psycho killer,' I said.

'That's exactly what I was thinking.' Matthew laughed. 'But don't let your imagination run wild. He's probably not a murderer. Just your garden variety child-molesting guidance counselor.'

At last we reached the street on which Mr Chambers lived. Matthew parked at the end of the block.

'Grab the flashlight,' he said.

'Yes, sir,' I said.

We walked through the dark empty street until we got to the house. All the lights were out, there wasn't even a porch light turned on. But there was just enough moonlight to see that the house desperately needed some serious TLC. Curls of peeling paint hung beneath the windows of the one-story house, and a moldy smell seemed to emanate from the basement.

'I told you,' I said. 'Smell that? He's got bodies down there.'

'Hush,' said Matthew. 'Be serious.' We tiptoed around the house until we were pretty sure we'd located Mr Chambers' bedroom.

'Stay down,' Matthew said.

He crept up to the window and tapped very lightly on the glass. Three short taps, three long taps, three short taps.

SOS.

No one answered. Nothing happened.

'Maybe he's not home,' I said, half-hoping he wasn't.

'His car is in the driveway.'

Matthew tapped a few times more, and again nothing happened.

'Okay, on to the second phase,' he said. 'Ready?'

'Ready!' I felt giddy, like a little kid, playing a thrilling game of pretend. This was definitely a different kind of role-playing than I was used to with Matthew, but I loved every second of it. It was almost as if I'd forgotten whose house this was, and what we were really doing.

Matthew switched on the flashlight to the highest beam and shone it into the window while banging on the glass as hard as he could.

The lights came on suddenly, scaring me. I jumped back. Mr Chambers' fat, sleepy face appeared at the window. Swollen and bloated from sleep, he looked a million times uglier even than he had at lunch.

'Who's there?' he said. 'Who is it?'

'Police,' said Matthew. 'Open up. We know what you've been doing here.'

I wanted to laugh, but I was too scared. Too scared and too excited.

'The girls,' shouted Matthew. 'We're here to rescue the girls.'

'What girls, you fucking idiot kids?' Clearly, Mr Chambers thought we were high school students, playing a prank on him, trying to scare him. Had something like this happened to him before?

We heard noise coming from inside the house, then footsteps running toward the front of the house.

We went around to the porch and stood on the front walk. I didn't know what we were going to say if Mr Chambers came out to confront us, but I assumed that Matthew had a plan.

A few moments later, Mr Chambers appeared, pointing a rifle at us.

'It's loaded,' he said. 'I'm warning you.'

He switched the front porch light on, and we stood in the wide circle of light.

He squinted into the darkness, then raised his rifle higher. It seemed to take forever until he saw that it was us.

'Isabel, what the fuck?' he said. 'What the fuck are you doing here?'

'Language, please,' said Matthew.

'You shut the fuck up,' said Mr Chambers.

'Merry Christmas,' said Matthew.

'You nasty little shit,' Mr Chambers said. 'You little motherfucker. I should call the police.'

'Go ahead,' said Matthew. 'And we'll tell them what you've been doing to those girls you've been ... mentoring.' You could hear the sneer in his voice as he pronounced that last word.

'Yeah, go ahead,' I said. 'And I'll make certain that the school board knows what you did to me. I'll bet I can find dozens of other girls who had the same experience, who you did the same shit to. Isn't that always the way?'

'Get the fuck out of here.' Mr Chambers pointed his gun straight at us. 'No one would blame me for shooting two intruders who came to my house in the middle of the night, Christmas night. Guys get off on cases like that all the time. Sorry!' He cocked his gun.

Matthew grabbed my hand. I could feel him shaking. I wanted to tell him that Mr Chambers wasn't really going to shoot us, he was probably just bluffing. But Matthew was so clearly agitated. Terrified, it seemed. And suddenly I had the definite feeling that Matthew's panic was about something besides Mr Chambers. I remembered him saying that he was gun shy, that he hadn't wanted to go shooting with Val...

'Come on,' I said. 'Let's get out of here.' And we ran back to his car.

Matthew was still shivering as we sat in the front seat of his car.

And that was when he told me about what had happened when he was a kid. Sitting there in his car, parked at the edge of an Iowa town, in the middle of a winter night, he told me how he and his little brother Ansel had gone for a joy ride and he shot his brother by accident. Of course he hadn't meant to do it. He loved his brother very much.

He'd had a thing about guns ever since.

'Every time I see a gun—even in a film—it brings back memories of that night,' Matthew said. He kept looking away from me and out the window.

I held his hand. We sat there for a long time in silence. I felt closer to him than I had in all the months I'd known him. For the first time I saw him as something other than some kind of sex god, making me do things that excited and scared me. For the first time I understood that he was a real human being with a history, a past, with his own demons and nightmares.

'Let's go back to my mom's,' I said. 'We've both had quite a day. Do you want me to drive?'

Matthew didn't answer. He turned on the ignition, and we drove all the way back to my mother's without saying a word.

I felt joyous, and at the same time very strange. I'd seen a new side of Matthew: tender, vulnerable, frightened.

And he'd put himself in danger and gone to a lot of trouble to pay a man back for something he'd done to me—to me—all those years in the past.

I thought: I'm ready to go back to New York. My life isn't here anymore.

It's there. In New York. With or without Matthew.

Back at my mother's, we kissed goodnight, another sweet chaste kiss.

'Thank you,' I said.

'Thank *you*,' Matthew said.

I don't think either of us was exactly sure what we were thanking the other for. But I knew that I did feel grateful. And if I didn't exactly feel at peace, I could imagine how some day it might be possible to feel peaceful.

'Goodnight,' I said.

'Goodnight,' Matthew said.

We each went to our separate rooms. I lay down in the bed where I'd slept as a child, as a girl. And I slept like a baby.

Matthew left the next day. I was glad he had a car and could drive himself to the airport. I don't think either of us had processed everything—or actually, *anything*—that had happened during his visit. Neither of us felt ready to be alone together, just the two of us.

Something had changed. The balance of our relationship had shifted. Maybe it would shift back again when we got back to New York. Maybe we'd forget the closeness—or whatever it was—that had brought us together in Iowa. Maybe as soon as Matthew got back under Val Morton's spell—an influence that I had begun to see as more and more evil—he would become the old Matthew, the cool seductive one who'd walked into Doctor Sleep, the one who was so secretive about his life that he'd let me think he lived in his boss's Brooklyn Heights apartment.

Meanwhile I had enough to do, trying to sort things out and repair whatever damage I might have done to my relationship with my mom. We were careful, even wary, around each other for the next few days. Mom had a lot of errands to do in town but judging from the way she dressed and looked when she left the house, I had the definite sense that none of those errands had anything to do with Mr Chambers. At least I was glad about that. But was Mom?

On New Year's Eve, Mom came home with two bottles of excellent champagne—and we drank them both. It opened the floodgates. Mom apologized to me for having withheld the truth about how my dad died. She hadn't wanted me to feel guilty, and then it became too late and too difficult to change the story she'd told me.

'I just didn't know what to do,' she said as she wiped the tears pooling in her eyes, 'I didn't want to reopen an old wound, to make you feel responsible for something so awful that truly wasn't your fault.'

I nodded. Now I was crying, too. I didn't know what to say. I didn't ask why she'd told Mr Chambers. I didn't want to know how close they'd gotten.

During the intervening days there had been no sign of him, no calls, no messages. Mom let the house get a little sloppy, and I was thrilled to see the newspapers and magazines piling up in the living room, the way they always used to. She traded her uncomfortable new clothes for her comfortable old ones, and though I didn't like to think of my mom alone again, that seemed preferable to her being with a sleazy, sketchy guy like Mr Chambers.

By New Year's Eve, Mom could laugh about what had happened, about her latest 'bad boyfriend.'

'I don't know what I ever saw in him,' she said. 'I guess I was just grateful to meet a man my age who wasn't looking to meet a woman in her thirties.'

'Thirties?' I said. 'Thirties was probably too old for him. He probably had all the teenagers he wanted. His *mentorees.*'

'Oh my God,' said Mom. 'I hate to think about that. I'm so sorry, honey.'

We hugged each other and laughed and cried and hugged each other again.

By the time I left on New Year's Day (flights were cheaper then) no one would have known that there had been the slightest wrinkle in my smooth, loving relationship with my mother. But I knew. The information about my father's death had unsettled me, no matter how reassuring Mom had tried to be. I couldn't help feeling guilty, responsible, like a criminal. I felt that my whole personality—being the nice girl, the sweet girl, the good girl—was all an act, just a false front, meant to conceal something darker underneath. Maybe that's why I'd always loved acting so much. Maybe that's why I loved the kind of 'acting' Matthew asked me to do. Matthew had helped expose that darkness, but this wasn't all about Matthew. It had started at a very young age—when I'd killed my dad.

And no matter how often I told myself that none of that made sense, that you can't blame a four-year-old for a fatal accident, that I was still the nice person I'd always believed I was, I couldn't even manage to convince myself.

It was snowing lightly when I got back to New York. In addition to the check she'd given me, Mom had pressed five twenty-dollar bills into my hand when she drove me to the airport, and I used half of that to take a cab from La Guardia back to my apartment.

I hoped that Matthew would call. He knew when I was getting home. But he didn't.

I'd learned something more about him in Iowa, and he'd learned a lot more about me. But in some very important ways we were still strangers, and maybe we always would be.

# Matthew

After I got back from Iowa, I slept for days. I didn't know exactly why the trip had turned out to be so stressful, exactly—maybe it was our little encounter with that creep and the gun bringing back buried memories of that long ago incident with my brother. I'd always been gun shy, and I'd always known better than to be around them. Or maybe it had nothing to do with that. Maybe it was just being with Isabel and her mom in a normal house, seeing what it was like to live with even one normal loving parent. I slept straight through New Year's Eve and woke up in the new year with a message from Val Morton on my phone telling me he was getting back on the 2nd and wanted to see me at nine o'clock that evening.

New year, new start, I kept telling myself as I crossed the park to Val's apartment. Maybe all the weird tension I'd been feeling between Val and me would have dissolved, washed away by the sea and sun of Val's vacation. Maybe we could slip back into our former relaxed situation, drinking brandy, Val smoking cigars and ranting about all the people who'd crossed him and what he'd like to do to them and how he'd like to see them pay.

Val's new butler, Miguel, answered the door and told me to go on up to Val's study. Val was lying on the couch, his face covered by a wet washcloth. I was shocked when he removed the cloth and I saw his skin—red, blistered, peeling.

What happened to you? I wanted to ask, but I knew better. Was I supposed to pretend that nothing was wrong? That he always looked like a crustacean boiled in a pot?

'Don't pretend you don't notice I look like a fucking lobster,' said Val. 'Shoot me before I ever agree to go to one of those fucking islands again. I don't care how much Heidi pleads and begs, I don't care how often she promises to blow me if we go. Night after night, sitting around with the same dull phonies, so-called celebrities, the type you know all drive Priuses when someone's watching and Lincoln Navigators when they know no one's around to see. Half of them I didn't recognize, but they knew who I was all right, and right in front of me they'd have these boring, ridiculous conversations about how great New York used to be before the developers got hold of it and ruined it. As if I wasn't there! As if half of them didn't live in brand new condos, some of which I'd built.'

'Sounds grim,' I said.

'Grim is not the word,' said Val. 'The only way to deal

with it was to drink until their voices fuzzed out into one big drone. And hey, as long as I was drinking all night, might as well get a head start on it, start drinking in the morning. And the afternoon.

'Which is not a great idea if you're on the beach lying in the sun and you drink so many umbrella cocktails and tequila shots and God knows what else that you pass out cold and the next thing you know you wake up with your face on fire. Did Heidi rescue me? Did Heidi even know what was happening? Heidi was off somewhere getting an ayurvedic yoga treatment, paying a fortune for some guy to put hot stones on her butt. Or *up* her butt for all I know. I couldn't get out of that hellhole soon enough, I booked a private jet to get me back early. Like an emergency rescue! It cost another fortune, but if I'd had to stay there one more day I would have shot myself, and you would have been out of a job, pal.'

'I'm glad you made it out alive. My God, Val...'

'God had nothing to do with it,' Val said. 'This fucking face of mine is proof that there is no God.'

I thought of Isabel's mom. How could two such different people exist on the same planet?

'Hand me that tube of goo,' said Val, and I watched him apply ointment to his burned skin.

'So...' he said after a while. 'What's new with you and ... the girl?'

'Isabel?' I said

'No. Marilyn Monroe. Yes, Isabel.'

'I went to her house in Iowa for Christmas.'

'You *what?*'

'I went home with her. For the holidays.'

'What the fuck?' said Val. 'Are you fucking engaged? Are you about to buy her the fucking ring? Because this was totally not in the playbook. Were you asking her dad for her hand in marriage, or what?'

'Her father's dead. And no, it was nothing like that. Nothing's changed.'

Could Val tell that this last part was a lie? Val was smart about things like that, but I thought I could get away with it. Something had changed between me and Isabel, but even I didn't know what it was.

'Did you do anything ... fun?' Val asked.

By *fun* he meant *dirty*, I knew that. I thought a moment. What did I want to tell him and what did I need to keep private?

'I did her in the shower at her mom's house. The shower walls were covered with baby animal decals from her childhood, little ducklings and whatever. And her mom was right next door, listening to her scream when she came.'

I added the part about her mom being next door for extra added excitement. Often when I told Val about me and Isabel, I had the feeling that he was watching a little porn film in his head, a film starring the two of us. But

275

now I sensed that a couple having sex in the shower of a house somewhere in Middle America was not the porn film he wanted to watch.

'I'm still thinking about what I need the two of you for,' Val said. 'About when and how exactly I want to deploy you as my secret weapon.' He chuckled softly to himself. 'But meanwhile I've got another idea. Something that might be fun.'

# Isabel

A week or so after I got back from Iowa, a solid week of fretful, anxious waiting, Matthew called.

I'd tried not to get into that crazed state of waiting for him to call. That was my New Year's resolution. I told myself that I had a lot to think about, to work out for myself. What I'd heard about my dad's death, and what had happened between me and Mom, and seeing Mr Chambers again, and what, if anything, had changed in my relationship with Matthew. Especially when I was thinking about Matthew, about what had happened with Matthew, it was helpful not to be obsessed with where he was and what he was doing, why he hadn't called me and would he ever call me again.

But the fact was, I was totally obsessed. I couldn't stop thinking about him. And I felt an almost overpowering sense of relief when 'out of area' finally came up on my phone, and I knew that it was him.

He asked if I had recovered, and I said yes, I thought so. I didn't have to ask: 'Recovered from what?'

'And you?' I said.

'Yes,' he said. 'It took a while, longer than I expected. I slept a lot.'

'Me too,' I said.

The silence lasted so long I was afraid he'd hung up.

Then he said, 'Listen, why don't you meet me ... Saturday night, ten o clock. On the corner of Hancock and Wilson.'

'Where is that?'

'Bushwick.'

'I have no idea how to get there.'

'Use your GPS, Isabel. You live in Brooklyn. Don't play games.'

That seemed like a funny thing for him—the world's biggest game-player—to say. But I didn't have the nerve to point that out.

I got to the corner, which turned out to be the corner of nowhere and nowhere. I was surrounded by vast industrial buildings and low concrete-block warehouses of some sort. I'd arrived fifteen minutes late in the hope that Matthew might already be there waiting for me. But there was no one around. I almost begged the Lyft driver to let me stay and wait in the car. I'd pay him extra. But some vestige of pride—and courage—kicked in. I thanked him and got out of the car.

The cold wind gusted through the dark street. Picked

up by the wind, garbage rattled against a wall. A guy came running toward me, loping like a wolf. I felt myself go rigid. My heart was pounding. I told myself, all right. Either I'm going to get murdered or raped or mugged, or else nothing bad is going to happen. I might as well be brave and stand my ground.

The running man was yelling something I couldn't make out. As he ran past me, I heard him shout, 'My feet were stolen. I lost my feet.' How could Matthew leave me here like this? Didn't he care about me at all? I thought what happened In Iowa proved he actually had some feeling for me. But I must have been mistaken. I'd known it wouldn't last once we got back to New York.

Finally Matthew's car drove up. *Get in* he said.

What a sadist he was. Why couldn't he have picked me up somewhere more crowded? Less scary. Why couldn't he have come and got me at my apartment like an actual boyfriend. Why? Because he wasn't my boyfriend, because he wanted me to be shaken and unsettled before I got in the car.

'Where are we going?' My voice sounded reedy and high.

'I know this fabulous bar,' he said. 'You'll love it.'

The bar was even further out in Bushwick, but at least the street was relatively populated. When we got close, I saw that a high percentage of the people walking toward the lit doorway were women, in couples, arm in arm, and in groups of friends, all laughing and talking.

One by one, couple by couple, they disappeared inside. The sign over the door said: *Nell's*. A very large butch woman, heavily tattooed and with a brush of yellow hair bisecting her scalp, sat outside the door on a high stool and vetted the new arrivals.

I said to Matthew, 'Oh, it's a lesbian bar.'

'Brilliant deduction, Sherlock,' he said.

'And is it okay for you ... I mean, do they let men...?'

'Gender tolerant,' Matthew said. 'Just as long as you leave your prejudices at the door.'

I couldn't imagine leaving my prejudices with the butch bouncer. I couldn't imagine letting her know I *had* any prejudices. And I didn't, really. I was just curious to know what Matthew had in mind, why he'd brought me here. I knew that it was going to be more complicated than just his wanting to have a good time in a fun place.

Matthew and I went in, swept past the bouncer and through the door along with a crowd of tall, beautiful black girls.

The room was dark and it took a while for my eyes to adjust to the low light. It was decorated like a Victorian bordello, with red flocked wallpaper and dark blue velvet settees and booths, with little tables in the center. Up front, alongside the bar was a little stage. Loud music was playing, a disco version of Christmas carols, and on the stage by the bar, two young women, in Santa hats, Santa jackets and nothing on beneath the waist but leather thongs, danced go-go style to the music, sometimes dancing alone, sometimes turning to dance back to front, bent over, clasping each other tightly, like two lesbian Santas having sex doggy-style.

'Cool,' Matthew said.

'It's like Santa Con with no red pants,' I said.

'A Santa con wet dream,' Matthew conceded.

I saw a few straight couples, scattered around the room. And there were lots of customers whose gender was almost impossible to figure out. I found it fascinating and thrilling to be in a place where there were so many variations on being a man or a woman, and it took all my self-control not to stare as I tried to decide who or what they were. I saw one person who seemed to be literally divided in two, with long hair and makeup on one side, while the other was bald and had a little goatee. That is, half a goatee.

The crowd was mostly female, women with little moustaches and baseball caps, with leather jackets and designer dresses, with blue hair, long hair, no hair. Some had on heavy make-up with dark-rimmed eyes and bright red lipstick. There was one woman dressed like Betty Boop, another in a catsuit. Everywhere couples were chatting, vaping (no smoking aloud) and pressing up to the bar where the bartender, whose short-sleeved white T-shirt revealed muscular arms completely covered with tattoos, was mixing drinks. Her hands flew from bottle to bottle, pouring long streams of alcohol, shaking the cocktail mixer with theatrical displays of high energy.

Passing through the crowd with little trays held high above their heads, the waitresses wore short black uniforms with little white aprons and fishnet stockings, like maids in a nineteenth-century whorehouse. The décor and the clientele could have come from totally different centuries, but everyone seemed to love it—to love being there. Everywhere couples were sprawled in the banquettes, crowded around tables, dancing close, leaning against the walls. Everyone looked happy.

No one was looking at Matthew and me. It was as if they knew we were tourists, sightseers in their world. No one was paying any attention to us, but still I felt self-conscious about being there with a guy.

'Want a drink?' Matthew said.

'I'd love one.'

'Well, this may be one place where you'll have better luck getting served at the bar than I will,' he said. He pressed some money into my hand. I had to hold it up close to my eyes to see that it was a hundred-dollar bill.

'Start a tab,' he shouted in my ear.

'Okay,' I mouthed back. The music was too loud for him to hear me.

He leaned down and whispered in my ear. 'I may have to leave. In fact, I'm almost sure I'll have to leave.'

'What?'

'I may have to leave you here.'

'That's what I thought you said.'

'It's one of those nights,' Matthew said. 'I have the definite feeling that Val is about to text me and summon me.'

'Can't you drop me at the station,' I said. 'Or I could call a Lyft.'

Matthew said, 'Let's not worry about it till it happens.' I was growing more and more certain that he had some kind of plan in mind, that he wanted me to be here without him. That it wasn't about Val needing him.

That it was more likely about sex.

'You go ahead. I'll wait here,' said Matthew.

Now I really wanted a drink.

'Where will I find you?' I hated how wimpy and insecure I sounded.

'I'm not going anywhere,' Matthew said.

We were a long way from the bar. I pushed my way through the mob of women. I smelled perfume and sweat, I heard laughter and picked up random scraps of conversation. Every so often one of the women looked at me, and her gaze lingered an extra beat. Or someone would turn to watch me pass. I tried to look relaxed, open and not unfriendly, but without lingering or communicating anything in a way that might be interpreted—misinterpreted—as a signal of sexual interest.

A very tall and attractive black woman took the stage, or maybe it was a guy in drag, I couldn't tell. The lights went even lower as I approached the bar. The performer announced, in a soft, breathy voice, 'Ladies and gentleladies, I'm going to sing you a medley of songs originally done by the greatest chanteuse of the last century or any other, Dionne Warwick.'

I recognized the first few bars of 'Anyone Who Had a Heart.' My mom used to play it all the time, and I knew that it was the expression of all her sadness and loneliness. I didn't want to think about my mom, alone now in Iowa, probably missing me and without even the small comfort she seemed to have gotten from the awful Mr Chambers. I tried to think of something, anything else, and after a while, I just closed my eyes and listened to the music, to the man or the beautiful woman or whatever the singer was, singing that anyone with a heart could look at her and know that she loved the person to whom she was singing. I could have been singing that song to Matthew, I thought. Anyone who had a heart could look at me and know ... that it wasn't just sex, wasn't just the thrill of doing strange sexual things in new places for the buzz or the 'acting' challenge. I was growing more and more attached to him, I wanted him to care about me, to love me the way I loved him. Anyone who had a heart—

'What'll it be?' said the bartender, bringing me abruptly back to reality.

'A scotch on the rocks and a Grey Goose martini, extra dry with olives.'

'Scotch?'

'Right.'

'What brand?' the bartended asked, impatient now.

'I don't know.' How could I not have paid attention to what kind of scotch Matthew drank? I didn't even know that much about him. 'Something good.' I held up the hundred dollar bill.

'Got it. We can do that,' the bartender said, noticeably friendlier now.

While I waited for the bartender to pour the drinks, I noticed a tall slim woman with long red hair standing beside me at the bar. When she turned to look at me, I saw that she was extremely beautiful. And I had the feeling that I'd seen her somewhere before. But I couldn't place her, I couldn't imagine where...

She looked at me and I looked at her. She was staring at me now. An unmistakable spark traveled back and forth. She was so lovely. I wasn't gay. But wasn't everyone a little gay? I looked away and focused on the bartender as she poured vodka from a shaker into a very large martini glass.

I felt a finger trail slowly, seductively, up the length of my arm, from my wrist to my shoulder. It was the woman beside me, the redhead. Was this really happening? I was confused, disoriented. I didn't know what to do or how to respond.

Just at that moment the bartender handed me our drinks.

'Should I put it on your tab?' she said.

'Please,' I said.

The redheaded woman watched me pick up the two glasses. Obviously I was getting one for someone else. She seemed to take it as a sign that I was unavailable, and she went back to her own drink, some kind of tropical concoction, thick and white, with a tiny pink umbrella ironically tilted against the glass.

By the time I got back to Matthew, the singer had segued into 'Walk on by.' I gave him his drink.

'Perfect,' he said. 'Thank you. How did you know my brand?'

I smiled.

We sipped our drinks, listening to the singer. Her voice was so affecting and sweet, and the lyrics seemed like a description of how I would feel after Matthew left me— which for some reason was beginning to seem more and more inevitable—and I saw him when I passed him on the street.

Walk on by.

The singer was telling Matthew to keep walking, to not stop, to pretend not to notice how devastated by the sight of him I would be. I longed to lean against him, to feel his warmth, his nearness. Especially if it was only going to be for a little while.

'Nice voice,' Matthew said.

'Beautiful,' I said.

I finished my drink before I was even conscious that I was drinking.

Matthew looked at my empty glass.

'Good,' he said. 'Let's start this thing. Ready?'

'Start what?'

'You didn't think I brought you here to hear Dionne Warwick's greatest hits, did you?'

'Then what…?'

'Go to the ladies' room. Take off your panties and tights. And bring them back to me.'

'Okay,' I said. 'Whatever.' It certainly wasn't the first time he'd asked me to get naked under my skirt, and as he said, I'd never wanted to ask for my money back. This time, it was winter. Cold outside. I wasn't looking forward to going back outside, basically unprotected against the cold, from the waist down. But Matthew had never disappointed me. Sexually, that is. And once again I was staying to find out where he was going with this—what role would I play this time?

There were two ladies' bathrooms and no men's room. Were guys supposed to piss outside? Was this a sign that, despite the official policy, they weren't entirely welcome?

I went into one of the ladies' rooms. One of the stall

doors was shut, and when I heard noises coming from inside, I bent down low enough to see under the door. I saw four feet—or actually, two pairs of shoes. Heavy boot soles faced the door, and on either side of them were high heels, the pointed toes facing forward. From the sounds they were making I could tell that a woman was giving another woman head in the stall.

I slipped into the stall beside them. I took off my lace underpants and peeled off my tights. Chilly air curled up my legs. The sounds were still coming from the next stall, and they were exciting, along with the expectation of what Matthew wanted, what was about to happen. For a moment it crossed my mind that he wanted me to do something public—something up on stage. I really hoped not. That wasn't the kind of theater I had in mind. On my way out I lifted my skirt and looked at myself in the mirror. Then I turned around and looked over my shoulder at my ass. All right. I could do this. No matter what it was. Fortunately, no one else came in and the women in the stall were too occupied to know or care what I was doing. And that's what I told myself as I made my way back to Matthew through the crowd. No one here knows I'm naked under my skirt. No one knows I have my tights and underwear balled up in my purse.

When I got back to Matthew, he seemed to have gotten another drink. He knocked it back in one swallow.

He put out his hand. The tights were bulky, and it was

awkward for him stuffing it into his pocket. But finally he succeeded.

'Mmm delicious,' he said. 'Okay, here we go. I need to leave. I'll be back in exactly ninety minutes.'

'Exactly?'

'Precisely.'

So this really didn't have anything to do with his needing to go see Val. This was our next act.

'Where can you get to from here, and get back from in ninety minutes? What's going on?' I asked.

'It's about Val,' said Matthew. Maybe he meant to reassure me—this wasn't about me, or about the two of us—but in a way it was the worst thing he could have said. Once more I felt as if I was in Val's control, as if he was pulling the strings that controlled every aspect of my life with Matthew. Had he told Matthew to take me here? Had he decided what was supposed to happen after Matthew left me in the bar?

'Wait for me,' said Matthew.

Something about the way he said *wait for me* made me realize that, against my better judgment, despite my common sense, I would have waited for him forever.

'Oh,' he said. 'I almost forgot. Here are the conditions for the scene.'

With Matthew, conditions meant sex. I was more conscious than ever of being naked under my skirt. The performer had left the stage, replaced by a disc jockey playing techno dance music. Beside me a couple was dancing, fast and hot and close, the women had their hands all over each other's asses.

'Ninety minutes gives you plenty of time,' he said. 'Find a girl. Flirt. Charm her. Seduce her. Have some kind of sexual thing with her. Find somewhere to do it here in the bar.'

I gulped.

'Ninety minutes. In other words, a quickie. There's an alley that starts in the middle of the next block. I'll pick you up in the alley block. He looked at his watch. At twelve-thirty exactly.'

'You want me to wait for you in an alley? After midnight? Are you kidding?'

'You need to trust me, *Isabel*.' I was his when he said my name. I had lost all self-respect. I didn't recognize myself. Going home to Iowa had made me think I'd gotten my old self back. But obviously I hadn't.

'Oh, wait,' said Matthew. One more condition. I almost forgot.'

I braced myself. Here it was.

Matthew said, 'I want to taste her on your fingers.'

I took a deep breath. 'All right. But how do you know I can't just...'

He read my mind.

He said, 'I know what you taste like. I'll know if it's you or someone else.'

My breathing quickened.

'I've never been with a girl.'

'I know that,' he said.

'How do you know? We've never talked about that.'

'I know that,' he repeated. 'Oh, and one more thing.'

'What?'

'The redhead at the bar,' he said.

'I didn't think you were watching,' I said. 'You were all the way across the room.'

'I saw,' he said. 'She likes you. It'll be easy.'

'How do you know she's still there?'

I stood on tiptoe, but I couldn't see. There were too many dancing couples between us and the bar.

Matthew craned to see over the heads. He was tall enough so he could.

'She's there,' he said. 'Waiting for you. No one else.'

'He gave me the claim check for my coat—and another hundred-dollar bill.

'Ninety minutes,' he said. And he kissed me goodbye.

I wove my way through the crowd to the bar. Even after a martini, it hadn't gotten any easier. I was half-sick, queasy with nerves and excitement and on the edge of desire.

The redheaded woman was still sitting at the bar. I went and stood next to her. She looked up at me, hesitated a moment, then went back to her drink.

The bartender was crazy busy, and this time it took longer to get served. But at least the music had died down if only for a few minutes. I could hear myself think.

What I thought was: an hour and a half.

I edged in close to the redheaded woman. I pressed my shoulder against hers.

'Another martini,' I said.

'Put it on my tab. And another pina colada. A hilarious drink, don't you think. Only in this country would they serve such a drink.' She had a foreign accent. French, I thought. 'So you're back.'

She put her hand on my forearm. Her nails were long and carefully done, an almost purplish red. Now I was sure I'd seen her before. In a film. A French film. She'd played a sexy, ambitious candidate who was murdered halfway through the film. I was pretty sure I'd seen the film with Luke not long after I first got to New York. I didn't want to think about Luke and Marcy, who would disapprove of what I was doing. But why was it so different from going on auditions? I supposed because the redheaded Frenchwoman wouldn't be in on the script.

'I'm Clemence Marceau,' she said. That sounded right. That was the name of the actress. I remembered it clearly now. She wouldn't have given her real name if she was hiding the fact that she hung out in lesbian bars.

I said, 'You're an actress.'

She liked it that I knew.

'I'm Isabel,' I said.

'A French name,' she said.

'My mother was a Henry James fan,' I said.

'In that case it was probably a good thing that she didn't have a boy.'

I laughed. I hadn't expected to laugh. I hadn't expected her to have read Henry James. I hadn't expected to like her. It made this easier and more difficult.

Ninety minutes.

I said, 'People have said things about my name before, but never that exactly.'

A French movie star who was probably smarter, richer and more interesting than Matthew. My being attracted to her didn't seem strange. The strange thing was that she was attracted to me. I felt some of the old power and charm come back. Maybe this wouldn't be so different from my Tinder and Bumble dating games. I was surprised at how easily I sprung back into the routine. I could become whoever she wanted me to be. Whoever I wanted to be for her. For ninety minutes—even less now.

She said, 'I thought you were here with someone. Two drinks.'

'He left,' I said. That at least was true.

'I see,' she said.

I said, 'Do you live in New York?'

She'd said she'd come to New York to audition for a part in a film being directed by a well-known indie director whose name I would know. She said she probably didn't get the role, they wanted someone younger. It would have been ridiculous for me to say I'd wanted to be an actress.

On the other hand, I was acting now. So which one was the actress?

'Male directors are bitches,' she said.

I raised my glass to that.

We ordered another round of drinks. She switched from a rum drink to straight-up rum.

This time I tried to pay.

'I've got this,' I said. 'It's on the guy who left. The one who got away, ha ha.'

'Keep your money,' she said. 'Was that your boyfriend?'

'No,' I said. Once more I wasn't lying. I also knew it was something she wanted to hear.

'Good,' she said. 'I don't like girls with boyfriends.'

After another round of drinks, everything began to seem funny. For one scary second, I thought, this is how it feels to get roofied, to have someone slip something in your drink. But Clemence hadn't given me drugs. It was just the vodka, mixed with fear and strangeness and lust.

'Why are you looking at your watch,' she said. I heard her though a fog.

'I don't know,' I said and giggled. But I did know. An hour and a half. I had an assignment. Those facts stayed solid and hard despite the melting feeling I kept having.

'I'm new at this,' I said. It was a gamble—would that turn her on or turn her away?

Clemence shrugged in a very French way. She said, 'Everyone is a virgin once. Until they're not.'

Something seemed funny again, and it was in the midst of a laugh that she leaned over and kissed me and I kissed her back.

Her lips were soft, and she began to kiss me with more and more intensity. For a moment I couldn't breathe. I pulled away and buried my face in her neck, where I inhaled the scent of her perfume: expensive, musky, French.

She ordered another round of drinks, and we alternated sips and kisses. I was turned on, I was drunk. But I wasn't so drunk or turned on that I wasn't aware of the time. I couldn't lose track. No matter how carried away I got.

After a while I said, 'I need to pee.'

She said, 'I'll go with you. I don't want to lose you in the crowd.' Holding hands, we threaded our way through the bar. I could tell that some of the women knew who she was. Maybe she came here whenever she was in the country, and they were looking at me to see what lucky girl had wound up with the hot French movie star.

We both knew where the bathroom was. Matthew had sent me here. He wanted me to know where it was. He wanted me to know that girls went there to have sex in the stalls. He wanted me to go there with Clemence. He wanted this to happen, but I was way too turned on to consider the meaning or the implications of that. I wanted her, I wanted whatever was about to happen in the bath-room of the lesbian bar in Bushwick. I wanted to meet Matthew afterwards. And Matthew wanted to taste her on my fingers.

The bathroom was empty.

'You first,' she said, though both stalls were free. She knew what was going to happen.

'No, you first,' I said, and we both started laughing again.

We squeezed into the stall and shut the door behind us. She pushed my back against the door, and we began to make out again. She touched my breasts, and I put my hands up under her soft cashmere sweater. She put her hands on my ass to draw me in closer, then felt up under my skirt.

'*Mon dieu*,' she said, when she realized I wasn't wearing underwear. 'You came prepared.'

Her hands ran up and down my body. I lost track of what I was doing. It all felt so good. I put my hand under her skirt. I almost came when I touched her thigh, but I made myself hold back and ran my hand up to her crotch. I slipped two fingers under the lace edge of her underwear, and then put them inside her. She was soft and wet, and I was gentle, as gentle as I wanted someone to be with me. It was like touching her and myself at the same time. I stroked her gently, insistently, until she put her head back, closed her eyes, and moaned. I couldn't tell if she'd come. I didn't ask.

'Now you?' she said after a moment. 'Tell me what you want.'

I laughed. 'I think I need some air,' I said. 'I need my asthma inhaler.' I was improvising. I had no inhaler. And if I had, it would have been in my purse, which I had with me. She must not have been thinking.

I said, 'Let's go back out to the bar.'

'Are you sure?'

'Yes. Let's wait. We have all the time in the world.' I was only dimly aware that I was quoting Matthew. Matthew! I looked at my watch. An hour and twenty minutes had passed.

Clemence sat down and peed, and I did the same. When we got out of the stall, she washed her hands.

But I didn't. Of course.

'Come home with me,' she said. 'I'm staying at the Pierre. I have a car waiting outside.'

For a moment, I was tempted. A beautiful hotel room, I was sure. A car. I must have been crazy to say no. But somehow I knew that things would be over with Matthew if I went with Clemence and stood him up. He would never forgive me.

*Why don't you?* I asked myself. She's better than Matthew in so many ways. She gets you hot. Spending the night with her would be amazing, and Matthew is only going to tease you and disappoint you and best case, drop you off at your sad little apartment in Greenpoint.

I don't know why I didn't do the sensible thing.

'I can't,' I said.

'The boyfriend?' she said.

I didn't answer.

'I knew it,' she said. 'God, I hate straight girls. I hate it when straight girls come cruising here, looking for a little excitement. For something to tell their boyfriends about. For a little something to spice up their sex life.'

Clemence said all that in her sexy accent. And she was right. I almost changed my mind.

'I'm sorry,' I said. 'I really am. But I've got to go.'

'Right,' she said. 'Fuck you.' And she said something else which sounded like French for fuck you. There was no way to apologize, no way to make her understand. I didn't understand myself. What kind of hold did he have over me? Why was I so ready and eager to do what he asked me?

As I left the bar, I felt awful. I knew I'd done something really wrong, and I knew that the things that Matthew was asking me to do were getting worse and worse. More and more wrong. This was worse than stiffing a waitress, worse than watching my friends act their hearts out in a Shakespeare play with a vibrator buzzing away inside me. This was worse than trying to scare the guidance counselor who'd betrayed my trust and who was probably betraying my mom. Our performances had consequences—the other players were real people. What I'd done to Clemence was like rape in a way. I'd behaved like one of those frat boys who have sex with a girl not because they care about the girl but only so they can tell their frat brothers all about it. It's not about the girl at all. But I liked Clemence, I'd been attracted to her, I'd—

I grabbed my coat and ran out the door to the bar. The same bouncer was eyeing me disapprovingly, and though I knew it wasn't possible, I had the feeling that she knew what I'd done.

The streets were empty. I took a deep breath and started walking. What if Matthew wasn't there?

I found the alley exactly where Matthew had said it would be. Matthew was waiting for me. Exactly where he said he'd be. Exactly when.

I was so happy to see him that it cured my guilty conscience in an instant, which only made me feel guiltier than ever.

He pushed me up against the wall, gentle and rough at the same time. I was thinking about being with Clemence in the bathroom, how her hands had felt on my skin, how it felt to touch her.

'Which hand?' Matthew said.

'Right,' I said huskily.

Matthew took my hand and put the middle three fingers into his mouth and sucked on my fingers. I felt the familiar sensation of warmth stirring between my legs. I wished I'd let Clemence make me come, maybe it would have given me some defense against Matthew. But I was glad that I hadn't come and that I had no defenses.

I was his...

A group of women, I guessed from the bar, passed by the alley, laughing and talking. They looked down the lane and saw Matthew and me, pressed together, writhing against each other.

'Hetero,' someone said. 'Bor-ing.' They laughed. Oh, if only they knew. But I was glad they didn't know—didn't know that I'd just deceived and mistreated a woman I'd met in the bar, a sister, someone who'd done nothing to deserve becoming the victim of my bad—my unforgive-able—behavior.

The passing women probably thought that we were going to have sex, up against the wall of the alley. But I knew we weren't.

Matthew took my hand out of his mouth. My fingers were sopping wet. Holding my hand in his, he pushed my hand up under my skirt and rubbed me with my own hand until I came. I screamed when the orgasm ripped through me. But now there was no one around to hear.

'Good girl,' Matthew said. 'I forgot to tell you not to come when you're with her. She can do anything to you that you want, but you can't come. The final condition. But I guess I didn't have to mention it.'

'No,' I said. 'You didn't.'

'Let's go home.' But he meant our separate homes. He

dropped me at my apartment, kissed me goodbye, and drove away.

My job at Doctor Sleep had become almost unbearable. Everything about it depressed me, and all the things that had once seemed like a joke—the decor, the medical jackets, the way Steve practically stood on my feet when he talked to me—no longer seemed funny. Every time I went to work, I felt like a failure. A woman who couldn't act, who couldn't get a real job, who couldn't find a boyfriend who cared about something besides weird sex in weird places. A woman who would do anything he asked her to do—by a guy who, after all this time, she hardly even knew.

One morning, not long after my visit to the bar in Bushwick, I walked into work and Steve said hello to me with a funny smile on his face, a secret smile, knowing and sly. My mom would have said that he looked like the cat who swallowed the canary.

He said, 'Someone was in here, asking about you.'

'Matthew?' I hadn't seen him in days, not since our date to the lesbian bar in Bushwick. The last time he'd come to my job, he'd left me the vibrator to wear to the Shakespeare performance. Once the idea of him being here, leaving me a message or a gift, would have excited me. But now it only made me feel tired.

'Guess again,' said Steve. 'Someone super famous. A

household name. What kind of people are you hanging out with, Isabel? How come you've been holding out on us about your famous fancy friends?'

I knew what Steve was going to say before he said, 'Val Morton.'

I felt slightly sick, and there was a funny taste in my mouth,

'What did he want?' I said.

'He just said to say hi,' said Steve. 'To tell you he's thinking about you. Do you mind if I ask why exactly Val Morton might be thinking about you?'

Something about the way Steve emphasized *you* made me so despairing and angry that I suddenly didn't care whether he fired me or not. I'd rather be unemployed, I'd rather starve than submit to one more day of his insinuations, his creepiness, his breathing in my face as he asked me questions that bordered on—that crossed the border into—nosiness and prying.

'Steve, do you mind if I ask you something?' I said.

Steve took a step backward, and I remembered how my life outside the store—my life with Matthew and now, it seemed, my life with Val Morton—gave me power. The kind of power that no sensible person would want, but power nonetheless. At least over Steve.

'Ask me anything,' said Steve.

'Where do you go at lunch every day? You leave and you come back and you never say anything.'

Steve swallowed hard. I was sure he was going to lie to me about the dominatrix he was going to see.

'I go see my mom,' said Steve. 'She lives two blocks from here. She's bedridden. I bring her food and sit and chat with her. Look.'

He took out his phone and showed me a picture of a sweet looking old woman, wrapped in a crocheted pink blanket, sitting in a wheelchair.

'That's her,' he said proudly. 'I don't know where she'd be if it wasn't for me. In a nursing home, I guess. But she wants to live on her own, to be independent. So I help her keep it up for as long as we both are able.'

I knew Steve was telling the truth. I was certain. No way was he lying to me. I still had some of that ability left, it seemed, that gift for knowing what someone was thinking and feeling. I knew Steve was being honest. And I was ashamed of myself for having thought he was going out to lead a sketchy double life. A secret sexual life. I was the one with a sketchy, secret sexual life. Not Steve. And my own guilt and shame was making me project it all over him.

'That's wonderful,' I said lamely. 'How kind of you. What a good son you are.' The man I'd suspected of doing something shady was in fact doing something honorable. I'd gotten it all wrong. I was the shady one, the guilty one, the one who could never ever tell anyone what I had done and what had happened. The one who had to hide—even from myself—who I really was.

Steve shrugged. I could tell he was sorry he'd told me, that he'd given me even the slightest glimpse of his life outside the store.

'Whatever,' he said. 'You do what you have to do.'

Or you do what Val Morton tells you to do, I thought. You and Matthew and I—we all do what Val Morton tells us to do. And I shivered, even though the store was, as always, overheated.

# Matthew

Val Morton was messing with me. I don't know why or how it started, or whether he was tired of me, of what he had in mind. But I wasn't dumb or naive enough to miss the signs that said: Someone is screwing with your head.

One night, not long after I'd taken Isabel to the bar in Bushwick and I was feeling sort of confused, unmoored, waiting for further instruction, Val summoned me to his house. I found him, as always, in his study, drinking brandy and smoking a cigar.

But there was something different about the scene, some subtle change. It took me a minute to recognize what it was, the way it always takes a while to notice something disturbing in a familiar setting. What was wrong with this picture?

Here's what was wrong with the picture:

There was a gun—a revolver—on the coffee table.

Val saw me looking at it, and he saw the fear in my

eyes, and he saw the years of being gun shy that hadn't gone away during all that time since I'd accidentally shot my brother Ansel. In fact, that fear had gotten even stronger since the pervert guidance counselor in Iowa had chased me and Isabel away from his house with a rifle.

Val saw that I was afraid, and he liked it. He enjoyed the fear in my eyes.

'Oh, sorry,' he said. 'I forgot that guns are *not your thing*.' He was imitating me, sort of. 'I was getting in some target practice this afternoon, and I forgot to put it away when I got home.'

But I knew he hadn't forgotten. He wanted me to see it, he wanted to see my reaction. But why? What had I done?

Still chomping on his cigar, he got up, picked up the gun, pointed it at me and laughed.

'Of course, it's not loaded,' he said. 'Gun safety 101.'

He walked across the room, put the revolver in a desk drawer and closed it. The he returned to his couch and picked up his brandy. He swallowed deeply, then put down the glass and poured me a snifter, then drank a few more sips, sighed contentedly and said, 'So how did it go with your little friend among the big bad lesbians of Brooklyn?'

'I think Isabel actually liked it.'

'All the better,' said Val. He raised his glass. 'Here's to Isabel's ... what? What should we toast to, Matthew?'

'I don't know,' I stammered. I could feel the color rising in my face, and I despised myself for it.

'Wait,' he said. 'Do you mind if I tape record this? It's the kind of thing that Heidi and I sometimes like to listen to ... in bed. It's like our own little podcast, you could say. You know, I think that's a huge market waiting to be explored. The porn podcast, pod porn ... Let's figure out what to call it.'

'I think it already exists.' I hated the idea of his tape recording my conversation about Isabel. What if she found out? Would she ever forgive me? And yet I didn't feel I could say no. Despite everything, I still liked my job. I especially liked my salary, paid in cash, my apartment, my car. And I couldn't imagine (though I'd been thinking about it) what else I could do after this. Val had already told me that this was off the books: no reference letter, no proof that I'd worked for him, no evidence that this job had ever existed. Anyway, how exactly would I even describe my position on a CV? Personal assistant? Errand boy? House manager? Sexual ... what?

I told Val how, on the ride home from Bushwick, I'd gotten Isabel to tell me everything she'd done in the lesbian bar.

'Fabulous,' he kept saying. 'I love it. Heidi's going to *adore* this.'

Something about the way Val said that sent up a little alarm, raised the tiniest red flag. Had he found out that Heidi had come to visit me? Was *that* what the trouble was? It was all too weird. No matter what, I didn't like the way he'd turned my life into some kind of porn film-soap opera to amuse him and Heidi. At the same time, I didn't have the energy to lie or invent something other than what had actually happened.

So I told Val about making Isabel come in the alley behind the bar. I told him exactly what we did. I felt as if I was giving up something, but I gave it up.

'So that was that,' I said.

He turned off the tape recorder and leaned back. After some time he said, 'You know what? I think your little friend is ready. I think it's time for the little ... prank, the little ... joke I've had in mind for quite some time.'

So this was it. The true purpose, the secret mission that Val Morton had been hinting about, all along.

'Cool,' I said. Part of me wanted to know what Val was planning for us, and another part of me was afraid to find out.

Val went back to the desk where he'd put the revolver. I felt my whole body tense. Was he going to draw a gun on me? Shoot me? Why would I even think that? Because anything seemed possible, I suddenly thought.

Maybe it was me. My fault completely. Maybe I was getting paranoid. But Val wasn't helping. I drank my brandy in a few swallows and poured myself more from the decanter.

But instead of a gun, Val produced a photograph. A black and white picture of a very ordinary man, with a large, round, bald, slightly bulbous head, wire-rimmed glasses, a pinched little mouth and nose, and a double chin. He looked like the kind of actor who would play a bank teller, or a bank president, in a film from the 1930s or 40s.

'Who's that?' I said.

'You don't need to know,' said Val. 'All you need to do is memorize the picture. All you need to do is be able to pick this little slime ball out of a crowd—let's say a crowd at a hotel bar, though my sense is that this hotel, this bar, the place where a guy like this hangs out, won't be all that crowded. Not exactly a hot spot.' Val chuckled mirthlessly. 'And all you need to do is to be able to take a photograph of this guy on your phone.'

'All I need to do is snap a picture of this guy in a hotel bar?'

'Well, not exactly in the bar. By the time you'll be taking his picture, he'll no longer be in the bar. He'll be up in his hotel room.'

'Slow down, Val, please. Let's take it one step at a time.'

'You'll go to the bar at a particular hour and day with your little friend, who will be all dressed up like an expensive hooker. A top-drawer call girl. She'll pick him up in the bar and make a date to go to his room. You will leave them alone in the room long enough for ... let's say, things to heat up. Then all you need to do is knock on the door and say *room service* and walk in and apologize for being in the wrong room. Then you need to snap some pictures of him, and get the hell out of there. He's fat and slow and out of shape, and he won't be wearing pants.

'And I'll take it from there. Do you think you can do that, Matthew? That's not asking too much, is it?'

I didn't like the tone of these last questions, but I nodded anyway. In fact it didn't seem all that hard. The guy looked like a harmless nerd, scared of his own shadow. All I had to do was send Isabel to get the guy in some kind of compromising situation, and then get in there and take some photos that I assumed Val would use to blackmail him. I didn't ask what Val planned to do with the photos. I didn't have to.

'Wait.' I said. 'Wait a minute. I just want to be sure about something. The guys looks like a total dweeb, but … tell me he isn't some gangster or Russian Mafioso or somebody dangerous who's going to be a problem for Isabel and me to handle.'

'Look at the guy,' said Val. 'Does he look like a Russian Mafioso? Does he look like a gangster? If you insist on knowing, the guy's a science reporter, okay? A science reporter! And as far as I know, there's still a world of difference between reporters and contract killers. Well, maybe not a *world*. Let's say there's enough difference for you and your little friend not to have to worry too much about it. Trust me, this guy is meek as a little lamb. A pussycat, as they say. He's got a vaguely hot, much younger wife and three kids, and—surprise!—the marriage is on its last legs. As soon as he thinks there's been a photo taken of him with a hooker, an *expensive* hooker, you're going to have to talk him out of jumping out a window, that's how dangerous this guy is. To himself.

'Oh, and by the way, I've made sure that you'll be given a room right next door to wherever our bald loser friend from out of town is staying. So you can fade in and out of the scene. Now he sees you, now he don't. He can run to the door and look for you after you've gone, but you'll have vanished into thin air. Or into the room next door.'

'And Isabel?'

'She excuses herself and leaves. Cameras make girls like her nervous. And this guy is not going to try and prevent her from leaving. Not after what's happened, believe me. And he's not even going to think about maybe connecting the dots until it's way too late.'

I thought for a moment, or perhaps I just went through the motions of thinking. Because really there was nothing to think about. Either I wanted to work for Val or I didn't, for as long as this job was going to last.

'It's a little joke,' said Val. But the word I was thinking wasn't joke. It was *blackmail*.

I wouldn't say that to Isabel. I would act like it was all about the sex—the consummating performance all our other acts had been leading up to.

I thought about it, I worried a little, but not for very

long. I didn't like the feeling it gave me about myself. But it was what it was.

When all was said and done, I guess I must have wanted the job more than I wanted the woman.

'All right,' I said. 'I'll have to talk to Isabel.'

'You won't have to talk to her for very long,' said Val. 'From what I've gathered about your hot little romance, all you'll have to do is tell her what's going to happen. What you need her to do. That's why we've waited for so long. That's why we took our time. That's why you put her through all that, as far as I can tell. We wanted to be sure that she would say yes to anything.'

'I guess…' I said. Somehow hearing Val put it so plainly like that brought the sheer awfulness of it home to me. I'd been thinking about the whole thing a little differently, telling myself … Isabel liked it, she knew what she was getting into it, she wasn't a clueless victim, she … I didn't know what I was telling myself. But I was trying very hard *not* to tell myself that I'd taken an innocent young woman off the floor of a mattress store, bought her like one of their cheaper models, except that I didn't even have to pay. I'd bought her with sex and uncertainty, with seduction and with an appeal to a dark part of her psyche she never suspected she had. All I had to do was tell her that she wasn't a failure, that she could still be an actress, someday, in some new way. And now she was mine, like a doll, a puppet, mine to do whatever I wanted with.

I half-wished I'd never started this game. But I couldn't stop it—not now anyway. I really wanted to keep my job.

Manuel, the butler, came in.

He said, 'Mr Morton, Mr Frazier is here to see you, sir. Should I ask him to wait?'

Mr Frazier? *I* was Mr Frazier. Was Manuel slipping? He hadn't been with Val all that long. So maybe he still got things wrong. But no one who worked for Val got things wrong—or they didn't work for Val very long. And besides, Val never double-booked. No one had ever interrupted one of our meetings before.

'No,' said Val. 'That's fine. Send him in, Manuel.'

A tall, good-looking guy, maybe a few years younger than me, wearing a suit that was way more expensive than anything I was likely to afford, walked into the room. He looked so much like me that it was a little like looking in the mirror ... only seeing myself grown younger. It took a bizarrely long time for me to recognize my own brother. Ansel hadn't looked that much like me when we were young, but it was as if we'd grown towards each other, grown to resemble one another. And I hadn't seen him in so long ... I'd had no idea.

'Ansel, I said. 'Jesus Christ ... good to see you, man.'

'Good to see you too, Matthew,' Ansel said.

Neither of us sounded as if we really felt like it was all that good to see the other. I don't think that either of us knew what to feel, or what we were feeling. My head was spinning, and my chest hurt. I thought of all the times I'd tried to get in touch with Ansel, and how he'd always refused to take my calls. I'd tried to call him at the office; his home phone was unlisted, and I didn't know his cell number. He hadn't acknowledged the Christmas cards I used to send him when we were younger.

Why was he so angry at me? What had I done?

I'd missed him. I knew that now. And I hadn't let myself miss him, or even think about him for long periods at a time. It had all been too painful.

Val laughed mirthlessly. 'I believe you two know each other.'

My brother and I hugged awkwardly and slapped each other on the back, for Val's benefit mostly.

I said, 'Hey. What the fuck is going on here, Val?'

'What the fuck is going on,' said Val, 'is that I've decided that it's always best to keep things in the family. So I'm hiring your brother, who, in case you're not aware, has been doing very well in his architecture practice on the eastern end of Long Island. I assume you know what end of Long Island I mean, Matthew.'

'Of course I know,' I said. Val had never been mean, in quite that way, before.

Val said, 'I'm hiring your brother to design the top-of-the-line apartments, real gold-standard stuff, for the new condo I'm building in Long Island City. As soon as those fuckers on the City Council and in the EPA finally come to their senses and allow the deal go through.'

'*If*,' I couldn't help saying.

It was the most rebellious thing I'd ever said to Val, and I could see the fury glittering in his eyes. He wasn't used to being contradicted—not one word of anything remotely resembling back talk. Well, let him fire me. Things were heading in that direction, anyway, I could tell, and I was sure that my brother had something to do with it. And if Val fired me, I wouldn't have to do that awful little ... thing ... he'd ordered me to do with Isabel and the stranger in the hotel.

'You must have heard me wrong, Matthew. Not *if*. *When*,' Val said. '*When* the deal goes through. *As soon as* means *when*. Okay, big guy. That about wraps it up for now. You can be on your way. I need to talk to your brother.'

I was being dismissed.

'Let's catch up some time,' I said to my brother. 'Sooner rather than later.'

'Definitely,' he said, his voice so flat I knew that we never would.

For just a second before I told myself that I was *really* getting paranoid, the thought crossed my mind that Val and my brother had been conspiring against me all along.

Just as I was leaving, Val said, 'Ansel, have you met your brother's girlfriend? Isabel? The young lady is very attractive. Want to hear something funny, Ansel? I caught your brother and the girl fooling around on my bed. I didn't mind. I thought it was hot. I told Heidi all about it.'

Ansel smiled uneasily. It would have made anyone uneasy. It certainly made *me* uneasy.

My brother and I hadn't spoken in fifteen years. And this was our reunion? In the home of a rich, powerful man who thought it was hilarious to tell my estranged brother a story about spying on me having sex on his bed?

Val could do it because he could. He could get away with it because he could, because he *was* rich and powerful.

My brother and I were working for him.

Val was like the neighbor whose car we stole, coming back all these years later to take his revenge. He was worse than our neighbor, the doctor who kept the gun in his car. Val was much, much worse.

It was a lot to process at once, and only now did the full implications of what Val was doing and saying kick in. He'd known I was gun shy. But he'd kept inviting me to go to target practice with him. And he had a gun on the table where he knew I could see it! Now, it seemed, he knew *why* guns bothered me so much.

Ansel must have told him. Except that he hadn't needed Ansel to tell him. Val knew things. He had his sources. He always had...

Then I thought: *Isabel*. I hadn't believed her about Val

watching us from the doorway. Isabel hadn't imagined it. She hadn't lied. She didn't lie. Her mother was right about that. It was Val who lied, and I was the one who'd been lied to. Fooled. A wave of shame and regret washed over me.

And, the most surprising thing was I had a wholly new feeling of tenderness toward Isabel. Of affection, maybe, or at least of wanting to protect her. I wanted to be with her. I wanted to treat her more kindly than I had before, I wanted to make it up to her. To talk to her. To put my arms around her. I wanted to say I was sorry. Sorry for not believing her, for not trusting her.

But I wasn't going to say any of that to Isabel. It just wasn't going to happen. I couldn't make myself that vulnerable. That weak. It wasn't anything I was going to do. I was kidding myself about that.

I had all these confused feelings even as I prepared to tell Isabel that I wanted her to pretend to be a prostitute and to get herself in a possibly dangerous situation from which I would save her.

I hoped.

# Isabel

I was scared when Matthew told me what he wanted us to do. He wanted me to pick up a stranger in a hotel bar and agree to go to his room. I'd get the guy hard, get him down to his shorts, or maybe even naked, and Matthew would burst into the room and save me.

Matthew said, 'Remember when you said you'd play any role I gave you, Isabel? This is it. The one all the other small games have been leading up to. I think you're ready for it. I think we're ready for it.'

And there was that *we* again. It was all I wanted to hear—more than the stuff about this being good for some kind of 'career.' It was frightening how little I cared about acting these days. I wanted Matthew more than any career. And I would play any role to get him.

It was by far the most dangerous thing, the only *really* dangerous thing that we had done together. We'd done some mildly risky stuff, sure, but this was a whole different level of riskiness from playing around in a mattress store.

It was certainly way riskier than having sex on Val Morton's bed, and in the shower at my mother's. There would be sex involved, I knew. Matthew hadn't said what it would be exactly. But I was staying in to find out.

Besides, I told myself, these crazy things that Matthew and I were doing actually were bringing us closer together. I'd felt the closest to him I'd ever felt after we'd gone to Mr Chambers' house in Iowa. Since then we'd ... regressed a little. That night in the bar in Bushwick made me think we'd slipped back into playing those same old weird games. But I wanted to believe that, at some point in the future, we would feel Iowa-close again.

And maybe this was it. Matthew made it sound like so much fun, so thrilling, so daring, it made me feel like a teenager again. A teenager who doesn't care about consequences—who doesn't *think* about consequences. A teenager who doesn't object when her friends drink too much and drive. A lucky teenager who has gotten away with it. So far.

On the night Matthew told me about it, he'd asked me to meet him in the bar near Doctor Sleep, a bar where we'd gone before. He was waiting for me when I got there. His scotch glass was empty. He asked the waitress for another scotch, and a vodka martini for me.

Matthew told me the plan.

I took a deep breath. I hesitated. Then I heard myself say, 'Sure. Okay.'

Matthew said, 'Excellent. And let's add in another challenge. When you pick this guy up, why don't you pretend you're Russian? A high-priced Russian hooker giving him a bargain rate for one night.'

'Why would I do that?' I said.

'That's up to you.' Matthew said. 'Maybe you think he's cute.'

I took Matthew's hand, but he pulled it away.

'You're the real actress here, Isabel. I'm sure you can do an impressive Russian accent.'

I loved it when he called me an actress. Sure, I could do a Russian accent. We did *The Seagull* in high school, with Russian accents, and later even the drama teacher agreed that it had been a dumb idea. But my accent hadn't been all that bad. I'd streamed YouTube clips of Russians and practiced.

He said, 'Here's another idea. Let's go shopping. I'll take you shopping. It'll be like *Pretty Woman*, only in reverse. Richard Gere took the gorgeous prostitute to buy respectable clothes and I'm taking the gorgeous respectable girl to buy prostitute clothes.'

Matthew had called me gorgeous. For a moment that was all I heard, all I wanted to hear. Then I thought: He sounds as nervous about this as I am.

This was all about Val. I worried this was something Val had told—ordered—Matthew to do. Ordered *us* to do. I worried it had nothing to do with any immersive theater 'opportunity.' Something told me that immersive theater project was made up from the start.

I knew it, and I didn't know it. I didn't want to know it. This was how it had always been since the day I met Matthew. Had Val told him to get on Bumble? Had Val told him to find me and play this theater game with a failing young actress? But it could only have been Matthew who knew that I would do what he asked. It could only have been Matthew who knew that I would *want* to do what he told me to do.

'Why would I want to do this to some total stranger who hasn't done anything to me?' I said. Matthew had pushed me pretty far, but never this far. Stiffing a waitress and making out with a woman I had no intention of going home with didn't seem half as bad as seducing, tricking, and humiliating a total stranger. But maybe all those things were preparation for this. Maybe this was what that had been leading up to. Maybe this was something Val wanted. I forced the thought from my mind.

'Because,' Matthew said, 'I've done some research on this guy. He's like your Mr Chambers, only worse. He was a high school basketball coach who molested a lot of girl students and got away with it. Now he's legally changed his name, and he pretends not to be that person. But I know someone who knows someone who tracked him down.'

'Was that someone Val Morton?' I said.

Matthew flinched, which worried me. I could tell I'd struck a nerve.

'This was entirely my idea,' he said. 'Val had nothing to do with it. You know what, Isabel? I got this idea after we came back from Iowa. And I realized that what we'd done to your Mr Chambers wasn't nearly bad enough. After he chased us away, after we left town, he's probably gone right back to doing whatever evil shit he was doing before we got there.

'I thought about how there are millions of guys like that out there. And I thought, let's find one and at least have a little fun with him. A little fun at his expense. Let's fix something that's broken and no one's willing to do anything about.

'That's the story of this guy we're going to mess with. He pretends to be a science reporter but he's not, really. He's ... I don't know what he really is, except a pervert.'

A funny look came over Matthew's face when he said: science reporter. There was something going on there, behind his eyes, but I couldn't read it.

'And finally, I thought it would be a pretty incredible experience for you—back in Iowa, we couldn't exact the revenge on Mr Chambers I'd had in mind. And you deserve to get revenge, Isabel. So I thought, wouldn't it be productive for you, for your career, to be able to act out the scene where you finally *do* get some revenge? Where you have the power to take back your life, and destroy his?'

For some reason I believed Matthew. I decided to believe him. Or maybe I just wanted to believe him. Or maybe, he was right—maybe there was some dark part of me that wanted revenge. There was always that.

'I have one more condition,' he said.

By now I had an almost automatic reaction to that word: *condition*. In a word, that reaction was lust.

Matthew said, 'After you meet the guy in the bar and arrange to go to his room, you tell him that you have to do something first. Tell him you'll be there in an hour.

'I'll have a room right next door to his. And before you go to his room, you come to my room and spend the hour in bed with me.'

'Okay,' I said warily.

Matthew said, 'I want to fuck you, Isabel. We've waited long enough.'

It was as if the bottom dropped out of my stomach—and didn't come back.

'Let's go shopping,' I said.

Matthew took me to a store on Bleecker Street. I decided not to wonder how he knew it was there, if he'd been there with another woman, bought something there for another woman. I told myself, most guys notice these things, even if they're not actually planning to dress their girlfriends up like hookers.

The sales girl was young and sort of pretty, heavily

tattooed and pierced. She looked me and Matthew up and down. I had the feeling she thought she'd seen our type before. Straight couple into role-playing, maybe trying to keep the spark in their relationship. But she knew nothing about us.

Matthew asked the salesgirl if she could tell what size I wore. She looked harder at me, at my breasts, my hips, my ass.

'Yes,' she said. 'Though with the bra size, it sometimes needs a little trial and error.'

Matthew told me to go wait in the dressing room. He would bring me things to try on.

The dressing room was bigger than you usually found in stores, but it was more softly lit, and there were two comfortable chairs and a huge mirror. There was some kind of perfume in the air: rose petals, I thought.

I sat in one of the chairs and waited for what seemed like an eternity until Matthew appeared, bunches of hangers in his hands, dozens of lacy garments draped over his arm. Ribbons and straps hung from everything he carried.

Matthew hung the items he'd brought in on hooks and sat in the other chair.

'Stand up,' he said. 'Take your clothes off. I was hoping I'd find you naked, waiting for me when I came in.'

'I'm sorry, I...'

'No matter. Hurry up. I want to see you in these.'

I tried on one thing after another. Tiny lace panties that opened up between my legs, sheer red underwear slit up the back, bras with holes cut out for the nipples, a kind of corset with stays and ties and straps that ended just above my hip bones..

When I put on a delicate white lace bra and a ribbony white garter belt, thigh-high lace stockings with a thin thong under the garter belt, Matthew said, 'It's so hard not to touch you. It's torture.' And a feeling of warmth surged through me.

Matthew told me to turn around as he stared at me in the mirror. I could see his reflection, over my shoulder, his face slack with desire. The ribbons on the garter belt pressed into my thighs, but it felt good. It *all* felt good. I felt woozy with excitement and desire, and for a moment I was able to forget what all this was for. I told myself: it's for Matthew. It's for me and Matthew.

Matthew opened the curtain and stuck his head out.

'Miss, would you mind coming in here for a moment?'

He wanted her to see me. He wanted a stranger to see me, and he wanted to see how I reacted. The pierced, tattooed salesgirl stepped into the dressing room. She gave me a long, cool look. I was embarrassed for her to see me dressed like that, but she didn't blink. She'd seen it all before.

'Actually,' Matthew said, 'we're looking for something similar, but in black—and maybe with red ribbons?'

'I guess you know what you want,' she said.

Matthew looked at me. I blushed.

'I do,' he said. 'We do.'

Matthew didn't have to explain to me that he was thinking of what I'd worn to the party that night we'd fooled around in Val Morton's bathroom. I hated the thought of Val creeping into my brain at this moment, but I liked the idea of there being a history that Matthew and I shared.

The salesgirl returned with the black lace and red ribbon ensemble. As soon as she left, I stripped naked, and put the garments on, first the thong—

'Stop,' said Matthew. 'I want to look at you just in that.'

I stood before him, wearing just the tiny thong.

'Now the garter belt,' he said. 'Let me help you fasten it.'

His hands accidentally, or not so accidentally, brushed against me as he fastened the hooks.

He stopped me at every stage, until I stood before him in the bra and panties, the garter belt and stockings.

Matthew sighed. 'I want you,' he said. 'I want you now.'

Electricity sparked all through me.

'The only thing that helps,' he said, 'is to think that this is what you'll be wearing when you come to my hotel room.'

For a moment, wrapped in the fog of shiny silk garments and the warm, perfumed cubicle, I'd forgotten the hotel, the stranger that I had to seduce in the bar, the pretense of being a Russian prostitute. And it was as if I'd taken some kind of pill, a muscle relaxant.

What I had to do no longer seemed so frightening. I could do it if Matthew wanted me to do it. It would be safe if he said so. And I would have that hour, alone in a hotel room with him.

We'd waited long enough.

I hadn't seen Luke and Marcy since I got back from Iowa. On Sundays, when we usually got together at Cielito Lindo, I'd pretended to be busy. I suppose they thought that I was seeing Matthew. But I wasn't. I was just too overwhelmed and confused to see them. I knew they would want to help me sort out what had happened—how it felt to see Matthew together with my mom, what it had been like to spend Christmas with him. I wanted to tell them about Mr Chambers, and about what Matthew and I had done. But I hadn't sorted it out for myself. At all. And I wanted enough clarity—at least in my own mind—to be able to give my friends some idea of what I thought and felt.

I used to be a person who knew what other people thought and felt. And now I didn't even know it about myself. All I knew was what I thought and felt when I was with Matthew..

Anyhow, I wanted to see them just once before I did

this ... thing ... Matthew wanted. Before I pretended to be a call girl and ... why had he asked me to do this? What could possibly be in it for him? Why couldn't we just have a normal relationship?

I had been feeling increasingly anxious about going to a stranger's hotel room. What if something went wrong? What if he tried to attack me before Matthew got there? What if he called the cops? I had so many dark fantasies that I finally decided it would help if I talked it over—or at least talked some of it over—with Luke and Marcy.

I could tell immediately that neither of them were in very good moods. Maybe their holidays had been as weird as mine. They seemed a little bored and distracted when I told them that Matthew had come home with me for Christmas. They weren't all that interested in hearing the details. It was as if their love affair with Matthew was over, and they didn't understand why mine was still going on.

I decided not to tell them about Mr Chambers. I'd need a really sympathetic listener for that story, and at least for the moment neither Luke nor Marcy seemed to be that person.

So I decided to cut straight to the chase.

'Listen, you two. I know this is kind of an innocent question but ... have either of you ever gone home with someone you met in a bar?'

Luke said, 'Let me get this straight. You're asking a

young gay man in New York City if he's ever gone home with a guy he met in a bar. Sometimes it seems I've done nothing but have sex with strangers. Gee, Isabel, you can take the girl out of Iowa, but...'

Marcy laughed, not that kindly, I thought.

'Marcy? What about you?'

'Honey, I work in a bar. Where else am I going to meet guys? Who else am I going to go home with?'

'So what did you do?' I said.

'What did we do?' chorused Luke and Marcy.

'I mean about keeping safe. About not getting into trouble. I mean do you know...'

'How do you know you won't get raped and murdered?' Marcy said. 'You don't know. You have to trust your instincts.'

My instincts are going to have nothing to do with this, I thought. I'm going to have to trust Matthew's instincts. And do I? Do I trust them?

'Why are you even asking us this?' said Marcy. 'I thought you and Matthew were ... exclusive.'

I didn't know what I could have said to have given her that idea. Exclusive? I thought of the time when I'd shown up at Matthew's apartment and I could tell that he had a woman with him.

'We are,' I said. 'Sort of. But I keep wanting to do something a little crazy. A little risky.'

'Okay, here's one piece of advice,' Luke said. 'I have my

biggest, strongest, most loyal friend on speed dial. So if anything goes badly south, and things start to seem even vaguely dicey, there's at least a chance I can call him and he'll find me and show up and somehow get me out of trouble. Actually, it's never come down to that, but there's always that possibility. In fact, I don't know why you're doing this, Isabel. I'd advise you against it.'

'Me too,' said Marcy. 'I'm sure there are better, safer ways to meet guys. I just haven't found one yet.'

'You guys are probably right,' I said. 'I don't know why I even thought of it. It was just a fantasy I had.'

Matthew was the biggest, strongest guy I knew. And this was his idea.

The Atlantic Hotel was on West 44th Street and 10th Avenue, and it certainly wasn't the Pierre. It wasn't even the Marriot. It struck me that it was a leftover, with only a surface renovation, from when the old Times Square was full of hotels that hookers and their pimps worked out of. *That* Times Square had been gone long before I got to New York, though I knew it was part of what my mother thought about when she kept warning me about the dangers of the big city.

But now it seemed that the old Times Square was alive and well—or anyway, half dead and not so well—in the Atlantic Hotel.

I walked into the bar. I hoped—more than hoped—that

the bar would be empty, that the bald guy with glasses whose photo I'd studied and memorized wouldn't be there. I could have a drink, wait for him a while, and then go home and tell Matthew I'd tried my best.

I should have been more upset or alarmed. But I'd taken a happiness pill. The last one in the bottle I'd taken from Val and Heidi's bathroom. As it kicked in, I felt the familiar, welcome edge of euphoria. Everything was manageable and nearly everything was funny.

If I was lucky, no one would be there. No such luck. There were people in the bar. Two businesswomen talking in the corner, an elderly Chinese man in a business suit drinking alone.

And there he was. I saw him.

He was sitting all by himself in a booth along the wall. Bald head, fringe of hair, glasses. The tiny chin and bulbous nose. He was the guy I was there to meet, I'd been told he'd he be there. And at the same time it seemed strange that he should be there at all.

Couldn't Matthew have picked someone handsome for me to seduce? There must have been a semi-attractive child molester out there who needed to be taught a lesson. Why did perverts have to look like perverts?

Isabel, I thought. That's unfair. You used to be a nice person. You used to be the girl people wanted to have coffee with after yoga class, the girl people called when the babysitter stood them up.

I was still that girl. Wasn't I?

Maybe Matthew didn't want me to pick up a really handsome guy. Maybe he didn't want competition, maybe he'd be jealous? That thought made me happy.

But ... how did Matthew know that this guy would be at this bar on this day and this time? What was really going on here? I wanted to know, and I didn't.

Val, I thought. This is about Val ... I should have gone home. But I stayed. I was going to meet Matthew upstairs in his room. I stayed.

I could feel the garters pinch, under my skirt. Matthew. I needed to trust him.

I was glad I'd taken the last Euphorazil.

On top of the black and red ribbon underwear I wore a red silk blouse cut so low you could see the tops of my breasts. Also a very short black skirt, and high black boots. For a moment I was afraid that the bartender would take one look at me and ask the obvious hooker to leave.

What was I worried about? This was a New York hotel. Hookers worked them, high and low.

No one on the staff acknowledged me. It was as if they didn't see me. They didn't want to see me.

I walked directly over to Mr X's table.

Matthew had said that any name this guy would give me wouldn't be his real name.

'May I sit down,' I said, in my best Russian accent. He didn't seem to think it was unusual to have a Russian hooker approach him in a hotel bar. Maybe that was why he stayed in this hotel.

He looked up at me, then down at my legs and stockings and boots.

'Absolutely,' he said. 'Have a seat, please.'

I slid in across the booth.

'Would you like a drink?' he asked.

'A Grey Goose martini,' I said. 'Straight up, extra olives.'

'Coming up,' he said, already signaling the waiter. 'I like girls who know what they want.'

I pretended to think that this was a cool, sexy thing to say. The happiness pill helped me pretend to be amused by the whole situation. Or maybe I really was amused.

He put out his hand. 'Wilson,' he said. 'Wilson Pickett.' Was he kidding? Even a dumb Russian girl would know that that was the name of a famous American soul singer. Though maybe I only knew because he was another singer my mom liked. In any case, it wasn't this guy's name.

I'd keep on thinking of him as X. It was easier that way. I didn't want to think of how far down I'd come if I'd stopped caring if people had names and had started thinking about them as letters of the alphabet.

'And you?' X said.

'Me what?'

'Your name, dear lady.'

'I'm Anastasia Romanov,' I said.

'That's a joke,' he said. 'You're not Anastasia Romanov.'

'And you're not Wilson Pickett.'

'Pleased to meet you, Anastasia.'

'Enchanted, Wilson,' I told X.

'Where are you from?' he said.

'Originally? A little village north of Volga.' I'd prepared my character, but I was improvising. 'Little village you never heard of.'

'I've been to Moscow,' X said.

'What were you doing in Moscow?'

'Research.'

I didn't want to ask what kind of research.

'My hometown is a million miles from Moscow.'

'A million?' he said.

'I am exaggerating,' I said.

'I like you,' said X.

'Thank you,' I said.

'I love your English,' X said.

'Thank you,' I said.

'So Anastasia,' said X. 'What brings you here?'

The small talk was over.

I said, 'I want to have some fun.'

I couldn't believe this corny exchange, nor could I imagine that anyone could believe that a pretty (or pretty enough) young woman would come to an empty, dark, desolate hotel bar for fun. It was as if we were performing a script written long ago.

'Fun sounds good,' said X. 'And you know what? We

could have more fun in my room than we could here.'

'I'd love to,' I said. 'But I have some business to take care of ... oh, and I need a loan. I have a sick sister in Florida who needs medical care...' If I'd had a real sister, a healthy sister, I would never have said that. I would have been way too superstitious. But being an only child made it easier. I was improvising again. I'd decided to not over think it and say what came into my head. Matthew hadn't told me to say this. I was writing this part on my own.

'How much does your sister need?' X said.

'Three hundred dollars for the first doctor's visit,' I said. 'Medical care is expensive these days. She's uninsured. No Obamacare for Russian girls. '

'That's a lot of money,' he said.

'The doctors usually charge twice that much.' I wanted him to think he was getting a bargain. 'My sister is a pretty girl.'

'Like you,' said X, as if I was some sort of child.

I thought of Mr Chambers.

'Three hundred dollars for first consultation,' I said.

'I think I could help with that,' X said.

'That would be great,' I said. 'Spassibo.' The only Russian word I knew. 'The thing is ... I have an errand to run first. Can I meet you in your room in an hour?'

X didn't like it. Too bad. He should have had me right then, no waiting. But he could tell that he didn't have any choice.

I was good as the Russian hooker. I could act. I could still act. It was all coming together. I'd been acting in the bar in Bushwick. In the supermarket and the diner. Matthew brought my talent out in me.

'Fine,' X said. 'I could freshen up.' The creepy way he said *freshen up* made me physically queasy for a moment, but I overcame it.

'I'll be waiting for you,' X said. 'On pins and needles.' He wrote his room number down on a cocktail napkin. I took it and put it in my purse. But I already knew the number. Matthew had tipped the bell clerk.

Matthew would be next door, waiting for me.

I ordered another drink for X and left him with the bill, making sure that he stayed there when I went up to Matthew's room.

What if Matthew wasn't there? What if the whole thing was an elaborate joke on me? Matthew would never do that, I told myself. We'd done too much together, shared too much. But what exactly had we done and shared?

I knocked on Matthew's door.

An eye appeared at the peephole. Matthew opened the door.

He pulled me into the room.

In all this time, I had never been happier to see him. It had never been more of a comfort, a thrill and a relief. Here he was, waiting for me, where and when he promised.

He seemed happy to see me too.

Something was different. I could feel it. He *saw* me.

It was almost like (I thought now) he'd never trusted me before. Not since that lunch when I told him I'd seen Val watching us from the doorway. Matthew had always been looking to see if I was just another crazy girl. If I was toying with him like I had been with all the Tinder and Bumble first-date-only boys before him.

And now it was like a switch had flipped. When Matthew looked at me, he *saw* me.

I sensed it right away. He put his arms around me and kissed me hard, then tenderly, then hard again. This was different too. We'd done so many sexual things—-but we'd never made out, like kids. We stood there, by the doorway, kissing and embracing. He was shaking as he bent down to kiss the tops of my breasts.

He said, 'That's quite an outfit.'

'You should know. You chose it,' I said.

He unbuttoned my blouse, then took off his shirt. We pressed against each other. We stumbled over to the bed, giggling because it was so hard to walk. Then we fell onto it, touching each other, tearing at each other's clothes. When he'd taken off my skirt and shirt, and he looked at me in my new hooker underwear, he said, 'It's way hotter here than in that store, and that was hot. I knew that it would be.'

He'd bought the underwear for me to wear for *him*. I understood that now.

'Thank you,' I said. And we laughed again. We were so glad to be together.

The weird thing was, after everything we'd done, it was still the first time we'd actually made love. And it wasn't totally smooth. In fact, it was almost, maybe not quite, as awkward as any first time.

Every so often he'd stop. He'd look kind of sad and say, 'I'm sorry, Isabel.'

He could have apologized for so much. I didn't know what exactly he was apologizing for. It seemed a little strange that he would choose this moment. Except for how easy it was to turn his attention back from apologies to sex.

He was making love to me like a man in love. I knew it.

As he slipped off his pants and shorts, I saw that he had a huge hard on. He touched me between my legs but I was too hot for foreplay, I moved his hand away and pressed against him. I drew back, spread my legs.

I groaned with pure pleasure when he entered me. This was what I'd been waiting for. Nothing had ever felt so good.

I was glad I had taken the happiness pill. It made everything more intense.

Matthew stopped and said, 'Shh. Listen.'

We heard a door shut hard and someone walking around the room next door.

'These walls are so thin,' I said. 'Thin as paper.' It was

strange, having a semi-normal conversation with Matthew inside me. And yet it seemed so natural, as if we'd been lovers forever. We could start again, any time.

Matthew pointed at the wall behind the bed.

'He's there,' he said. 'Your boy. How noisy we are is up to you. It's going to make him hotter. Maybe that's not what you want.'

Until the door slammed, I'd forgotten or *almost* forgotten the guy next door, and what I had agreed to do, after I was with Matthew.

For a moment I was so distracted that the heat ebbed away. But Matthew moved inside me and the feeling came back, full blast. I didn't care about anyone else, anything else, the past, the future, all I cared about was having it at last, of seeing what happened next.

We rolled over, with me on top. I arched my back and watched Matthew's face, his eyes closed, his shoulders tensed and hunched. He almost seemed to be somewhere else, but when I hesitated, with just the tip of his cock inside me, he looked up at me. He knew I was there all right, he knew who I was. He was right there with me. It was where we wanted to be.

We couldn't believe it.

Time passed, I don't know how much. We came. I wanted to scream, I tried not to scream.

It was so intense I laughed because I seemed to have hurt my jaw.

For a first time, it was amazing.

And we had all the time in the world for it to get even better.

I rested my head on Matthew's chest, he put his arm around my shoulders. Our bodies still felt tingly. From time to time he kissed me on the top of my head.

Was it the happiness pill? Or was this what happiness felt like? If only for the moment, I was too happy to tell. Or care.

'I'm sorry, Isabel,' he said.

'Stop saying that.' I could say that now. 'There's nothing to be sorry for,' I lied. Who cared? All the problems had been solved by what just happened. By how he'd made me feel. The way we'd made each other feel.

I must have dozed off, because I opened my eyes to hear Matthew saying my name.

'Isabel,' he said. 'There's that thing we need to do,' and he motioned with his head toward the wall beyond which I knew that X was waiting.

I no longer saw the point of playing a weird sex game when we'd just had the best sex I could ever imagine. And that worried me. Was the sex just a freak? We were about to go back to the same old relationship in which Matthew told me to act out his fantasies and I did what he told me. Because I liked the challenge. Because it felt good. Because it was fun, and I was curious to see what happened next.

I don't know why I kept thinking that it had something to do with Val Morton.

Or maybe I only thought that later. Memory is a funny thing. Maybe later I convinced myself that I'd thought it at the time.

'I have to take a shower,' I told Matthew. 'Even with all my clothes on I'd...' I was too shy to say: I'd smell like sex.

'Good idea,' said Matthew. 'Good thing we're in a hotel, because you need to keep your hair dry. Use one of those stupid hotel shower caps, and dry off really well. He's going to be suspicious if he thinks you've just taken a shower. He'll think your so-called errand meant doing another guy in the hotel.'

'Wasn't it?' I said.

'Not the way he thinks.' Matthew said. 'The last thing we want is for him to put two and two together and figure out you spent that hour having sex with the guy next door.'

'Who would think that?' I said.

'This guy would,' said Matthew. 'And he's not going to like it.'

I got dressed. Hooker bra, panties, garter belt, stockings, skirt and blouse. My make-up was a mess, and it took me a while at the sink to fix it.

'Don't worry,' Matthew said. 'I swear to you. You're not going to have to fuck him. You're not going to have to fight him off. You're not even going to have to touch him. I'll be there before that, I'll save you. Your knight in shining armor.'

'How will you know when to come in?' I said.

'Knock on the wall,' Matthew said. 'These walls are made of paper. As you know.'

'Okay,' I said.

'You look great,' he said. 'You look totally hot. The guy's lucky just to get to look at you. To be in the same room with you. Remember. Knock on the wall when you want me to come in. Or maybe a couple of minutes before you want me to come in.'

'I want you to come in now,' I said. 'Before I get there.'

'Not an option,' said Matthew.

Matthew and I kissed goodbye for a very long time. He looked sadder than I'd ever seen him. I wanted to comfort him, but why? This was his idea. Or was it?

He pointed toward the bathroom and made a sucking motion. I went in and gargled with the mouthwash that Matthew must have brought with him.

No matter how passionate he got, he would never lose his head. I would know that going into this, and I would no longer be surprised. Or disappointed.

This was who he was. I could choose if I wanted to be with him or not. And for the moment I did. *I wanted Matthew.*

I'd become his robot. Sex Robot Girl. I would still do whatever he said.

I knew it wasn't really like that. I told myself: You're still your own person. But sometimes that was how it felt.

I put on my high heels and short fake-fur jacket and toddled into the hall. I closed Matthew's door very softly and tried to walk noiselessly up to the next door on the left.

# Matthew

As soon as I opened the hotel room door and saw Isabel standing there, I knew that I loved her. I had always loved her. All I wanted was to be with her.

My knees went so weak I could hardly stand, and I was glad when we tumbled back on the bed. I thought about our shopping trip, about the items she'd tried on, about what I knew she was wearing. But I would have been just as hard without any of that. It was the thought of making love to her that got me so hot.

I wanted to tell her how sorry I was, though I couldn't think of a way to explain what I was sorry for. I was sorry I hadn't believed her about Val watching us from his bedroom doorway. I was sorry I'd lied to her about why we were role-playing; about the imaginary theater career Val could give her that didn't exist and never would. Or at least, not the kind of theater she wanted to be a part of. But I wasn't ready to say Val's name yet. And besides, it wasn't what she wanted to hear. She just wanted to have sex with me—normal sex, hot sex, without weird games and conditions. And that's what I wanted too. I wanted her more than I'd ever wanted anyone in my life.

It was better than I'd imagined when I'd jerked off, thinking about Isabel, during all those weeks I'd gotten her hot or made her come and left her.

Finally being with Isabel now was so sweet, so slow and passionate. It was the best sex I'd ever had. I came, with a blinding, soul-rocking orgasm that shook my entire body. And a few minutes later, I was ready to start all over again.

After it was over, I wanted to tell her what was about to happen to her—and why. I wanted to confess to how much of what we'd been doing had been orchestrated by Val. How much Val was still pulling the strings.

When she got into the shower to get ready to go to the stranger next door, I wanted to follow her and do again what I'd done to her in her mom's bathroom in Iowa. But I didn't. There wasn't time.

Then I made the mistake of looking around the gritty hotel room. And I knew that if I lost my job with Val, if Isabel and I didn't do what he wanted me to, I'd lose everything: my apartment, my car, the life I was currently enjoying. I'd be lucky to be able to stay in a room like this.

Isabel reappeared in the bedroom, then left again, then returned. How beautiful she was! How desperately I wanted to protect her, to make her happy, to give her a life in which she could have everything she'd ever wanted.

But we needed Val's help for that. I couldn't do it on my own. I needed his money, his power. I needed my job.

'You look great,' I said. 'You look totally hot. The guy's lucky just to get to see you. To be in the same room with you. Remember. Knock on the wall when you want me to come in.'

And I sent her on her way.

It was the biggest mistake of my life.

# Isabel

After a moment Mr X answered the door.

'Right on time,' he said. 'I like punctuality in a woman. I've heard that you Russian girls are always late.'

I would have been insulted if I was a real Russian. But I was glad, because it reminded me to slip back into my Russian accent. Having sex with Matthew had discombobulated me.

'Thank you,' I said. 'Thank you very much.'

X smiled. 'Come in. Can I get you something from the mini bar?'

I could have drunk every little bottle in the bar if I thought it would help calm me down. On the other hand, I needed to keep my wits. I asked for a club soda.

I said, 'I don't want to fall asleep.'

'We wouldn't want that,' X said.

He poured my soda into a glass.

'Ice, Anastasia?'

I nodded. That's right. That's who I was. Anastasia.

He was drinking something honey-colored, on the rocks. It wasn't his first bottle, either. And he'd gotten a head start down in the bar.

His room was more or less like Matthew's. Not the most expensive room, not the cheapest. The hotel was pretty basic, but of course I hadn't noticed that when I'd been next door with Matthew.

X sat on the edge of the bed, I sat in the desk chair. I let my knees fall open to move things past the boring conversation.

His gaze kept tracking to the V between my legs. I let him look. I was trying to do some yoga-like thing and somehow leave my body. If there was ever a good time for an out-of-body experience, this was it.

He was portly and so out of shape that he had to heave himself off the bed with both hands. He came over to me and clumsily bent down and kissed me.

I pushed him away, but gently. I tried to make it teasing and seductive rather than horrified, which was how I felt, despite the soothing effects of the happiness pill.

'Later,' I said. 'We have time for that. We have all the time in the world.'

'I like your attitude,' X said. 'I hate it when a girl acts like she's got a taxi waiting downstairs with the meter running.'

'No taxi,' I said. 'No meter. Sit down on the bed. Get comfortable. Take off your pants. Let me watch.'

'Love it,' he said.

He sat back down on the edge of the bed and unbuttoned his belt, unzipped his fly. It was not a pretty sight, him wriggling out of his trousers and grinning.

I really hated doing this to another human being. But I believed Matthew when he'd said that X was like Mr Chambers on steroids, that he'd gotten away with it, and that we could make him suffer in this embarrassing but basically harmless way. I didn't especially like this idea of myself, as some kind of sexual vigilante. But X had gotten away with crimes, years of crimes, and something had to be done. And if I was honest, I wanted some revenge.

Somehow I knew that X was going to be wearing those awful old-guy thin white shorts. And black socks. The nerdy perv from central casting. If he was an actor, he'd be a natural to play the horrid old pedophile on *Law and Order*.

'Now come over here,' I said.

I stood up to embrace him. It took all my self-control to take him in my arms, and kind of pull him, or dance him across the room. I let him think he was backing me up against the wall, the wall between us and Matthew.

I kicked the wall with my heel, three times. I made it seem like I'd done it because my leg was twitching with passion. X must have thought it was something Russian girls did when they got hot.

As his face came closer, it seemed to get bigger. In just

seconds his lips would smash into mine. I braced myself, hardened my mouth.

There was a loud knocking on the door.

'What the hell is that?' X mumbled to me.

'Hello,' he called shakily in the direction of the door. Did he think it was his wife?

'Room service,' said a voice.

It was Matthew.

'Mistake! I didn't order anything,' X cried.

'A hospitality basket from the management,' Matthew said.

X couldn't turn down a gift.

'Coming,' he called.

Then to me, 'Would you mind waiting in the bathroom?'

'Not at all,' I said. 'That's fine.'

I went into the bathroom and shut the door, but I left it a little open. Just enough so I could watch the room without X noticing that I was watching. Anyway, he was focused on the door.

X opened the door a crack, and then flew back as Matthew barged into the room. I came up behind X and leaned against his back. I draped myself all over him with my skirt hitched up and my ass—garter belt, stocking, thong—toward the camera. Matthew stepped back and took a picture of us with his phone, then stepped back further and took another.

'Smile at the camera,' Matthew said.

'What the fuck?' said X. 'This is a set up. I should have realized something was wrong when she said her name was Anastasia Romanov. Like the dead Russian princess. That should have been a tip-off right there. Look, guys, to be honest, I'm married. This is the last fucking thing I need. What do you want? Money? Because if this is a money thing, I can pay you to take those pictures off your phone. Unless they're already uploaded. In which case I'm going to sue your fucking ass. '

'No,' Matthew said. 'They're not uploaded. And there's no need to sue. As for the money...'

I could tell what Matthew was thinking. As long as he was doing the right thing and having fun, why not get paid to do the right thing and have fun? If the perv was offering us money, we might as well take that too.

'Five hundred bucks, and you get the pictures,' said Matthew.

'Deal! I'll pay you,' said X. 'Let me go get my wallet.' That he was still wearing his shorts gave the conversation an element of shaming that I had to admit I enjoyed.

He reached into his jacket pocket. It took me a weirdly long time to realize that he was holding a hand gun, and that he was pointing it at Matthew.

I wanted to hurl myself between Matthew and X. But I didn't. I told myself it would be unwise to startle a man with a gun in his hand.

351

'Who the fuck are you really?' he said, taking aim at Matthew.

I was still convincing myself that this wasn't a bad dream. It certainly seemed like one.

'Hey,' Matthew said, 'Relax. It's just this crazy sex thing I like to do with my girlfriend. I am really and truly sorry that you got caught in the crossfire. Collateral damage, whatever. I assure you there's no threat involved. What happens in this room stays in this room.'

He laughed. X didn't.

'You think this is funny?' he said, advancing on Matthew,

'Can you please put the gun down,' Matthew said. 'This is not a life and death matter.'

'Who are you?' X repeated. 'Why are you doing this?' He meant Matthew.

He really had forgotten I was there or what he'd planned on doing with me. Maybe I should have felt insulted. But I was just relieved. And his being unaware of me was actually very useful.

I crept up behind him. I don't know why I pushed him as hard as I could. It was the totally wrong thing to do. It was instinct, but the wrong instinct. What was I thinking? He had a gun in his hand.

A shot rang out. Matthew tried to grab the gun, but X held on to it with surprising strength, given the difference in their age and height and physique. Given how buff

Matthew was and how flabby and out of shape X was.

All that X had going for him was the fact that Matthew hated—and was scared of—guns. And there was really nothing that I could do to help. I looked for something to hit X over the head with, but anything I did would have made him turn around and focus on me. Could Matthew have jumped him if that happened? I couldn't think, I couldn't figure anything out. It was all so chaotic and scary.

X stood there, stunned, not moving. He almost seemed to have forgotten that he was the one with the weapon, and it seemed increasingly clear that he wasn't actually going to use it. Or at least he didn't want to.

Matthew lunged for the gun again.

X woke from his trance. His face turned dark red. The two men struggled.

I kept thinking it was like a play.

Only now did I see the giant drawback of the happiness pill. I was having a very hard time convincing myself that this was actually happening. That this nightmare was real. It kept seeming like a play being performed for my entertainment.

Both men grabbed for the gun. A shot rang out, then another. I heard the bullet strike the wall.

Didn't anyone hear? What kind of hotel was this? Didn't someone come running when they heard gun shots? Didn't someone call the police?

I crawled behind the bed and hid there, raising my head from time to time to watch the fight that went on and on. Another shot. Someone shouted. Was it Matthew or X? Why couldn't I tell? The yelling and motion and violence got louder and faster and scarier. I picked up the phone, put down the phone. I screamed, but no sound came out.

'Isabel, go lock yourself in the bathroom,' Matthew said. 'Now!'

But I didn't. I was afraid to crawl out from behind the bed, where I felt a little safe at least.

The two men were grappling on the floor, and as they rolled near the door, I made a break for it, and did what Matthew told me. I ran into the bathroom and locked the bathroom door.

I heard another shot, then another.

Again I wondered, was there no one else in this hotel? How could no one have heard and reported shots from X's room? Was it true what people in Iowa said about people in New York? They wouldn't help you if you were in trouble. Well, we were in big trouble now.

Then I heard nothing. No shots. No noise. No words. No motion.

And that silence was the scariest sound yet.

I opened the door, very carefully and slowly. Matthew and X were lying on the rug, near the door. Blood was everywhere, on the walls, the carpet, the bed. Especially the carpet.

I walked gingerly across the blood-drenched carpet. I picked up the house phone and called downstairs to the desk.

'There's been an accident,' I said.

The EMT guys arrived in what seemed like no time. Just long enough for me to stop shaking and start breathing again. Just long enough for me to check and see that Matthew and X were both still alive. Just long enough for me to realize that I had no idea what else to do. I knew how bad it looked, with me in my hooker outfit and both men wounded and covered in blood.

The ambulance guys said that both men were badly hurt. Both had been shot. But when I pressed them, they said they thought both guys would probably make it. Were they just trying to calm me down, or did they believe it? What did *probably* mean? I didn't like the sound of it.

'Why should I believe you?' I said.

One of the guys said, 'Because we're taking them to the hospital and not the morgue. How about that, for a start?'

Even though they sounded brusque and impatient, I was grateful for the reassurance. But I couldn't stop trembling. I had a funny feeling in my chest, as if my heart kept stopping and starting again.

It was amazing how fast the happiness pill had worn off.

I prayed, a prayer for which I knew I would be punished

someday: if one of them has to die, let it be X. Don't let it be Matthew. Save Matthew. Please let Matthew be all right.

I was no longer the same person—not just the nice girl but the decent human being—I was when Matthew met me. But still I wanted to be with him.

After this, we would change. No more games, no more risks. A life of quiet contentment. I'd learned my lesson— and somehow, I felt sure that Matthew would have, too.

The cops arrived, right behind the EMT squad. Two male cops. When they saw me and the bloody mess in the room, they called in for reinforcements. A man and a woman cop came. The female cop asked me what happened.

At first I saw myself from the inside. The Isabel I knew. Then I saw how I was dressed and must have looked to her. Isabel the cheap hooker.

I asked the woman cop if she and I could talk in private, in the bathroom or the hall. I motioned at the male cops. I was embarrassed to talk in front of them. She seemed friendly and sensible, and for the first time I thought that I might be okay.

The lady cop and I went into the hall. I told her how sorry I was. How ashamed I felt.

I felt myself blushing as I explained that my boyfriend and I played this sex game. We'd done it before. The game was, I pretended to be a whore. And he pretended to be my pimp who stormed in just before the action started. It wasn't a blackmail thing, just theater.

The gun wasn't ours. It belonged to the guy, a random stranger whose name I didn't even know. My boyfriend and I had played the game a couple of times, and there was never trouble before. In fact mostly everyone had a good laugh, and we went home and had sex.

That was the only detail that was a lie—the part she would least expect to be a lie. The part about our going home and having sex.

I wasn't a whore. No money had ever changed hands. No money would. And there would be no sex with the stranger. It would never get that far. I repeated—it wasn't blackmail, it was just pretend. Fun. Just fun.

Were there actual crimes we were guilty of? Misdemeanors, at most, I thought.

The cop shook her head.

'Some people have a pretty weird idea of fun,' she said.

Her saying that helped me see our situation—the past months—from the outside. What had we done? How could I have gone along with what Matthew told me to do? Then I remembered what had happened in his hotel room before I went next door—and I knew why.

I'd let sex derange me, delude me. I'd let the allure and thrill of sex trick me into being someone I wasn't. I really wasn't.

Then it hit me again, what had happened. Matthew!

X! Would they be all right? The two men rolled by me, strapped to gurneys. Neither one was conscious. Both were still covered with blood.

I began to cry. I cried and cried. I couldn't stop. I thought to myself that these were tears I should have started crying months ago, the first time I met Matthew, the first time I realized I had surrendered my independence and was willing to do whatever he said. Whatever a man I hardly knew told me to do. And why? Not for my career—like I'd told myself so many times. But for sex.

'Two men were seriously hurt because of your little game,' said the cop.

That was when I fainted. I woke up on the floor of the hotel corridor. I looked up to see three cops and some of the EMT guys gathered around, looking down at me. Looking down *on* me.

I said, 'I'm so humiliated.' I could tell the female cop thought that was truly weird and inappropriate. My boyfriend and a stranger had just gotten shot and all I could think about was myself and my own embarrassment.

'We could charge you with something,' she said. 'But we have to figure out what it is. So for now ... don't leave town, okay? Don't go far.'

I said, 'I have an apartment and a job. I'm not a flight risk.'

'Flight risk.' The cop rolled her eyes. 'Everybody watches the same shows on TV.'

I heard myself say, 'I work in a mattress store.' As if that meant that I was a decent responsible citizen, gainfully employed, with a life. As if that meant anything at all. As if I was anything besides a young woman dressed like a cheap hooker who'd just seen her injured pimp wheeled away.

And I began to cry again.

Both men wound up in the hospital. For some reason they were sent to different places. Matthew was in New York Presbyterian, and the man—whose name turned out to be Randolph Blaine, not X, nor whatever Matthew had told me it was — went to NYU.

That night and the next, I watched the local news for a story about the scuffle and the double shooting in a midtown hotel. But there had been several spectacular murders that day, and those stories took precedence over Matthew and X's—Randolph Blaine's—fight. Besides, there was another new illegal recreational drug that had people overdosing and staggering in the streets like zombies. So two guys rolling around on the floor in a Midtown hotel didn't make the cut, even though shots were exchanged.

It took a day or so for the awfulness of it to sink in. Matthew was hurt! Matthew was in danger. It still seemed possible that he might die. I missed him terribly.

I had believed, as he always said, that we had all the

time in the world. I thought that meant we had time to get past the games. To be honest with each other. To realize that we loved each other. To get out from under the dark spell of Val Morton.

I'd thought we'd have forever to get it right. But it turned out we'd had no time at all. Something tragic had interrupted us when we were still getting it wrong.

I was painfully conscious of how few mementos of Matthew's I had. How little I knew. How few normal-couple things we'd done together. He'd never spent a night in my apartment, nor had I slept over in his. He'd never left a T-shirt at my house by mistake, something of his that I could treasure now, press my face into, smell him.

I clung to the bracelet I'd gotten from him for Christmas. But the crazy thing was, I stopped wearing it. I was too afraid I might lose it.

By now I was more obsessed with Matthew than I had been when we'd first met. I thought about him constantly. I cried on and off all day. I missed him with all my heart. I thought I would die from the pain.

Even Steve was understanding. When I began to weep, he'd gently suggest I retreat to the broom closet 'staff lounge' so I wouldn't have to deal with customers. Either Steve had gotten nicer, or I saw him as a different person since I'd found out that he went to visit his elderly mother on his lunch break. And he gave me more space, more physical space—he no longer wanted to stand practically on top of a woman in grief and mourning.

I visited Matthew in the hospital, but it only made me feel worse. And it certainly did nothing for him. He had tubes all in and out of him. He was in a medically induced coma. He didn't recognize me. He didn't even know I was there.

The sad thing was, no one else came to see him.

Only once. I met his brother there.

His brother looked like him—enough so that my heart started beating very fast when I first saw him, and it took me a moment to calm down and tell myself it wasn't Matthew.

In fact his brother was extremely attractive in much the same way Matthew was. But I pushed that disloyal thought away as soon as it entered my mind.

'You must be Ansel,' I said.

'Yes. I'm the brother.' He didn't ask who I was, or what I was doing there. He was very cold to me, and it seemed clear that he held me responsible for Matthew's tragic situation. But who was he to judge me? I knew that he and Matthew had been out of touch for years. To say the least. His brother had refused to see him, all because of some childish mishap involving ... a gun. Maybe Ansel secretly thought that Matthew was finally being punished now for what happened then. And now that Matthew was helpless, his brother decided to come around? What kind of brother was that?

*Carrie Blake*

I never once saw Val Morton anywhere near Matthew's bedside. There wasn't a card or flowers or anything with Val's name on it to be found anywhere in the vicinity of the man I'd loved and may have lost.

Soon enough, I found out why.

# Isabel

A few days after Matthew was shot, an article ran in the *New York Times*.

It turned out that Randolph Blaine, the man I'd tried to seduce and Matthew had shot, was not some unrepentant pervert masquerading as a reporter but a respected scientist who worked for the EPA and who had come to New York to testify before the City Council about the extremely negative environmental impact of a group of high rises that the Prairie Foundation was trying to develop on the Long Island City Waterfront.

He was married. He had children.

The Prairie Foundation. The Long Island City waterfront. I knew who that was. I knew what that was.

Val Morton had known who Mr X was. Val had known exactly why he was in town. And Val had probably also known that the guy had a weakness for Russian hookers.

It hadn't been about sex or theater or some big joke. It had been about blackmail. Val was planning to use the pictures of me and this married scientist to persuade him not to testify against Val's development plans.

According to the newspaper, the identity and the motives of the other male involved in the struggle was as yet unclear.

Matthew Frazier, 32, was described as 'unemployed.' Clearly he was not on the record as a Prairie Foundation employee, and there was no one involved in the case who was about to tell them that he worked for the guy whom Randolph Blaine had come to testify against.

No one was more shocked by the news than me. I'd suspected the truth about how often Val was pulling the strings. That is, I'd suspected something close to the truth, and then again, I hadn't. Countless times it had crossed my mind that the man I wanted to love me and want me was merely his boss's puppet. And I'd always put the thought out of my mind, as soon as I thought it.

I had no one to blame for that but myself. I wanted to have sex with Matthew—and something romantic with Matthew—enough to ignore my own intelligence, common sense, and even my most basic instincts.

I was so angry—at Matthew, at Val. At myself. I felt so betrayed. I considered going to the police with the truth. But the sensible part of me knew that I would only make things worse for me and Matthew. Attempted blackmail would be a much more serious charge than an attempted sex game gone wrong. And Val would hire the very best lawyers to keep him out of it, or clear his name, or make it seem like the whole thing was Matthew's idea. The scenario would go like this: a rogue employee who knew he was falling out of favor with his powerful boss dreamed up one last crazy stunt to try and demonstrate his loyalty. To prove that he was indispensable to the Prairie Foundation.

As the days wore on, I couldn't help wondering, had any of it been real? Had Matthew ever really desired me? Had any of the things he'd said to me been true? Had he just pretended to enjoy his time in Iowa with me and Mom?

Far away in his induced coma, with a bandage around his head and tubes hooked up everywhere, Matthew, oh poor Matthew, was in no shape to tell me the truth. Had everything we'd done together been some little drama planned and stage-managed by Val Morton?

One afternoon I went to see Matthew and someone called to me from a long black limo parked outside the hospital.

'Isabel!'

I knew who it was before the back window slowly rolled down.

*It was Val Morton.*

Turning his head only as much as he needed, he looked out of the window.

Was he waiting for me? How did he know I was going

to be there? Were he and Steve conspiring against me now? Once more I told myself that I was paranoid, but since so many things had turned out to have sinister explanations, nothing seemed paranoid any more.

Or even unlikely.

'Get in,' Val said.

A glass partition separated us from a driver. All I saw was the back of his shaved head.

'Soundproof,' Val said. 'Don't worry.'

'I'm beyond worrying,' I said.

'Sorry about that,' said Val. 'Circumstances beyond my control etcetera.'

The look I gave him must have flashed pure hate, because Val shrank back slightly and said, 'Let's take it easy. Talk this through. There's more here than meets the eye, I can tell you.'

'I'll bet there is,' I said.

Val said, 'I need to talk to you. It's extremely important. We need to have a longer conversation than we can have in a car circling the block in traffic.'

On the one hand, I wanted to tell him to go to hell, to stay out of my life—and Matthew's life—forever. On the other hand, there were so many questions I wanted answered. So many mysteries that I knew that only Val Morton might be able to solve.

'All right,' I said.

He took out his phone and texted me the address of a

restaurant in Brooklyn Heights. It took me a few seconds to recognize Pierre and Menard as the name of the French restaurant where I'd gone with Matthew. After we'd fooled around on Val's bed. After Val had watched me from the doorway. It wasn't the most tactful choice for Val to make. But Val had all the power. Val didn't have to be tactful.

'Tomorrow night,' he said. 'Will seven o'clock be convenient? I can send my driver around to pick you up at Doctor Sleep.'

It shocked me to hear Val say the name of the store. Of course he knew where I worked. He'd been there to talk to Steve. But it was somehow painful to be reminded of just how much Val knew about me. Maybe he knew everything—that's what I was going to find out.

The driver was waiting for me, exactly when Val said he would be. It occurred to me that the only fun part of the evening would be watching Steve's face as I went outside and got into the chauffeured limo.

The ride over the Brooklyn Bridge was beautiful, but I couldn't appreciate it. Feeling slightly sick, I closed my eyes and leaned back against the seat—which only made me feel sicker. All I could think of was how weak and helpless Matthew looked beneath those bandages, hooked up to all those tubes, alone in his hospital bed.

And I was going to have a civilized conversation with the man who had put him there.

Val was alone at the table. Even though it was relatively early, the restaurant was already quite full, but the tables around his were empty. I had the feeling that he had made this happen. That he had paid the restaurant to give us plenty of space.

He rose and shook my hand. All business, no nonsense, not like a friend or a seducer. Not even a hint of flirtation.

He said, 'I've ordered us Grey Goose martinis, straight up with extra olives. I hope that will be all right.'

He even knew what I liked to drink. It was weird, being alone with a famous movie star. With the former governor of New York. But I didn't feel even an edge of the thrill that you were supposed to feel around celebrities. I felt none of the excitement that I'd felt the first time Matthew introduced me to Val, at his and Heidi's apartment. And all I could think of was how much I hated Val for what he'd done to us.

'That would be fine,' I said.

After a silence, Val said, 'How are you holding up, Isabel?'

I hated how he said my name. Like he knew me. *Like he owned me.*

'I'm all right,' I lied. In fact, I was a total mess. Some mornings I found myself at work with absolutely no idea how I'd gotten there from home. Sometimes—often, actually—I looked in the mirror and didn't recognize myself. It took me a really long time to figure out who I was seeing, the young woman who looked like me, staring back at me. The person I used to be and who didn't seem to know what I had become.

'It's a tragedy,' said Val. 'Matthew was like a son to me.'

Was he? I thought. Then why did the paper not even say that Matthew worked for him? Why had Val refused to acknowledge him, why had he covered up the fact that Matthew was connected to him in any way? A son? *Seriously?*

'And Mr Blaine?' I said. I suddenly couldn't remember his first name, that's how out of it I was.

'Randolph Blaine is expected to make a full recovery,' said Val. 'They've put off the hearing until he does. But it hardly matters. I've decided to drop my plans for the Long Island City project. Out of respect. Even though it's going to cost the foundation a fortune.'

'Respect for whom?' I said.

'For Matthew,' he said. 'Who is also going to recover ... but perhaps not so completely.'

At that I began to cry again. Tears came so easily these days. Val offered me a monogrammed handkerchief, but I shook my head and blotted my eyes with the table napkin. Reflexively, I looked to see if there was mascara on the napkin. But I hadn't worn any makeup. Not for Val.

'Matthew cared a great deal about you,' said Val. '*Cares* a great deal about you.'

'Did he?' I said.

'He does,' said Val.

I wondered, how did Val know what that man in the hospital bed was feeling?

He finished his drink and waved to the waiter for another. I sipped mine slowly. I needed to stay sober, clear, alert.

'When Matthew recovers,' Val said, 'I'm prepared to make him a generous offer. A very generous offer. I feel I should tell you that this offer will involve a major ... relocation.'

'To where?' I said.

'To the Dominican Republic,' Val said. 'I'm planning to branch out. To develop some resort property down there.'

I knew what was coming next, but I had to ask anyway.

'And will I be included in this relocation?'

'I'm afraid not,' said Val.

'Matthew will never agree to it,' I said, though I wasn't nearly as sure as I sounded. I wasn't sure at all. I didn't know what Matthew would agree to, or not. I didn't know him that well.

'I'm afraid you're wrong. I think Matthew will be very grateful for the chance to make a whole new start,' Val said.

'Was Matthew working for you?' I said.

'Of course he was working for me,' said Val. 'You know that, Isabel. I don't quite understand what you're asking me.'

'I mean, was he working for you when he got shot?'

'Of course he was,' said Val.

My mind raced through the details of our relationship, wherever Val showed up. 'And the whole immersive theater project—was that a real thing...?'

'Never,' Val said, brushing the idea away, before I could even finish it, with a swipe of his hand. '*That* was all Matthew's creative genius. I had nothing to do with that special detail. But I think you knew that too, Isabel.'

Val was right. I did. I'd known it all along. Too many times, I'd found myself wondering how often Matthew was doing what he wanted to do—and how often he was following orders from Val. How much of what we did together was what Val instructed him to do? And how much had he kept for us, how much had he told Val?

I'd tried to tell myself that I was just being borderline crazy and paranoid about Val and his power, but now I realized that I'd not only been totally sane, I'd been right: power was power. For some people—including Matthew, I realized now—power was everything. Stronger than affection, than love—stronger even than sex.

I was finally being realistic. Sensible. The sensible girl my mom had raised me to be. I didn't want to think about Mom at the moment, or about the girl I used to be—the person I hoped I still was. No, not *hoped*. The person I *knew* I still was, deep inside, beyond where Val—or even Matthew—could reach me.

But as I looked back over the last months, I was no longer sure about anything. How much of what had happened was Val and how much was Matthew? Had Matthew cared about me at all? Had he just been a puppet—and turned me into a puppet too?

Val's lips were moving, but I couldn't make out what he was saying.

'Excuse me? What was that?'

'I want you to come work for me,' Val said.

'*What*? Doing *what*?'

'Doing more or less what Matthew did. Emphasis on the *more*. I want you to consult on how the Prairie Foundation might best market our high-end condos to women, who, as you may know, are more and more often making real estate decisions—high-end decisions—on their own. I want you to do everything Matthew did and more.'

'Making sure the gas jets are turned off in your apartment when you and Heidi go away?'

It was a direct challenge. That was what Matthew was doing that day when Val surprised us on his bed. Or at least made it seem like a surprise. Had Matthew known he'd been there?

Val rose to the challenge. He didn't blink, didn't flinch. He gave no sign of remembering what had happened that day.

'I can get someone else to check the knobs on the stove.

I need you for more important things. Matthew told me about your little games—the ones you played on Tinder Box or Buzzle or whatever the fuck they're called—before you met him. You've got a special talent, and you've been wasting it. You can find out what people want in a matter of seconds—and you give them exactly that. I need more people like you. You'd be well compensated, believe me. I'm prepared to offer you ten times as much as you're making at Doctor Sleep. No, wait. Twenty times as much. How does that sound?'

I was about to say no, to tell Val that I never wanted to see him again, let alone work for him. I was about to say a million things all flooding into my mind at once when Val held up his hand.

'Wait. Before you decide, I want to show you something that might help you make up your mind.'

'I don't...'

'Wait. Just go over there. To that table.' He pointed to a table most of the way across the room. I could vaguely make out three women sitting there.

'Go talk to them,' he said. 'They know you. They'll help you decide.'

Who were they? How did they know me? How could they help me decide? I had no idea, but once again, I was staying long enough to find out.

I walked across the room. I had the strangest feeling of fear. Of shyness. Of having been here and done this before.

Even when I reached their table, I wasn't looking directly at them. Wasn't focusing. I stared down at the floor, then glanced up again, then back at the floor. I couldn't bear to look at more than one of the women at a time.

I'd seen the first one somewhere before. Latina, heavyset, with close-cropped hair dyed a striking bright yellow. But where had I seen her?

She said, 'Hola, chica. How's that baby you were carrying? That unborn child that was actually a steak? Did you eat it for dinner? Was it delicious?'

Now I remembered. She was the cashier from All Foods. The one who'd been fooled when Matthew and I shoplifted the steak. The one who'd *pretended* to be fooled.

'I'm sorry,' I said. 'I...'

'Don't worry about it, she said. 'Good for you. Hope you guys enjoyed the steak. It wasn't my steak, my money, or even my job. My bosses were very understanding.'

She gestured vaguely at Val, across the room. 'Oh, and I'm sorry to hear about your boyfriend. I hope he gets better soon.'

Normally, it was the kind of sentiment that would have made me burst into tears. But I was too shocked to cry.

Sitting beside her was the waitress from the diner. Dyed black hair, red-rimmed eyes, the wart on her nose. An actress, just as I'd thought when I saw her in that car insurance commercial.

'You still owe me twenty-four thirty-six,' she said. 'Plus

a twenty per cent tip. You knew better than that. Your mom used to be a waitress.'

How did she know?

'I'm sorry,' I said. I couldn't stop apologizing. I remembered how Matthew had tried to apologize that last time we'd made love in the hotel before I went next door, before he got shot. I'd made him stop ... but oh, if I'd only known the truth about how much he had to apologize for.

For the first time, I felt really, really angry at Matthew. Furious. It wasn't as if he didn't have a choice. As far as I knew, Val had never put a gun to his head and forced him to do the things he did with me. *To* me. The way he manipulated my dreams for a career as a legitimate actress to keep his illegitimate, sleazy job for Val. Matthew had done whatever he wanted to keep his job, his salary. I was just a ... thing he was using to ingratiate himself with Val. I didn't know if I could ever forgive him.

But then again, no one had forced me to do what *I* did, either. It never really had anything to do with acting opportunities. I'd wanted to do what we did together. I had myself to blame, along with Val and Matthew.

It had been completely ... consensual.

But at least Matthew had known what he was doing, what was being asked of him. He didn't have to take it this far—make it this staged. I never had any idea, any real choice. I never had the necessary information to make that choice. No one had taken the trouble to tell me. No one, including Matthew, had considered me worth telling.

Even before I looked directly at her, I knew who the third woman at the table was going to be.

The redheaded Frenchwoman from the lesbian bar in Bushwick. Clemence.

She leaned across the table and reached for my hand. I stepped closer and gave it to her. Her hand was cool and very soft.

She stroked my palm, intimately, seductively.

'Everyone has her price,' she murmured.

I don't know what I'd expected, but it wasn't that. I pulled my hand away.

'Not me,' I said. 'I don't.' But at that moment I wasn't entirely sure that I believed it.

I stumbled back to the table where Val was waiting for me. He'd ordered me another martini, which was also waiting for me. It looked cool and delicious and inviting. I took a sip. Then another and another.

Now I finally understood that what I'd thought of as a normal life—well, a *sort* of normal life—was actually a fun-house life, staged inside a hall of mirrors. Had Val Morton engineered *all* of it? Had the master puppeteer pulled *all* the strings that made everything happen?

I must have been crazy to think I was having a love affair with Matthew. All along, Matthew and I had both been involved in a weird business partnership with Val.

Now Val said, 'Will you, Isabel? Will you come work for me?'

Why did he want *me*? Was it because I was someone who would do anything that someone else told her to do? Or was it really because I could figure out what people wanted, and transform into whomever they wanted me to be? The Perfect Girl for everyone. Even *The Perfect Girl* for Val.

I should have said: My mother raised me to be an independent woman. The kind of woman who knows when to say no. A decent, compassionate person. A nice person. A woman of substance. A kind, thoughtful, generous person with a clear sense of right and wrong.

But Matthew had slowly, stealthily, purposely changed all that. Now I felt almost as if I was floating high above my former self. I could see her, but I couldn't touch her. I didn't know who she was. I had no idea what she was thinking, or how she would respond to what Val was asking her to do. Why couldn't I transform into the Perfect Girl for me, the one I wanted to be?

I was no longer the same person. I'd been changed, changed forever. Or had I?

Val leaned across the table and took my hand. He stroked my palm with one finger, just the way the redheaded French actress had done. Had he instructed her to do that, too?

And that was when I knew. This was where everything

had been leading, all along. I didn't ask: What happens now? I didn't ask: Why me? I didn't ask: What will I have to do? I didn't ask: How bad will I have to be?

I waited for him to speak.

He didn't have to explain. He gently stroked my palm. His hand was smooth and as cold as the devil's.

'You're perfect,' he said. 'Perfect.'

I said, 'Give me a few days. I need to think it over.'

'You'll find I'm very patient,' Val said. 'Up to a point.'

That was when things really started falling apart. I couldn't eat. I couldn't sleep. I got on the subway to go to work and rode one stop and got off and turned around and came home. I couldn't bear to be in my apartment. I'd look around and think about how differently I would be living if I took Val's offer. But I didn't want to work for Val. It would be like working for the devil.

My mom hadn't raised me to work for the devil. Maybe that was why I stopped taking my mom's calls. I didn't want to ask her what I should do. I didn't want to hear her opinion. I already knew what her opinion would be.

After a few days of trying to call me and not getting through, my mom texted me: Worried. Are you ok?

I texted her back: I'm fine. Busy. Call you soon.

But I wasn't fine. And I wasn't busy. Or if I *was* busy, I was busy trying to not think about what I was being offered and what I would be turning down and what I knew I had to turn down.

Once more, Steve turned out to be unexpectedly understanding. I told him that I was having health problems, and he said he understood. Business was slow, he said. He could struggle along without me for a little while. That 'struggle' was a joke. In a moment of weakness I almost told him that I'd stopped sleeping. But I knew what would have happened. He would have sent me a mattress—probably a floor model he hadn't been able to sell—on the house, as a way of trying out his crazy theories about sleep problems all having to do with having the wrong mattress. I didn't want a new mattress. I felt as if the sheer bulk and weight of it would tie me to my apartment, my life, my dim future. I didn't even want to sleep. I didn't want to dream about Matthew.

After a couple of days I got a call from one of Val's secretaries saying that Mr Morton would like an answer to his inquiry within the next forty-eight hours. I almost told the woman (whose name I didn't catch) to tell Mr Morton what he could do with his inquiry. That was what I should have done. But I didn't have the heart. I didn't have the courage to slam the door on money, position, comfort, power—and find myself back in my bedroom in Greenpoint without even enough light to sustain a small plant.

Only now did I understand how much Matthew had

meant to me—not only as a lover but as a distraction and a promise. A false promise, maybe, but a promise nonetheless. The sex had been like a drug that took me away from reality, and Matthew had been like a drug that promised me that my whole reality might be about to change.

But it was never going to change. Matthew was never going to stop working for Val—not unless he got fired. And as long as Matthew was working for Val, I was too. I might as well take his job offer—at least the money would be going directly to me.

Without Matthew, I had no fantasies, no dream, no escape. My life was the dull dead end that I most feared it would become.

I didn't want to reach out to Luke and Marcy. In my heart, I knew they would be sympathetic. My boyfriend had been shot. I'd had a horribly traumatic experience. But I could never bring myself to explain how that experience had happened. I would lie to them, like I'd lied to so many other people

And especially like I'd lied to myself.

And what would they say if I told them how much I was being offered? By Val Morton? And that I was having doubts about it?

At night, lying awake, I told myself that maybe it would not be so bad, accepting Val's offer. I could always quit. If he was doing something I really didn't approve of, I could always tell him I was through. But where would I begin?

I didn't approve of anything he did. And I knew that from the beginning. I would be going into this with my eyes wide open, and already I would be seeing more than I wanted to see.

I thought of those three women in the bar. I would be an actress, like them, working for Val, acting out the evil script he'd put together. In the early days with Matthew, I had convinced myself that Val might be able to offer some opportunities for my career, but this was theater I would never audition for—a play written and stage-managed by the devil himself.

Val's secretary called again. I had till tomorrow to make up my mind. The clock was ticking. Time was running out.

I don't know why I decided to go see Matthew one last time. He was still in a coma. That's what they told me when I called the hospital. The nurse I reached said that his condition was improving, but I didn't know what that meant, exactly, and I didn't want to ask. She sounded vaguely disapproving. Why was I calling and not coming to visit? I tried to make my voice sound as if I was calling long distance—-from too far away to get there. But I wasn't fooling anyone but myself. Again.

I don't know what I expected to happen when I saw him again. Or, as I told myself, when I saw him one last time. Should I ask an unconscious man's advice? Should I take his job? Should I go work for his former boss? For the man who had gotten him into this state in the first place. Still bandaged, still hooked up to tubes and machines.

I have to admit that some superstitious sentimental part of me imagined that scene in the movie. The lover goes to the hospital bed of the comatose patient, and the nurse says, *Talk to him. He can hear you.* And the girl talks to him, and he finally opens his eyes, and ... some part of me imagined Matthew opening his eyes and telling me that he'd always loved me, that he was really and truly sorry, that he would never work for Val Morton again, that he and I would go away somewhere and start over and make new lives for ourselves together.

I imagined the scene a dozen different ways. But of course I imagined wrong. In none of the scenes I pictured did I go to Matthew's bedside to find Ansel there, standing by the side of his bed, looking down at his brother.

I said, 'I don't know if you remember me...'

'Of course I remember you, Isabel.' Ansel said my name just like Matthew did, and for a moment I wanted to turn and run from the room. It was all too intense. Too painful.

Then he said, 'Matthew would probably hate it if he knew I was here.'

I said, 'I'm sure if Matthew knew you were here, he'd be glad you came.'

Ansel said, 'He doesn't know.'

'Then why are you here?' I asked.

'For me,' he said. 'I want to look at him and make sure that I was right. I want to be able to see without him being awake and conning me, tricking me, bullshitting me, doing everything in his considerable powers to convince me that he was always the innocent one and nothing is ever his fault.'

'Matthew?' I said.

'My brother was not a good guy,' said Ansel. 'I don't know what you thought, or what he tricked you into thinking. But he was definitely *not* a good guy.'

I wanted to defend Matthew, who looked so helpless, lying there. But I didn't know where to begin ... I didn't know what I could say that would prove that Ansel was wrong about him.

'I don't know what Matthew told you,' Ansel said. 'But everything he told you, everything the two of you did, he also told Val Morton. I don't know if you knew that.'

'I suspected,' I said. But suspecting wasn't the same as knowing. I gripped the railing around Matthew's bed for support.

It seemed very weird to be having this conversation over Matthew's comatose body. But I couldn't bring myself to walk out. I couldn't tell Ansel that I didn't want to hear what he was saying. In fact, I was desperate to hear what he had to say.

'You suspected right,' Ansel said. 'He always was a liar, and a little bit of a sociopath, and you can't convince me

383

that he's any different now. He was born that way. And he'll stay that way. Val Morton saw something in him. Something cold and sick. He was the perfect guy to work for Val.'

Matthew was also sexy, I thought. You forgot that part. But I certainly wasn't going to say that to his brother. *Is* sexy, I corrected myself. But, strictly speaking, that wasn't totally true. A guy with his eyes closed and his face swollen and his head bandaged and machines and tubes coming out of him isn't naturally sexy. If I'd loved him, I would love him even more in his vulnerable, damaged state. But I was no longer sure I'd ever really loved him. And I was increasingly certain that he'd never loved me.

I wanted to wail. I wanted to burst into tears. I wanted to say something about how terrible life could be and how unfair it was and why did I have to meet a guy like Matthew? What had I done to deserve it? Was there something wrong with me? But I couldn't have said any of those things to his brother.

His extremely handsome brother. The younger brother who seemed kind and decent and honest. *Seemed*. As far as I could tell. I'd lost my faith in my ability to judge people, my confidence in my gift for knowing what others were thinking and feeling.

'People change,' I said.

Had Matthew changed? Maybe a little. I hadn't known him well enough to tell. I kept thinking about Iowa, and about the way he held me in his arms in that hotel room, what felt like ages ago now. There was tenderness and real care there. I wanted so badly for it to be true.

'Not my big brother,' said Ansel.

'How do you know?' I said. 'How can you be so certain?'

Ansel held up his hand, his palm turned outward.

The center of his palm looked as if it had caved in, as if someone had made a giant, raw, red, angry stitch and pulled the thread tight.

I remember Matthew saying that he'd shot his brother by accident.

'It's called a defensive wound,' Ansel said. 'My brother shot me on purpose.'

'Are you positive?' I said.

'I'm sure,' he said. 'I was the favored son. He hated me. He did everything he could to destroy me, to make me look bad, to get me into trouble. And when all that wasn't enough, when he didn't succeed in convincing our parents that he was better than me, more deserving, he tried to kill me. He lied, he cheated, he accused me, he ...'

'But how do you know he shot you on purpose?'

'If you don't mean to shoot someone,' Ansel said, 'you don't stare in their eyes and say "bye bye" before you pull the trigger.'

I felt a sharp stabbing pain in my chest, as if I was the one who'd been shot.

Of course it crossed my mind that Ansel was making

this up, getting back at his brother, who'd shot him by accident, just like Matthew said.

But I believed Ansel. I can't explain why. I believed him more than I'd ever believed Matthew. I told myself: *You hardly know him.* But it was Matthew I'd hardly known.

Ansel must have noticed the stunned expression on my face. He let the shock dissipate, waited a while, then went on.

'He and Val Morton were made for each other. And Val really is the worst. You know he's paying Matthew's hospital bills, but he's bribed the hospital to keep quiet about it? He's promised them a huge donation if they don't let one word slip out about who's footing my brother's medical bills. And the hospital is complying.'

'How do you know that?' I said.

'Val boasted about it. Just like he boasts about everything. If that isn't power, what is? Money talks, and you know what walks. You promise a donation, and in this economic climate you can do anything you want.'

It didn't feel right, having this conversation with Matthew lying there, but I still couldn't bring myself to leave him. I believed Ansel. But I hoped I was wrong to believe Ansel. That Matthew would wake up and tell me none of it was true.

A lot of things didn't feel right. Standing next to Ansel, even in this most unromantic setting, smelling of disinfectant and illness, so brightly lit that it hurt my eyes, I felt a funny charge: the buzzy, unmistakable awareness of an attractive body in close proximity to my own. It felt wrong, very wrong. But that didn't stop me from feeling it.

This is gross, I thought. Worse than gross. The guy's brother—my lover—is unconscious, comatose right in front of me, and I'm already thinking about how fast I can substitute one brother for another. But I wasn't, not really.

I wasn't thinking about much except how to process everything that Ansel had just told me.

Matthew's eyes stayed closed, his breath stayed steady. No fluttering eyelids or twitching fingers to signal waking. I moved over to one of the chairs by Matthew's bed. Ansel walked over to the chair on the other side of the room and brought it close to mine, leaving just enough room to make that buzzy charge between us get brighter. It felt ... what can I say? Normal. Comfortable. As comfortable as two regular people who happened to be a man and a woman, sitting in a hospital over a comatose man's body, can be.

Nothing had ever felt normal or comfortable with Matthew. Not even in my own house in Iowa. If I couldn't be comfortable there, where could I be?

I said, 'Listen.'

'I'm listening,' said Ansel.

And he was.

'Val Morton offered me a job. Matthew's job, I think. Only for more money.'

'Join the club,' Ansel said. 'He offered me a job too.'

'Doing what?'

'Being part of the design team for his Long Island City condos.'

'Did Matthew know? He never told me about that.'

'Matthew knew. I don't think Matthew liked it,' Ansel said. 'I think he was hoping it would just turn out to be a passing whim of Val's. A bad dream. I think he was hoping it would all go away.'

I thought, but I didn't say, 'And now it has gone away. Not in a way that anyone would want.'

Ansel said, 'And now it has. It did go away.'

Ansel looked suddenly very sad. After all, Matthew was his brother. But was he sad for Matthew? Or the project? I still wasn't sure why Ansel would have any contact with his estranged brother's boss.

But then the thought was gone. Drowned out by the real concern I heard in his voice.

He said, 'I think that Matthew will recover. And I think that, if he possibly can, he'll go back to work for Val. He'll go to whatever distant godforsaken outpost Val decides to send him.'

'You're probably right.' I hated to admit it. But he was.

'The Long Island City project has gone down in flames,' he said.

'I figured it would,' I said. 'At least we accomplished that.' We—Matthew and I.

I stopped myself. I still hadn't decided if I would go to work for Val. I hadn't decided how much I wanted to tell Matthew's brother. I hadn't decided what to say about what I'd done. About why I'd been in that hotel room with Matthew.

Ansel said, 'I turned Val down pretty soon after he asked. The next day, maybe. I don't think Matthew knew I'd passed on the job offer. I wish he had known. I could tell what working for Val Morton would mean. I didn't have to wait for the Long Island City deal to tank. I could pretty much tell what was coming. Not, of course, that Blaine would get shot. And Matthew...'

'And Matthew...' I said. 'It was a total surprise. A horrible shock.'

'I'm sure it was,' said Ansel, and we were silent again.

'Long story short: I couldn't do it,' said Ansel. 'Val Morton was going to destroy the waterfront forever. And he simply didn't care. That guy he got Matthew to shoot was going to blow the whistle on what was probably the biggest eco-disaster in New York history, and the bar's been raised pretty high for that.'

'Val didn't tell Matthew to shoot him,' I pointed out. 'It was the other guy's gun. Matthew didn't know he had a gun.'

'Still defending Matthew,' said Ansel. 'My brother must have had *something* special.'

I blushed.

'Sorry. That's not enough,' Ansel said. 'My brother's missing a body part. A heart. He was born without a heart. Matthew *would* have shot Blaine if Val had asked him to. Matthew was an icy soldier.'

There was an awkward silence.

'Matthew *is* an icy soldier,' said Ansel. 'Besides which, I don't need the job. I've got enough work on Long Island for people who can afford anything they want.'

'Lucky them,' I said.

'I intend to pay it forward,' he said. 'Make amends. Build houses for the poor.'

'I believe you,' I said, and we laughed, even though it wasn't funny. Was I imagining the edge of something— affection? friendship? Or maybe even desire?—thrumming in the air between us?

I had to get out of there. It was too much to process in front of Ansel, in front of Matthew. 'I need to take a lap. I think I'll go get some coffee from the waiting room. Can I bring you anything?'

'I understand. I'd love a coffee, if you happen to find some. Thank you,' Ansel said. Two words that, it suddenly occurred to me, I'd never heard Matthew say.

I walked out to the end of the hall, where the family waiting room was empty, save for a young man—not much older than me—asleep on a small, lumpy hospital-issued pillow. His legs were impossibly curled up in the chair, his full frame leaned against the thin metal arm rest, his head at a sharp right angle on the pillow nestled between his knobby knees and his ear. His hair was greasy and there were blue circles under his eyes, more than a day's beard creeping up his face. He looked exhausted. Heartbroken. Who was he here for? What news was he dreading?

I walked up to the single-serve, complimentary coffee machine in the waiting room, carefully pulling the Styrofoam cups from their plastic sleeves so as not to wake him. He barely moved. As I put each pod in, pushed the button and waited for each cup of watery coffee to fill up, I couldn't help but stare at the poor guy. I wanted to stay close to him, watch him. But it wasn't because I felt compelled to comfort him. As I listened to the coffee machine spit out the last few drops of the second cup of coffee, I realized why I couldn't take my eyes off him.

I wanted someone to be this guy for me.

But would Matthew be this guy? If the roles had been reversed, if I had been shot by that gun, instead of Matthew, would Matthew be glued to my bedside, or greasy and asleep in some hospital waiting room? Would he be torn about taking the new job with Val? Or would it always be about Matthew first? Would he just turn to me one day, like he'd supposedly done to Ansel, and say 'bye bye'?

But then again, I didn't know Ansel. His story didn't totally add up either. I still didn't understand why Ansel had spent any time with Val in the first place. Why would he know so much about what Val and Matthew were doing with me? Was Ansel in on Val's plans even more than Matthew? Why did he care about me?

I didn't know who I could trust anymore. I would have to start by trusting myself again.

The crumpled young guy moved his knees to the other arm of the chair, turning the other side of his face to the pillow.

I picked up both coffees and walked back to Matthew's hospital room, where Ansel sat, staring at his brother's bed. His face brightened the minute he saw me walk into the room.

'Only the finest,' I said, handing him his coffee.

He smiled, his fingertips brushing mine as he took the Styrofoam cup from my hand. My stomach flipped. 'Thank you, Isabel,' he said. And there were those two words again.

We drank our coffee in silence. The quiet—and the coffee—were soothing. I felt weirdly at peace. I was going to tell Val Morton no. I wouldn't work for him, I'd figure something else out. As soon as I thought about it, *really* thought about, I knew that was the right decision. How could I even have considered anything else? It felt good to recognize myself again.

Maybe it was Ansel's presence, encouraging me to be a better human being. Unlike his brother, who'd tried so hard to make me a worse one.

I wanted to tell Ansel what I'd just decided. I wanted him to approve of me, to like me for it. I wanted him to think of me as a good person. As good as he seemed to be.

But before I could speak, he said, 'Hey, I've got an idea. I know you don't really know me, but I feel like I know you. I've experienced my brother's bullshit so many times, but I can only begin to understand what he's put you through. And, well, I feel responsible. I want to make up for his behavior in some way.

'Come back out to Long Island with me. Have dinner. Stay in my guesthouse. No strings attached. Bring a book. Relax. You could probably use some time to chill out for a while. After seeing two guys get shot. To say nothing of imagining that at any moment my brother was going to turn from a monster into an actual human being. Like Frankenstein in reverse.'

I couldn't help it. I laughed.

'One condition,' Ansel said.

It brought back all the old memories. I lifted my coffee cup, not because I wanted any, but because I wanted to hide behind it.

What's that?' I asked.

'Tell Val Morton you're not working for him.'

'I already decided that,' I said.

He stood up and walked to the garbage can near the door to toss his cup in the trash.

'Tell him you've gotten a better offer,' Ansel said, playfully extending his hand to me. His smile was honest, friendly, warm. And also *extremely* attractive.

I wanted to take his hand. He wanted me to come with him. But I hadn't gotten up from my seat next to Matthew's bed yet. I smiled up at Ansel. But an offer for what? Would his offer end up being just like Matthew's? I looked from Ansel's hand, back at Matthew's own hand, lying limp at his side in the bed.

I was tired, so maybe it was just a trick of my imagination, or the way my eye caught the light when I blinked, but I swear I saw Matthew's pinky finger twitch. My heart leaped.

'Isabel?'